T0328756

ACCIDENT

ACCIDENT

Dawn Garisch

Published in 2017 by Modjaji Books
Cape Town, South Africa
www.modjajibooks.co.za
© Dawn Garisch
Dawn Garisch has asserted her right to be
identified as the author of this work.

Edited by Emily Buchanan
Cover text and artwork by Carla Kreuser
Book layout by Andy Thesen
Set in Palatino

Printed and bound by Creda, Cape Town
ISBN print: 978-1-928215-33-2
ISBN ebook: 978-1-928215-34-9

Thank you to the friends who read drafts of the novel, to Emily Buchanan my wonderful editor and to Colleen Higgs for holding the space open.

1.

At last the door labelled *Psychiatry Registrar* opened and a short, stout man dressed in brown trousers and a striped shirt stepped out. He looked down at the folder he was holding. 'Dr Trehorne?' he called, scanning the waiting room. His thick lenses, set into black spectacle frames, amplified his gaze.

Carol was seated at the back of the waiting room next to a dying pot plant and as far away from the other patients as possible. She ran a comb of fingers through her fringe, stood stiffly and pushed her way past various angled knees. The collective gaze followed her across the room, accusingly, assuming correctly that she had pulled rank and jumped the queue.

The registrar offered his hand. 'Good morning.' His head did a funny little bob. 'I'm Dr Ndlovu.' An earpiece of his glasses was broken and had been fixed back onto the frame by a wrap of white plaster.

Carol grasped his palm. It was warm and slightly damp. Just her luck to get an anxious psychiatrist. He waved her into his office.

She remembered the small room from the time she had worked as a medical officer in the emergency unit next door. In the intervening years nothing much had changed – the shiny white enamel paint, high industrial window, basin in one corner and large desk taking up most of the space. Whenever the alarm bell from psych casualty had sounded, it had been her job to grab a vial of sedative, a syringe and needle and to run with the security guards towards the mayhem, where a psychotic and paranoid patient had realised that the system had him cornered.

Dr Ndlovu closed the door. Carol had hoped for a woman. An older woman, someone who was a mother herself, someone she could relate to. Someone who responded to breakage with something more appropriate than plaster. But you couldn't choose who you saw in the state system. You got what you got.

'Have a seat, Dr Trehorne.'

'Carol. Please call me Carol.' Dr Ndlovu nodded, a crank of his head on the stiff hinge of his neck, but he did not offer his first name.

He sat behind his desk, put the folder down and opened it. Picked up his pen and sniffed as he perused the notes. An awkward silence hung in the room. Was there something he was struggling to tell her, something of which she was as yet unaware? No, it was probably the difficulty of their altered relationship in this setting. They were colleagues after all, although they had never met. He had no doubt attended to some of the patients she'd referred to the state hospital, patients too poor or crazy to be treated in a private institution. Yet here she was, of middle income and well cushioned by medical aid, being interviewed as a family member of a patient. She had been summoned from her son's bedside in the high care ward upstairs.

A turbulent yo-yo was disturbing her innards. Had a minute gone past? Five? Something had to happen, or she'd snap. She went through things she might say to put her colleague at ease, to get things going, when Dr Ndlovu turned to her and blinked his magnified eyes. 'This must be very hard for you,' he said. It sounded rehearsed, something registrars had been instructed to say to parents of kids in trouble.

Annoyance pushed in her throat. 'I know what it looks like but it's not what you think. I'm aware, of course, that patients who've harmed themselves are automatically referred to a psychiatrist, but Max wasn't attempting suicide, Dr Ndlovu. It was a prank, gone horribly wrong. Let's not forget he's an inexperienced young man. Young men sometimes play with fire. Literally and figuratively. Although,' she felt forced to add, 'as an artist I'm sure my son would see it differently.'

Dr Ndlovu adjusted his glasses on the bridge of his nose. 'How would your son see it?'

'Well, he's a performance artist. I imagine he'd say something like … he was making a statement about the world, making a visual display of how messed up it is. He really didn't mean to hurt himself.' The psychiatrist nodded, crank, crank. 'Apparently he took the precaution of using a barrier gel.'

Barrier gel was probably the wrong word – it sounded like a contraceptive product. What had the plastic surgeon called it? Fire retardant? 'If he'd done his homework properly,' she continued, 'if he'd protected his airway, if he'd got proper advice from a stuntman, or someone, if the stupid security guard hadn't sprayed the fire extinguisher right in his face, he probably would've got away with it. He has a social conscience, you know, and he's bright. He got a first in his finals at art school.' She was sounding mad, even to herself, but medics needed to understand that there was a whole world of people out there who didn't see things through scientific lenses.

Dr Ndlovu cleared his throat. 'The police want to lay a charge.'

That was unexpected. 'No, why?'

'For public disturbance, maybe arson.'

'Goodness! I didn't know that setting fire to yourself could be considered arson!'

Dr Ndlovu sniffed again, whether from allergies or disapproval, Carol wasn't sure. 'He put other people at risk by doing so in a public space. He could have set fire to other structures. It's a place where children or people with psychological difficulties could see him. It's very traumatic to see someone burning.' Carol flushed with embarrassed indignation, that this man at the beginning of his specialist career felt he had to spell all this out to her. She didn't know what to say, needing to defend her son, to defend herself as a mother, needing to barricade her heart against everything the psychiatrist was implying.

Dr Ndlovu inserted his forefingers behind his lenses and rubbed his eyes. He looked tired; no doubt he'd been up all night trying to talk people down from psychotic ledges, medicating them back to reality. He settled back in his chair and sized Carol up as though through a visor. 'We have to

3

look at why he has chosen public and violent displays to voice his concerns. This could have ended very badly.'

Performance art is public by definition, Carol wanted to object. Her cell phone erupted in her handbag; she probed around and found it. Peter's name on the screen. She silenced the phone, dropped it back. 'Sorry.'

'Do you mind if I ask a few questions?' Carol shook her head. Of course she minded but sometimes one had to comply. 'You're in private practice?' Was that a veiled accusation – that she was one of the lazy, entitled doctors who had abandoned the listing, understaffed ship of the state medical services in favour of self-enrichment?

'Yes, a family practice. I'm one of four partners.'

'You're divorced? From Max's father?'

'I'm his only parent.'

'His father's deceased?'

This was so annoying, to have to go into it all here with this man, for this reason. 'His father ... well, he's never been involved. In fact, he doesn't even know about my son. His son.' Carol shifted under Dr Ndlovu's gaze. This information wouldn't look good if it were plotted on a Normal Family Behaviour Chart. 'I met him overseas, while travelling after internship. I only found out I was pregnant once I was back. You know how it was in those days – or maybe you don't. It was almost impossible to get an abortion in the old South Africa. Besides,' she added quickly, 'I wanted a baby.'

Even if she had wanted to track Neil down, which she hadn't, it would have been difficult. By the time she'd discovered she was pregnant, he'd already left his rented accommodation in Paris and had returned to his home in the States. Nebraska, or Alaska, she couldn't remember.

Dr Ndlovu wrote something down. No doubt ticking off all the warning boxes: mother is irresponsible, narcissistic, manipulative, hyper-sexed, controlling. Unwanted pregnancy.

It wasn't my fault, she wanted to insist. Life can take strange turns. You should know that, as a psychiatrist.

The doctor leaned back in his chair and glanced at his watch.

4

'Has your son ever hurt himself before?'

Carol's mind went straight back to Max's end of year exhibition two years previously where final year students showcased their work.

2.

Carol arrived late at the art school exhibition. Normally she would avoid events where there were speeches, although in this instance she was curious to hear what the Professor of Fine Art had to say about Max's year in general, perhaps even about her son's work.

She was late because of an emergency. As she was leaving the practice – slinging her bag over her shoulder and locking her consulting room door – she had heard a wail and shouting from reception and Naledi had come running down the passage carrying an unconscious infant in her arms, a stricken woman following, someone she had not seen before.

They converged in the emergency room and Naledi poured the baby of three or four months out of her arms and onto the resuscitation trolley, where he lay, small and still. Pallor, eyes closed to a slit, floppy frog-legs, arms flung out. No obvious breathing. Stethoscope. No breath sounds. Zubeida arrived at Carol's side, handed her gloves, the small ambubag, connected the oxygen, applied electrode stickers to the tiny chest while Carol twisted the mouthpiece through the ashen gums and into position, suctioned, held the ambubag mask over the nose and mouth, squeezed the bag, small puffs, rapidly. No heart beat on the monitor.

'Get Trevor!' It was Ralph's afternoon off and she had just seen Xoliswa leave work. Trevor was the only other doctor in the building.

Tiny squeezes for little lungs, trying to get this child back.

'Naledi, get the history. Zubeida, cardiac compressions.' Zubeida had already slipped the small board under the child and was using stiff fingers to pump his sternum.

The mother was hardly able to speak. She managed to say that she found the baby wedged between the bed and the wall. He must have rolled over, she wept, he's never rolled over before. He was fine, she insisted, absolutely fine when he went to sleep. She found him about twenty minutes ago.

Sally, there too, handed Carol the smallest laryngoscope. Carol gave a few more squeezes of the ambubag, removed the mouthpiece, suctioned, inserted the flat blade. The back of the throat lit up – a tiny perfectly formed cavity, the little uvula hanging. Bluish tinge to the palate. Got to get oxygen in fast. Look for the tiny split membrane of the vocal cords. Sally handed her the smallest ET tube, gelled, in it went, sliding through the gap. The mother's sobbing receded through the swing doors – Naledi leading her out. Someone banged their way in, Trevor arriving beside her, thank God, but it was getting crowded round the bed, around the small body, so little substance to work on. He put a tourniquet round the tiny sausage of an arm. Tied the ET tube in place round the back of the head. Attached the ambubag to the ET tube, several breaths, the little chest rose, fell, rose, fell.

'What happened?' Trevor smacked the inside of the elbow, looking for a vein.

'Sounds like asphyxiation. Forget the arm. Here, try for the external jugular.'

'Five minutes.' Zubeida, keeping time.

Sally prepared a drip, running Ringer's through the drip set and Trevor was still pushing a needle into the baby's neck, again and again, searching for venous access.

Carol put her stethoscope on the chest to check for breath sounds. 'Stop,' she told Zubeida. Squeezed the bag. Again. Breath sounds on both sides, the tube in the correct position.

They all turned their heads to watch the monitor, all except Trevor, who opened a pack and was doing a cut down on the baby's leg. Got to get a drip up, somehow.

Flat line. Scrap of baby still flopped and cold on the bed. 'Keep going!' Carol instructed. Bag him, bag him. Sally brought a blanket and wrapped his body.

'I'm in!' Trevor connected the drip tubing, gave a bolus of bicarb. Zubeida continued, fingers straight, pressing his sternum, pushing his chest in, repeatedly, rapidly, towards his spine, hard, she must have been breaking ribs, trying to get this child going again, get him going, where has he gone? The little body was jerking rhythmically, an inert puppet, in time to her jabs.

'Ten minutes.' Zubeida swapped hands.

Carol gave another two breaths with the ambubag. 'Stop!' she said, looking at the monitor.

Flat line.

She put an index finger on the infant's eyelid, slid it up. Underneath, as she suspected, the pupil was dilated, the iris had shrunk back to a rim of intense blue. Using the laryngoscope, Carol shone the light into the deep black well of the child's eye. No response, the iris muscle didn't even flicker. She turned the baby's head, left, then right. The eyes kept looking straight ahead, totally still in their sockets. She straightened, looked round at the team, shook her head, sliced the air across with her hand, like the conductor of a symphony motioning the orchestra to stop.

They dropped what they were doing, stood for a moment, looking at the evidence of their failure, of life's failure. Carol slipped a pair of scissors out of Zubeida's top pocket and cut the tie digging into the baby's cheek and pulled the ET tube out. A long string of clear mucous was attached to the end of the tube, a thread of glistening fluid that clung for a moment, linking the tube to the child's mouth; then it broke.

Dread, like dark spillage, started to leak into Carol's chest.

There was a peeling sound as Zubeida pulled the electrode stickers off baby skin. 'I never get used to this,' Zubeida said in a tremulous voice. There was water dripping off her chin.

Carol ripped off her gloves angrily and threw them into the bin. The baby's curls were stuck, damp and stark, against the grey cold of his perfect forehead. He must have been dead already back at home, Carol consoled herself. They'd had to try, go through the motions for the sake of the mother. She pulled the blanket up to the little one's chin, as though tucking him in for the night. It didn't seem right to cover his face, the way one would with an adult. Besides the mother would probably want to come and sit with him, hold him, say goodbye.

This is how quickly things change, she thought. This is the tightrope we all walk every day, oblivious. Fall to one side and you live; to the other, you die. It happens every day in different ways, to someone or other.

She looked over at Trevor, wanted to ask him please, deal with this or I'll be late, but he was already washing his hands, giving her shoulder a squeeze and heading for the door. He was young, unmarried, had no kids yet, so he wouldn't be the right person anyway. Besides, she was first on the scene, so this was her patient.

It would be marginally better like this: breaking bad news, mother to mother. She realised she did not yet know the baby's name.

Naledi was giving the woman tea in the sisters' office. As Carol opened the door, they both looked up, the mother shifting forward in her seat, then standing with a slight lurch, momentarily going over on a heel, putting a hand out to the cupboard to steady herself, her terrified gaze locked all the while onto Carol's face, searching the doctor's expression for the single thing she needed. The woman looked like a child herself, too young, too vulnerable, her thin, pale arms angling out of a summer frock, her pretty floral dress the same one that she had put on this morning, without a moment's thought, at a time when all was well and nothing like this could ever happen.

The mother made her job harder, for there was something like a pin-point of hope in her eyes, a last ditch appeal, as if Carol were some kind of god who could make everything right, reverse the perverse course of nature, breathe life into dirt. Irritation passed briefly through her belly. *Surely* the mother *knew*?

'I'm so sorry … we did our best –'

The mother's face opened up in shock, disbelief, as though Carol had lifted her fist and punched her in the belly, hard.

There was no doubt about it. She was going to be late.

3.

By the time she arrived, there was a 'Full' sign on the boom at the entrance to the art campus, so Carol had to park in the street several blocks away. She checked her face in the rear-view mirror and tried to get her hair right, fluffing it with a comb. Her hairdresser had cut it too short, giving her a butch look, a don't-touch-me-with-a-barge-pole look. She tried to add some flair, to make herself look more available, by touching up with some coral-coloured lipstick. Her cell phone showed 7:05, over an hour late. Hurrying towards the main building, she saw that the crowd was already spilling out onto the veranda in a drift of cigarette smoke, laughter and talk, holding drinks in their hands.

She longed for her bed and the comfort of light crime fiction. A glass of wine would help to wash the day away. The mother had turned out to be older than she looked and her child was much wanted – the first successful take after many failed attempts at in vitro fertilisation. Somehow, Carol had to put the pain and fury aside and be present for her son's graduation show. She pushed her way through to the drinks table.

Where was Max? Carol had helped him by providing him with some medical stock for his sculptures but all she knew was that they were for mock-ups of the human form. Also that he was doing a performance piece, something that involved his sound-engineer-cum-photographer friend.

Catalogues, on a table. She picked one up, saw that Max's work was being exhibited in the Greek Building. He had called it *MIND/THE/BODY*.

'Hi Carol.' Tamsyn, a student a year below Max, who was unfortunately probably still involved with her son. Her face looked like a badly upholstered piece of furniture, held together with pins, studs and rivets. It was hard to see who she was behind all the hardware, the makeup, and the streaked strings of blonde hair hanging into her eyes. Since snooping in Max's diary earlier in the year, Carol had further reason to want to avoid these encounters. Max had referred to her nether regions in terms not found in gynaecological textbooks. Carol couldn't help wondering whether, like some of her more avant-garde young patients, Tamsyn was studded down there too.

What Carol had seen of her son's girlfriend's work consisted of paintings and collages of objects, buildings, landscapes and people exploding, a mix of images of war, suicide bombers, volcanic eruptions and *Tom and Jerry* cartoons. She was worried about what this preoccupation might say about her and, by extension, Max's preoccupation with her.

'Hi Tamsyn, nice to see you.' Carol gave her a quick smile. 'Looks like I missed the speeches.'

'Yeah. Didn't miss much. Same old bullshit, the university patting itself on the back, trying to persuade us that it's still relevant.'

'You're not getting a good education?'

'I learn more hanging out with homeless people than sitting in lectures.' The ring that pierced Tamsyn's upper lip was moving disconcertingly as she formed the words. 'Max'll be stoked you made it. He reckoned you wouldn't.'

Carol restrained the urge to raise her little finger, hook it into the lip ring and yank. 'I told him I'd be here!' She knew, with a twist in her gut, that her son was protecting himself against disappointment after the many times she had not arrived in time for a school play or a soccer match.

'He's doing his gig now.' Tamsyn pointed across the car park to a building with a long veranda and a façade of Doric columns. 'He's absolutely amazing!'

Why was it that the younger generation seemed determined to reduce the number of English words in use to about ten? Carol felt glad Max wasn't like that. He was well read, intelligent. He didn't speak often, but when he did he used words to good effect, with a certain erudition. What was he doing with someone like Tamsyn?

'Thanks,' she smiled. Tamsyn was making an effort but Carol was afraid of encouraging her. She waved her away. 'See you.'

She crossed the quad, scanning the crowd for anyone she might know, particularly for that familiar dandelion cloud of silver-grey hair. Peter had said he might make it.

Above the doorway to the room housing Max's exhibition was a huge sign: *MIND/THE/BODY*. Hanging on chains in the entrance was another smaller sign, positioned so that one had to duck in order to enter the room. It said: *THE THOUGHT*. She ducked and found herself in a large room where the floor was scattered with bodies, pieces of bodies. The corpses lay as though caught in the freeze-frame of a battle scene after the victors had withdrawn – amputations, beheadings, stiff with rigor mortis, none of them restful, relaxed. The few people inside were picking their way through the mess.

A repetitive mechanical sound permeated the scene – a copy machine? – over the faint sound of a heartbeat, the latter suggesting that amongst the felled corpses there might be one who was still alive. The room was wallpapered with pages of what looked like music scores, texts and poetry. She took a closer look at the ones nearby. Beethoven, Pinter, Ibrahim and Jonker.

The heartbeat was coming from an enclosed cubicle built against the far wall. To reach the dark curtain at the entrance to the cubicle, you had to find your way through the carnage.

The casts were cleverly fashioned from amalgams of plaster of paris – that she had provided – fired clay, beaten aluminium, fibreglass, wood, resin and wire mesh. Some looked like felled statues of overthrown political leaders, others were like the wire figures found in craft markets. A few resembled the plaster casts of the bodies found at Pompeii, curled to protect themselves from heat and ash or frozen in eternal death throes. The amputations were jagged and frayed, suggesting the massive violence of machetes, land mines, bombs. Bending to take a closer look, Carol saw that all the bodies were modelled on her son. Each was constructed around the same slender, muscular frame. The hands, some detached, had the long fingers of the classical guitar career he'd decided against. Inscribed into every forehead was a signature scar above the right eyebrow, a reminder of Max's accident as an adolescent when he came off a skateboard in front of a car.

Mass suicide. Carol thought back on the times she had been worried sick that her son was suicidal. After Daniel's death, and on finding Max's notebook. Perhaps this work was an exorcism.

At the curtained entrance to the cubicle stood a heavy man in a black cassock, holding what looked like a begging bowl. At first Carol didn't recognise him, because of the beard. It was Hedley, Max's sound engineer friend. He looked like Friar Tuck.

'Hello Hedley.' He ignored her greeting. It was probably the wrong thing to say, like calling your child by his name when he was dressed up as Batman. He gestured that she should wait beside a gaunt older man in a purple shirt and a beret. This was how it would be from now on, Carol mused – waiting in queues with strangers for a turn to see her own son. Her feet were aching from the long day but there was nowhere to sit. Typical young men, she thought. Inconsiderate.

Running alongside the pulse of heartbeat through the curtain, she could now also hear a soft and regular shush. The sound of breathing? Above the door was another sign in the same functional font as the first: *THE THINKER*.

From where they were waiting, Carol could see across the room to the entrance and observe people's reactions as they entered. The show was certainly making an impact. Those who ventured into the artwork were forced, as she had been, to pick their way through the strewn bodies, sometimes stopping and crouching to take a closer look. They reminded her of photographs she had seen of relatives searching for loved ones after a massacre, staring into each face.

She was about to turn to the beret man next to her and inform him, proudly: This is my son's work, when a chic young couple emerged from the cubicle. The woman was holding her scarf over her mouth and nose. 'Sies!' she exclaimed, giggling. 'What the fuck was that about?'

The man shrugged. 'Some pseudo-bullshit.'

Hedley indicated that Carol and the beret man could enter. As they stepped towards the curtain, he pressed his forefinger into the bowl which contained a wet sponge. Slowly, deliberately, as though performing an ancient sacred rite, he touched the middle of the man's forehead, chanting 'Reason is Godly', then repeated the gesture and intonation as Carol came to stand in front of him, anointing her too. A trickle escaped the wet spot on her skin and ran down the side of her nose; she caught a whiff of rose water. She wiped it away with the back of her hand, worried about bacteria breeding in what was essentially a Petri dish. She'd noticed previously that Hedley didn't have clean fingernails. She would have to speak to Max. There was nothing artistic about spreading disease.

She followed the beret man into the small enclosure. The heavy curtain dropped behind them and they were immersed in dark and heat and stink. Stale sweat, overwhelming foot rot. Was that urine? The immediate effect was claustrophobic, with a rush of nausea.

The only light source was shining directly behind the shaven head of a raised and seated figure in front of them. It threw his head into silhouette, creating a halo. As Carol's eyes adjusted to the semi-darkness, she saw that the man was her son and that he was naked, the contours of his beautiful, muscular, familiar body gleaming with sweat or oil. He was seated on what looked like a commode in the attitude of Rodin's sculpture *The Thinker,* leaning forward, his right elbow bent and resting on his left knee, his chin resting on the back of his right hand. Sweat bloomed and trickled at his temples but he didn't move, just kept staring down at the floor beneath their feet.

The smell was of someone who hadn't washed for weeks. Heat pricked in her armpits, soaked the nape of her neck; the smell hit the back of her throat with every inhalation. She glanced over at the beret, to gauge his reaction. He was gazing up at the living sculpture, like a tourist in a church or shrine, contemplating the sacred image of a deity.

ECG electrodes were strapped onto Max's chest and

abdomen, sprouting wires that wound round to the back. Peering around the side of the platform, Carol saw that they were attached to speakers. The light behind Max's head, she could now see, was an anglepoise study lamp. The skin on his shorn scalp shone pink and trickled wet from the heat. The amplified rhythms of his heartbeat and breathing, together with the shoosh-clack, shoosh-clack of the copy machine outside were a sound track of shifting syncopation; gurgling stomach noises added intermittent riffs to the mix. There were brief bursts of tinkling as he released spurts of urine onto the side of the commode.

As she turned to leave, unable to stand the fetid atmosphere any longer, Carol was annoyed to hear the trumpet and squeak of a fart. Could Max have seen that she was in the room and directed that part of the performance at her? He had always been a past master at generating farts and burps. As a boy, he and his best friend Daniel had had competitions – a veritable wind ensemble.

Did he really think that not washing and farting in public contributed to ideas about art?

Perhaps he was subverting Rodin's sculpture, wrenching it into the modern age where bodily functions and suffering intrude inexorably into the life of the mind.

Why had she not engaged in more conversations with him recently? They had both been too busy, preoccupied with their own concerns. On the few occasions she'd seen him, Max had evaded her questions about his work and had told her she couldn't see it until the opening. He'd said he wanted to surprise her. Well, yes, this was a surprise, not the kind she'd envisaged. She could see now that Max hadn't wanted her opinion on anything of late – not on his work, his relationships or his finances. He was excluding her from his life, extracting himself from her ambit.

She was losing him.

'What do you think?' asked the beret man, with whom she might, under different circumstances, have had a chat over a cup of coffee.

'I don't know,' was the best Carol could manage, afraid to hear his opinion. She needed to get outside, to breathe the night air.

As she stepped hastily over the corpses on the way to the exit, she inadvertently kicked a severed head, which rolled unevenly, then bounced to a stop against a torso. She couldn't bring herself to check whether she had inflicted any damage.

Once outside, she pushed through a clutch of people on the veranda, determined to get another drink.

'Quite something, isn't he?' Carol turned to find Peter beside her, his tall frame topped by thick clouds of snow white hair, his kind face framed by a manicured beard. She almost fell against him with relief.

'Oh, you're an angel, thank God you're here.' Then she saw the glass of red in his hand.

'Don't worry, darling.' Peter waved her concern away with an irritated flick of his cigarette. 'It's grape juice. Now, do you think we can try that again? Hello, darling,' He bobbed down in a quasi-curtsey so that his head was level with hers, squished his lips sideways and offered her a cheek. Ignoring his affectation, Carol captured his head between her hands and kissed him on the lips. Smoke, mint and wine. The wine breath must surely be hers. Surely.

Peter feigned a half-swoon. 'Oh, my! That was a bit forward, don't you think? I've only known you for … what? Ten years.'

'Eleven. Long enough for me to take all kinds of liberties with you.'

'Promises, promises! First,' Peter raised his glass and cleared his throat dramatically, 'to your son. May he bring us all to our senses.'

'You've seen it?'

'Just brilliant!'

'You think so?'

'Don't you?'

Carol patted the cigarette box in Peter's shirt pocket. 'Give me a smoke.' He shook one from his pack and lit it for her. 'I've had a hell of a day. Baby died. Maybe I'm not in the right frame of mind.'

'What happened?'

'Not now.' Talking about the child might loosen the knot in her throat. She couldn't risk wailing in front of all these people. Carol waved towards Max's exhibition, 'It's hard to relate when you've come from real death, real trauma.' She sucked hard on the cigarette, exhaled a long chute of smoke. 'Don't tell Max I said that.'

Peter lifted his chin and scratched his neck. 'I have to say I'm struck by how Max's work evokes authentic suffering.'

Carol looked at her friend sharply. Today she needed his support, not his clever arguments. 'At best it's a mock-up. Nothing close to the grief and anger when real people really die.'

'Max is making a political statement. Army generals, laboratory scientists, unscrupulous businessmen and political leaders, religious fundamentalists, petty bureaucrats, they're all capable of creating swathes of suffering out of some clever or doctrinaire idea that's cut loose from feeling.'

'Isn't Max's work itself just a clever idea? I couldn't see anything redemptive in there.' The cigarette wasn't helping. She stubbed it out in a pot plant.

'Oh Carol, I don't know. We live in a terrible world. Artists kick up dust, throw life in our faces, make us blink, rub our eyes, so we can see again, see ourselves. Max has done a good job. There's a world of ideas, violence, beauty, excrement, decay in there.'

'Beauty?'

'The beauty of what the mind is capable of, he's reduced to photostatted pages. The lack of feeling, of compassion, it's all there. What can happen when our clever fucked-up thoughts think they have no connection to our bodies. Destruction, meaninglessness.' Peter was waving his arm around, winding up enthusiasm for his own argument. 'Sometimes I think meaninglessness is the worst kind of suffering.'

'Okay, I get that. My patients are happily engaged in all kinds of self-destructive behaviours because they're not thinking about the effects they have on their bodies, not to mention the environment. My job is to keep up with the self-inflicted damage while I try to change the way they think.'

'Flow charts and diagrams. Do they get us anywhere? What we need is more art, more compassion.'

What was Peter talking about? Max was often so wrapped up in his own ideas and needs he often failed to notice her, his own mother, other than using her as a cheap laundry service. Yet as a small boy he'd stood up for a newcomer in his class who was being bullied, and had tried to care for a fledgling he'd found, putting it in a shoebox and feeding it from his mouth. His grief when it had died must surely mean something. 'Compassion doesn't arise out of intellect,' Carol asserted. 'Max still has to learn that.'

'Max has too *much* compassion, that's why he's compelled to make art like this. Go take another look some day when you're not feeling so fragile.' Peter put his glass down on the table with a little too much force. 'Tell the boy I'm proud of him.' He checked his watch. 'There's nothing I'd rather do than take the beautiful mother of the star of the show out for supper but I'm playing at the Twelve Apostles' from eight.'

'Good, you needed the extra work.'

'Yeah, well.' He laughed self-deprecatingly. 'As fast as bright young artists like Max wake people up, old failed ones like me put them straight back to sleep. Playing incidental, inconsequential music while les patrons quaff their Veuve Clicquot and schlurp their bouillabaisse.' Peter dipped in his pocket for his keys.

'How to explain it,' he mumbled.

'What?'

'Why some people are able to take hold of their pain and … use it, like … like a tool. They make something of it … something valuable, out of difficulty, things that happened to them. Whereas others,' he laughed again, a dry, cracked smirk, 'do everything in their power to bury the hurt, numb it, render it pointless, ineffectual.' Peter glanced again at his watch. 'Got to go.'

Her friend's face was an unhealthy colour, or was it due to the sparse light? 'You okay?'

18

Peter bent and pecked her forehead. 'No, not at all. I'm about to be late and if I'm late I'll get fired. *Au revoir, ma cherie*! Speak soon.' Carol watched as he walked across the car park a little too carefully for a man in a hurry. She scanned the table for Peter's empty glass. Which one was it? Had it been cleared away already? She picked up the one she thought was his, the one closest, and sniffed.

Wine, without a doubt. Red wine.

Carol drove home over the shoulder of the mountain, fretting about what she thought Peter had inferred – that Max was in some kind of emotional pain and that he used it as a tool to fashion his work.

Maybe he was making generalisations. Or it was the wine talking. Fuck it, she hoped Peter wasn't drinking. What to do if he was? She couldn't go down that plug hole with him again, even if he was one of her dearest friends.

She wanted to grip her old friend by the throat, force him to stop.

Maybe she'd sniffed the wrong glass.

Carol had hung around for about an hour after Peter had left, waiting for Max. She'd wandered anxiously through the exhibition spaces, barely able to concentrate. All she wanted to do was go home and cry; but first she had to put on a stable face and congratulate her son. Ask him … What? She hadn't found the words yet, not the right ones.

Had he been hurt in his life more than she realised? There was the matter of his father but that surely hadn't caused him sleepless nights. Perhaps his near-death experiences had left their traces. Daniel. And Jack. Were those old ghosts still plaguing him? His latch-key existence during his high school years had probably not been a good idea but as a single parent whose own parents had by then grown too old and frail to help, what other options were there?

When Max came up to her, freshly washed and dressed, a handsome and desirable young man, she reined in her anxieties and told him how proud she was, how even she could see that his work had merit, which was probably the wrong thing to say but it was a lot less wrong than many of the other things that had come to mind.

He shrugged and hugged her, while holding her at emotional arm's length. She could feel it, the way his embrace kept her at bay. Was this the usual manner in which a son needed to grow apart from his mother? Or did he keep her away, keep himself away, because she represented harm, or in some way was actually *harmful* to him?

There was no evidence for these mad thoughts. She was just tired and sad. A bit depressed even.

As she drove home, Carol recognised that there was a part of her that was *appalled*. That was not too strong a word, although she would never admit it to anyone. Her son's work filled her with dread.

4.

Carol didn't go into all that with Dr Ndlovu. She picked out a few facts about Max's final year work, choosing her words carefully, not wanting to appear either over- or under-anxious. She then realised that she hadn't addressed Dr Ndlovu's question. Her son had not actually harmed himself during that performance, he had only done violence to multiple copies of his body in the name of art.

'No,' she declared. 'Actually, no. My son has never injured himself. I mean, he came off his skateboard when he was a teenager, and he fell off a slide at preschool and was concussed. Obviously, those weren't on purpose. For someone so unafraid of danger, he's had very few injuries.'

Dr Ndlovu asked her a few more questions about drug use and family history of mania, suicide and depression, then he looked at his watch and closed the folder. 'Thank you. If there's anything else that occurs to you that would be useful, please let me know.'

As Carol stepped out of Dr Ndlovu's office, the patients in the front row of chairs in the waiting room looked up at her. A woman with thick, stockinged ankles and a cardigan stretched at the pockets; a restless young man in jeans and t-shirt despite the cold, his eyes set too deeply into his bony face; a large and lethargic man in a suit who raised his eyes to her but not his head. All three inspected Carol to see whether she had been altered in any way by her sojourn in the psychiatrist's office and whether she might be about to deliver good news from a place of salvation.

I'm normal, she wanted to explain. I'm not supposed to be here. I'm the one who sits on the other side of the desk.

A cup of coffee was what she needed before going back

up to Max's ward. Back in the days when she'd worked in the emergency unit, the coffee available from the little shop in the hospital hadn't been great but now she was surprised to see one of those coffee-making machines that look like a space craft behind the counter, and fair trade coffee advertised on the menu. Sign of the times, she thought. In a state hospital for the poor, this provision could only be for medical students and staff. She ordered a double shot in her cappuccino and took a seat.

A newspaper was lying on the table; she picked it up, needing distraction. On the front page were two photographs of a man on fire, one of him running towards the camera in agony with his arms outstretched, and one taken from the side, with him on his hands and knees, head hanging. The caption blared: 'Artist Self-Immolates'. Which was not true, she wanted to object, furious with the inaccurate reporting. Her son was, most fortunately, very much alive.

Carol glanced around, flipping the edge of the paper over to cover the photo, hoping no one else had seen. Of course they had, the whole of South Africa had been notified, it would probably be on television too, on the news. The spectacle of her son ostensibly burning to death horrified her. She could see Dr Ndlovu's point, that this went further than a prank. The images were reminiscent of the political strategy of necklacing and of Buddhist monks protesting invasion and persecution, but unlike poor and oppressed people in South Africa or the tormented people of Tibet, her son had nothing whatsoever to complain about. Max seemed to have taken his good fortune, which included excellent health, for granted. He possessed this wellbeing largely because she herself had ensured it, bringing him up safely, securely, with all the right vitamins and minerals. And now? That wasn't good enough, he'd had to create a problem, bring several problems upon himself by doing the most extraordinary thing of attacking his own body. It was against nature and she absolutely could not bear it.

Thank goodness her parents weren't alive to see this.

Carol forced herself to look again. The photographs reminded her of images she had seen elsewhere; this one, where Max was down on his hands and knees, looked like the front page photograph of that xenophobic attack on a Mozambican man a few years back. The other jigged a powerful emotion but she could not place the association. Vietnam? Hector Pieterson? Max must have carefully planned and reconstructed the scenes, together with the photographer. Who, she wondered, had stood casually by and photographed this? Hedley. It must be Hedley.

That morning, when she'd got the call from the hospital, she'd had to cancel her patients for the day. She had swerved through highway traffic, filled with the dread of not knowing exactly what awaited her. This was not the first time she had been in this position.

Now that she knew he'd done it on purpose, she was going to take him on before he had sufficient breath to argue back.

The cappuccino had come with a serviette which she pressed under her lower eyelashes, trying to save her mascara. She couldn't cry here, it was possible that someone medical who knew her would pass by and ask what she was doing at the hospital. My son is trying to kill himself, accidentally on purpose. She turned back to the paper.

Artist Self-Immolates
In front of horrified shoppers, Max Trehorne, a 26-year-old performance artist from Cape Town, set himself alight at the Waterfront this morning. He is in a stable condition in a city hospital. His manager, Hedley Anderson, released a press statement written by the artist: 'Now that I am alight, will you look at me?'

If she had paid Max more attention, could this have been prevented? Those times when he'd screamed at her: You never listen! For the life of her Carol couldn't recall what the fights had been about. But this, this wasn't about mothers. It was about the world. Buddhist monks, the plight of refugees, the insane, her son was commenting on what it takes for people to stop and take note.

So Hedley *was* mixed up in this. Two stupid young men, able to imagine all kinds of crazy things to do to attract attention, unable to imagine the consequences. Did they really think that if Max put himself at risk, it would achieve anything other than admission to hospital and a possible criminal record?

She remembered Peter's call, from earlier, found her phone and turned it on.

Voicemail: 'It's on the front page of the *Argus*. I'm on my way to the hospital right now.' Damn, that must have come through almost two hours ago. Another from her annoying cousin Stella: 'Carol, I've just heard, how terrible. Give me a ring.' From her good friend Katy: 'Carol, I can't get through to you. The hospital won't say much, only that Max is stable. Let me know, okay? Love you lots. I'm stuck in meetings all day but please message and I'll find a way to leave if you need me.' There were so many people she'd need to get hold of, to let them know that Max was okay, that the whole incident was a hoax.

Another from Peter: 'Where are you? I'm in the ward. Max's sleeping. Naledi insists you're here, at the hospital. I'll hang around a while.'

She paid for the cappuccino and ran up the stairs to the ward, hoping that Peter hadn't left yet. He'd know how to speak to her son.

Carol heard the commotion before she entered the ward. Over the metronomes of heart monitors a woman's voice rose and fell.

The nursing sister in charge was standing at the end of Max's bed with her feet planted apart, her knees locked and a fist on a hip, ordering two visitors to leave. Seated on one side was a young woman with an iPad on her lap; on the other stood an overweight young man whose face was partially obscured by a video camera as he filmed the argument. In the middle Max lay awake, silent behind his oxygen mask, with his burnt hair and strawberry-red face. His bandaged arms lay at his sides above the bedclothes, his chest rising and falling more rapidly than normal, his singed eyebrows twitching with either pain or amusement. Now and then he'd contribute to the exchange with bouts of coughing.

'Will you *stop* that?' the sister demanded, swinging her wrath towards the cameraman who carried on pointing the camera at her. It was Hedley.

Carol edged round to him, trying to stay out of the focus of the camera. 'Hedley, what are you –?''

'Do you know these … these *people*, Dr Trehorne?'

It was embarrassing to admit. 'For goodness' sake, Hedley, I'm *talking* to you.'

'Will you please ask them to *leave*?' The sister turned abruptly away to the nurses' station.

'Haven't you caused enough trouble for today?' Carol asked the three in general but Hedley in particular, her voice low with indignation. 'Look around you.' Max's was one of eight beds. All but two of the occupants were conscious and staring at the goings-on as though at a *Jerry Springer* show. Next to Max, a frail woman was lying with a frame over her legs and a drip winding into her arm; on the other was a middle-aged man with a bloated stomach on a cardiac monitor. 'There are sick people in here, this is no place –'

Behind her, the sister was shouting into the intercom. 'Security! To High Care stat!'

The young woman stood and put out a gracious hand. 'You must be Max's Mum.'

The sister flew back to the bedside and grabbed the woman by the arm, her fingers clamping into her flesh. 'I've told you already, journalists are not allowed into the hospital. All queries must go through HR. Now get out before you are thrown out.'

'Please leave,' Carol emphasised.

'Okay.' The journalist shrugged nonchalantly as though ultimatums were a normal part of her day. 'Cheers Max. Give me a ring when you're out?'

He nodded.

She left, followed by Hedley, who had slipped the video camera into its case. 'No offence, Mrs T,' he said. 'All in a day's work, just a different kind of office.'

Carol wanted to hit him as he passed. She had never warmed to Max's friend and flatmate but now she truly disliked him. He was as bad as that photographer who took pictures of the starving child with the vulture waiting in the background. People like him provided fodder for a bored world sitting comfortably in front of their TVs waiting for their next injection of sensational footage. The photographer as vulture, feeding off the misery of others in order to enrich himself. Convincing themselves that they are objective observers, refusing to intervene so as not to change the course of nature or of history, using whatever trumped-up justification. She wanted to run after Hedley and ask him: How can you be so heartless?

She sat down on the chair still warm from the stupid young woman's backside and turned to her son. 'Okay, Max, seeing you're awake enough now to give interviews, how about I throw you a few questions?'

'Not now, Ma.' Max whispered. He was trying to adjust the oxygen mask on the inflamed skin of his face with his bandaged hands. 'Help me loosen this, it's too tight.' His voice broke through briefly, raw.

She pulled the elastic through, lengthening it so that the mask didn't press against his skin. His breathing rate was still rapid despite the oxygen and she could hear a slight wheeze when he exhaled. But the oxygen saturation on the monitor was normal. Stupid, stupid boy. You give them perfect lungs when they're born and then they go and mess them up with cigarette smoke or performance art. 'Why didn't you tell me you were going to do such an idiotic –?'

'Ma –'

'What were you thinking!' Max closed his eyes, turned his head away. 'You realise, the police … you could end up with a criminal record, not to mention emphysema and –'

Someone was at her side – the nursing sister, tense with anger. 'Dr Trehorne,' she announced. 'I'm going to have to ask you to leave. There's been too much disturbance this afternoon and my patients need to rest. You're welcome to come back this evening at visiting time. Between seven and eight. When we've all calmed down and I'm off duty.'

Carol stayed sitting for a moment, holding her anger. She was a *doctor*, visiting rules didn't apply. Perhaps, on reflection, her voice had started to climb. She stood. 'I'll be back, darling,' she said and bent to kiss Max. His forehead felt hot and dry. 'I'll bring you some moisturising cream.'

'A friend left this.' The sister gave her a note, in Peter's artistic scrawl. *Got to go, speak later. Much love.*

At the door, Carol turned to have a last look at her son and caught him wiping his forehead with the back of his hand.

5.

'How's Max?' Trevor asked.

On her way home from the hospital Carol had stopped by the consulting rooms to make a few urgent calls to give patients their results. She'd whisked past Naledi in reception and dived into her room, not wanting to attract any attention about this event. Something in her was burning, a low conflagration. It was shame, she realised. Trevor had caught a glimpse of her in the passage and had knocked on her door.

'He'll be all right. Thanks. Sorry about today. You must've been busy.'

'So-so.' Trevor leaned against the door frame. 'Don't stress about work. Let me know if there's anything –'

Carol nodded and opened the first folder. 'I'm phoning some results, then I'll be going. I'm taking tomorrow off but I'll be back Wednesday.'

Just her luck, Ralph was standing at reception when she left an hour later, his hand on the shoulder of a female patient. She tried to hurry past but he spotted her.

'How's your boy?' he asked in a tone more annoyed than caring.

'He'll be fine. Thanks. Got to go.' Carol forced a smile.

'Bye, Doc!' Naledi called after her.

Carol drove home in a blur of tears.

Cousin Stella and her husband Greg were at Max's bedside when Carol returned to the hospital that evening. She hesitated at the door, but they had seen her.

'Hello, my dear!' Stella came over and pulled Carol into a tight embrace. 'Your young man here gave us all a big fright,' she smiled, tugging at Max's foot through the hospital bedding.

Max lifted an arm in a weak gesture of greeting and closed his eyes. Whether his grogginess was due to pain medication, or whether he was pretending sleepiness, Carol didn't know. She couldn't check what had been prescribed for him because hospital folders were no longer left at the bedside as they had been when she was a student. He was probably on pethidine. Partial thickness burns were very painful.

She could do with a hundred milligrams straight into her vein right now.

Greg stood and put his arms around her before she could avoid him. He always held on a moment too long for comfort, always tried to kiss her on the lips. She disengaged the moment she felt it would not initiate a struggle. 'Have my chair,' he offered.

'Thanks, this is fine.' Carol perched a buttock on the white island of Max's hospital bed, wanting to be close to her child, to his poor burnt body, distancing herself from these relatives and the kind of things she knew they would say.

'Tell me,' Stella asked in a stage whisper, 'why is Max in here? Why isn't he in a private hospital?' Stella made big eyes, swivelling them melodramatically around the socially and racially mixed crowd of patients and visitors. The notice on the swing door to the ward had a sign stipulating that there should be no more than three people around each bedside, so there was also a queue of relatives outside, carrying wrapped pots of fragrant curries and stews, packets of breads and parcels of sweets, waiting their turn.

'He's on my medical aid but the ambulance had to bring him here.'

'Transfer him somewhere else. It can't be hygienic.'

'The medical aid won't pay for a private hospital,' Carol said. 'Not if the injuries are a result of something that looks like suicide.' Her voice started to wobble. She was *not* going to cry in front of Stella.

'Oh my dear, what a trying time! Here, have a chocolate. I brought them for Max but he doesn't seem interested. But then, Max never did seem interested in the ordinary pleasures of life.' She gave a little laugh and popped one into her mouth. 'They're very nice.'

She offered Carol a tray that was half empty. It was seven o'clock and Carol had not eaten since breakfast. She took two swirled mounds and ate them one after the other, biting hungrily through the firm coating. The too-sweet, creamy fillings spilt and melted over her tongue, sliding into crevices. A rush of energy flowed out into her limbs. She felt dizzy.

'He's a very lucky chap,' remarked Greg, working his lips round a toffee. 'You're a doctor. I don't need to tell you that.'

Stella nodded her agreement and posted another chocolate into her mouth. 'You know, Greg tried to commit suicide once,' she remarked. 'You don't mind me telling Carol, do you, honey?'

Greg shifted uncomfortably. 'That was yonks ago, Stella. I was young and screwed up.'

'Max's wasn't suicide,' Carol corrected.

'It's exactly when you're young that you go and do silly things,' his wife insisted. 'Shame, Greg was in love with this girl, wanted to marry her even …'

'Stella, this isn't the …' Greg objected.

'She broke up with him. Why was that again honey? Was it your drinking, or your nose? Ha ha! Anyway, Greg couldn't get out of bed he was so depressed, only there wasn't a word for it in those days, so his father gave him a gun for his birthday, you know, to cheer him up! Imagine. Horrible man, Greg's father. So he tried to shoot himself, put the gun against his head.' Stella turned her hand into a gun, pointed the barrel at her own temple and pulled the trigger. 'Bam! Only my darling husband's got such a thick skull and his hand was shaking or something and the bullet –'

'Stella, please!'

'– tracked under his skin, all the way over the top!'

Greg slumped lower in his chair. 'There are some things you'd rather forget but your wife won't let you.'

'The man's never tried to kill himself over me,' Stella added.

Greg glanced up at her. 'The way you're carrying on, I might consider –'

Carol couldn't stand it. 'Ask Max, he wasn't trying to commit suicide, were you love?' She waited a moment but Max kept his eyes closed, not giving a flicker. 'He wanted to make a sort of statement, a protest. Artists do that kind of thing, nowadays. His method went wrong, that's all.'

Stella leaned over to Carol. 'You know, it's unbelievable what they teach at art school nowadays. What passes for art ... well, there's no decency any more, no *aesthetic*! When I saw the picture in the paper, I was having coffee with a friend whose niece is studying art history. You know what these professors teach? About so-called artists cutting off their ... private parts! Drinking their own, excuse me, *excrement*! Can you imagine! This niece, she's a young impressionable kid of nineteen! If the universities teach this kind of nonsense to the kids as *art*, for heaven's sake, of course they're going to be influenced and think it's clever to jump off a building, with a piece of hardware up their bums or something.'

'Waste of talent, if you ask me,' Greg chipped in, perking up now that he and his wife were on the same side of the argument. 'Any damn fool can forget to make their bed, or, what did that guy do? What's his name again? Heist. Hearse. Stick diamonds on a skull! Any idiot can do that if they're rich enough. But to call it art! There's no skill in cutting up a sheep and stuffing it in a tank. Now, a Monet, or a Rembrandt ... if you think what went into those works. The years of apprenticeship, the patience, the mastery. I hear they don't even teach painting any more at art school. Is that true?'

Carol was suddenly and thoroughly tired. She couldn't find the right words that would do to stick up for her son, partly because she half-agreed with their argument. 'Max needs to rest,' she suggested.

'He's a great kid,' said Greg, giving Carol's shoulder a squeeze. 'Should've done law, like I told him. He was always a great one for arguing. I told him, don't get mixed up with these bipolar, schitzo arty types. All the modern ones are con artists. Ha ha! Now there's a statement, if Max cares to make it. Artists, the galleries, art critics, they mess with your head until you end up believing that utter rubbish is worth a fortune, then they coldly relieve you of your hard-earned cash. Have you ever read Tom Wolfe's book? *The Painted Word*? You should give a copy to Max. People a few generations on are going to look back and wonder what the hell was wrong with the twentieth-century brain.'

6.

Carol persuaded Max to come home to stay with her for a few days after he was discharged. It was strange to have her son back at home as a guest.

Max had moved into digs three years previously in his final year at art school. Carol would wake up in the morning with an ache of loss, not knowing what it was until she remembered that she would be having breakfast alone. After months of failing to nag her son into sorting out the smorgasbord of random stuff he'd left behind, the ache had turned into annoyance. Carol had set about going through Max's cupboards herself. She'd filled boxes with broken torches, old cell phone chargers, a defunct computer, a damaged skateboard, clothes and shoes he had outgrown, school textbooks and half-used cans of shaving cream and deodorant. She'd given them to Pumi, her domestic worker, for redistribution.

Once Carol had taken the dark curtains down from the window and had applied several layers of white undercoat to the black walls, the room was transformed. The final coat she had chosen was a creamy colour called Picasso Sundae. Together with new lace curtains with a lilac backing, the bedroom had felt fresh and clean and a good deal bigger.

When Max had come for a visit a week or so later, he'd made no attempt to hide his disdain. 'You are so middle-class, Carol.'

'Funny that. Some people aspire to middle-class.' Her son was no longer brushing his hair. It hung in matted curls down his neck.

He opened the cupboard. 'Where the fuck's my skateboard?'

'You should give up skateboards, Max. They're middle-class, bourgeois accoutrements.'

'Oh you are so hilarious. So where is it?'

'If you think calling me by my first name entitles you to use bad language around me, you can forget it.'

'Come off it, Ma, you say "fuck". Where've you stashed it?'

'That old thing with a big ding in one side? Some happy child in Masi is no doubt putting it to good use after it lay around in your room for what? Six years?'

'Ma! It was a classic! Jack gave it to me. It was mine, it wasn't fucking yours to give away.'

Carol wanted to smack him. Her last patient had been a distraught man who had lost his business and his home because of ill health, and her spoilt boy was kicking up a fuss over a broken skateboard. 'I've told you to watch your language. I gave you fair warning about clearing out this room.'

Max kicked the cupboard door closed. 'Jeez, I've been working really hard! You don't have a clue what my life is like.'

'You think I've been sitting around? You think I have time to waste on your rubbish?'

'It's not rubbish! Why couldn't you wait until after my exams? You're such a control freak.'

'I live here, Max. I don't want a cockroach problem. Your room was a festering cesspit.'

'Cockroaches are among the most intelligent species on the planet, Carol. A fuck lot cleverer than most human beings.' Max pulled a desk drawer open. 'Where's my workbook?'

Carol had almost thrown the notebook away. Opening the drawer to empty it, she'd found a pile of scribbles and drawings, old exam papers, lists of things to do, old receipts, speeding fines and mind maps. Underneath was a ring-bound notebook. Flipping through it, she saw that it contained quotes, thoughts, poems and drawings. Strange hallucinatory sections. The content was artistically and provocatively put together, with doodled borders and occasional newspaper clippings and magazine photographs stuck in.

She sat down on the bed and went through it more carefully. Written inside the first page in Max's angular hand, floating alone like a boat drifting on an ocean:

interrogate
your past fate

On the opposite page was a cartoon of a man in front of a mirror screaming at his screaming reflection.

'I'm the one that's got to die when it's time for me to die, so let me live my life the way I want to'

This quote was scribbled under a photograph of Jimi Hendrix in performance, back-lit, the edge of his Afro a halo, his gaunt face dazed.

On the next page, a sketch of a crucifixion with Max in a loin cloth looking up to heaven with an expression of bliss. Except the nails fixing his hands and feet to the beams were large hypodermic needles. The caption read:

'A thing is not necessarily true because a man dies for it.'
Wild Oscar Wilde

I'm on my way Red Rover
hawk-mole
the sky tarred over
read me; I'm palm up,
my eyeballs crystallised, glazed closed
gypsy profit, anodyne toad

A sketch of a large number of many coloured helium balloons rising into the sky, all the strings tied around the necks of tiny hanged men. The caption:

'I've told my children that when I die, to release balloons in the sky to celebrate that I graduated. For me, death is a graduation.' Elisabeth Kübler-Ross

no way I'm gonna get wrinkled

A graph plotting the number of births in the world against the number of deaths over time, with the births far exceeding the deaths.

Another graph, of suicides by country, Japan leading the way.

'They tell us that suicide is the greatest piece of cowardice ... that suicide is wrong; when it is quite obvious that there is nothing in the world to which every man has a more unassailable title than to his own life and person.' Arthur Schopenhauer

'I decided to devote my life to telling the story because I felt that having survived I owe something to the dead and anyone who does not remember betrays them again.' Elie Wiesel

We crashed together but only I survived. I will not betray you Daniel.

Daniel. Max never spoke of him. Yet here he was, embedded in this book.

'Men fear death as children fear going into the dark.' Francis Bacon

Death in the carpet, reminds my every step. My days like ivory, hunt them down like ivory. Not for me the concrete life, castles of plastic dreams, moats of raw oil. Burn them all, go down burning.

Crucifixion
Suicide bombers
Extreme extreme sports
Consumerism
Capitalism
Addictions
Protest (Buddhist monks in Tibet)
Pharmaceuticals – death as side effect, overdose death.
Seppuku

'The timing of death, like the ending of a story, gives a changed meaning to what preceded it.' Mary Bateson

'I do not agree with what you have to say but I will defend to the death your right to say it.' You rock Voltaire!

'The reports of my death are greatly exaggerated.' Mark Twain (LOL!)

What thought could kill the thinker?
Can killing the thought kill the thinker?
The thought that precedes the act that kills the thinker.

The house of thoughts of death that Jack built. I miss Jack.
I miss Kraken. Kraken wakes to his death.
Do thoughts die with death?

Blown seed thoughts disperse from the dandelion mind

What do my bones think? Muscle reminisces
Limping lymph

My overblown gone-to-seed mind. Forget remembering
before I'm Alzheimered in.

ROAR!

How to Roger out of here.

'People fear death even more than pain. It's strange that they
fear death. Life hurts a lot more than death. At the point of
death, the pain is over. Yeah, I guess it is a friend.' Jim Morrison

You know better than we do, Jim, you Rider of the Storm.
Trailblazer.

Fears
1. Working for a bank.
2. Not being able to make art
3. Being with Tamsyn
4. Not being with Tamsyn
5. Sudoku
6. LOL! I meant Seppuku. (Shame killing belongs to the
   samurai; guilt killing belongs to Jesus)
7. Not making it, where it is incomprehensible.
8. The greedy trite trashy world. I DO NOT BELONG HERE.
9. That humans will eventually manage to destroy everything of beauty.
10. Pit bulls
11. Snotty partly-boiled eggs
12. Politicians, meetings, agendas, committees, develop-
    ment, fracking, nuclear power, the Dow Jones index,
    pyramid schemes, vomiting
13. I am afraid of how many fears I have if I start thinking. I
    think I will stop now.
14. Thoughtlessness. (Ha! How to not think in a not thought-
    less way.)

'There is no easy walk to freedom anywhere and many of us will have to pass through the valley of the shadow of death again and again before we reach the mountaintop of our desires.' Nelson Mandela

Desires:
1. Tamsyn and her amazing cunt

Were they using contraception? Carol worried.

2. To be on the cover of *Time* magazine for all the wrong reasons (LOL!)
3. To make like the Buddha and have no desires.

'Let us all be brave enough to die the death of a martyr but let no one lust for martyrdom.' Mahatma Gandhi.

What am I prepared to die for? Everyone should answer that question, every single fucking useless treadmill day people must stand grimacing in front of the mirror, brushing their holy teeth and ask themselves: WHAT AM I PREPARED TO DIE FOR?

An aerial drawing of a small estuary, in the style of Blake: on the sand two boys are lying with their torsos twisted so that each is holding the other's ankles forming a circular, mandala shape. The caption:

'For life and death are one, even as the river and the sea are one.' Khalil Gibran

'Death may be the greatest of all human blessings.' Socrates

'Remembering that I will be dead son is the most important tool I have ever encountered to help me make the big choices in life. Because almost everything – all external expectations, all pride, all fear of embarrassment or failure – these things just fall away in the face of death, leaving only what is truly important.' Steve Jobs.

Did you ever get to say sorry to all those slave labourers making Macs in China for you, Steve? But hey, thanks for my iPhone, it's awesome.

Carol's mouth had gone dry. That typo *dead son*!

What was this beautifully illustrated, poetic, disturbing amalgam of images, thoughts and quotes? She couldn't ask Max. Yet the drawer hadn't been locked. Would he take offence? Of course he would. He often seemed offended by her, ever since her relationship with Jack had ended, even before that, since Daniel had died.

That sentence *I miss Jack* stuck like a burr in her chest. Jack's loose, wild ways had been so attractive to Max. A risk-taker in all departments, a minesweeper looking for trouble, always thinking he'd be able to detonate it safely, at way too much cost to her. She had brought Jack into their lives at an age when Max had been vulnerable to his machismo. It was her fault.

She hadn't returned the notebook to the drawer but had put it in the linen cupboard in the passage, hidden away between folds of white sheets as though this violent manifesto could be soothed and rendered ineffectual by the soft fabric made for exhausted bodies, for rest, for dreams.

Finding the journal had precipitated the redecorating of his room as a matter of urgency, as though by rinsing the space through with light she could help to purge her son's mind of morbid thoughts.

Weren't most adolescents obsessed with sex and mortality? Max wasn't exactly adolescent any more, he was twenty-one, but they said that boys grew up more slowly than girls. Perhaps this preoccupation was a normal stage of development, especially in this devastating age – nuclear and environmental threats, AIDS, fiscal cliffs and general uncertainty. Carol felt her judgment skid and flounder. What was normal for young people nowadays?

She recalled wanting to throw herself in front of a train around that age when she'd gone home unexpectedly at lunchtime and had opened the front door of her flat to find her boyfriend Jeremy naked, his back to her, leaning forward over the seat of the sofa. He'd sounded as though he was in pain and had too many legs, the outer set bent the wrong way.

They'd belonged to Andrea, Carol's flatmate and best friend.

Killing herself was the only means she could imagine that would end the massive pain that had flared like a blowtorch in her chest. She'd wandered, stunned, away from the revelation and had found herself on the path next to the railway tracks at a point where the fence was broken. A train was up ahead, coming towards her, gathering speed as it pulled out of a station. It would have been so easy to fling her anguish down on the tracks and obliterate it but the train had passed by faster than she'd been able to act. By the time the next one came grinding down the tracks, she'd already lost her nerve.

She'd hidden Max's notebook away and had got down to scrubbing and painting the room, meaning to go back later and see what else his writings contained, yet she'd ended up avoiding it. For a week or two she had not even opened the cupboard to get a change of bedding.

Then Max had arrived unexpectedly and was standing in front of her demanding it.

'What workbook?' she feigned, hardly believing her own ears. 'I don't know anything about it.' Her damn voice had given her away. It came out tight and twisted, like a length of hangman's rope. A look came over Max's face, as though he was seeing his mother for the first time and didn't like what he saw. She wanted to grab the words back, stuff them back in, find other ones closer to the truth. But it was too late.

Other than Father Christmas and the Tooth Fairy, it was the first time she had ever lied to her son.

7.

Three years later, Max was back in her home, hurt, coughing and burnt. Carol realised with shock that she had concealed the workbook so well she had no idea what had happened to it. She had no recollection of destroying it, although she had been tempted to. The illustrations had been created with such care and craft she couldn't bring herself to consign it to the fire. She had been hoping that when Max was older she could pretend to find it behind the sofa and they could marvel and laugh at his crazy obsessions.

Yet here was her son, straight from hospital, having thrown himself right into the path of death. Better for the manifesto to have been burnt than her own son. The book had been a warning, yet at the time she had done nothing. Should she tell Dr Ndlovu? She was so ashamed of the machinations of her son's mind and of her own questionable actions.

She and Max needed to talk but she was afraid of what he might say and what might emerge from her own mouth. So she restrained herself, didn't wake him when she left for work and didn't phone home too often to see how he was. Fear stalked her. She was afraid of what he might do when left alone, afraid that he might leave if she was too fussy, afraid that he wouldn't ever go.

The burns were healing well; Max's epidermis was growing back in islands from his unaffected hair follicles, back over the shiny raw areas on his abdomen and arms. The plastic surgeon had decided that skin grafts were not going to be necessary, but there was a whole regimen they had to do daily to prevent infection and scarring.

'Don't ever do this to me again,' Carol said, trying to keep it light, as she buttered his wounds with cream.

A moment of silent irritation. 'I wasn't doing it to you.'

She couldn't stop herself. 'Max, don't be ridiculous, of course what you do affects other people. Especially me.'

'Yes, well, what you do affects me too but that never stopped you.'

She caught her breath, slapped. 'Like, like what? What are you referring to?'

'How long have you got?'

Had it been that bad? Surely not, he was deflecting. 'Careful what you say when you're right in front of me with your wounds exposed and I'm wielding a spatula.'

Max faked a smile. She applied clean dressings and stuck them in place. Took a deep breath. Tried again. 'No, really, tell me. I'm sure, I know, I mean, I must have made many mistakes as a parent. I'm sorry. The times I was too busy, you know, looking after other people, when my own son ...' To her surprise, her words got caught, her breath got stuck, there was a pricking in her eyes. She burst into tears.

'Stop it Ma.' Max sat up, awkward, embarrassed and pulled on his shirt. 'Don't get me wrong.'

'What?' she managed. 'What are you saying?' Just shut up and listen, she reminded herself. Try to listen, even if it's the hardest thing.

Her son shrugged. 'We all have to do what we have to do. Even if it affects other people. It's not personal.' He stood up. 'I'm going for a walk.'

When she got home from work that evening, Max had left. There was a knife and plate with a scatter of crumbs and a smear of jam on the kitchen counter and a note that read: 'I need to get back. I took the rest of the ointment and the dressings. Feeling better. Love you.'

This was a statement: he would no longer tolerate her mothering. He was going back to the flat he shared with that dreadful Hedley, where he dreamed his apocalyptic dreams, planned his next death stunt and where he slept with Tamsyn. Carol tried not to imagine the clanking it might entail.

42

Over the next few days he did not pick up her phone calls and only answered her text messages curtly, obliquely.

You okay, Max? she texted.

I'm cool, he answered.

Come for supper, tomorrow night?

Got something on. Speak soon.

He didn't initiate contact.

She phoned Peter. 'Please, talk to Max. I mean, he's been through phases of not communicating but now I'm scared.'

'Of what?'

'What might be going on in his head. What he might do next. He talked about "doing what he had to do".'

'Max's got a good head.'

'You think?'

'The police haven't followed through with charges. We can regard the episode as over.'

'Between you and me, I have half a mind to insist that the police do press charges. To discourage him.'

'He would never forgive you.'

'I would never forgive myself if something happened to him. Better to have a son in jail than dead or in ICU.'

'Have you ever been in a South African jail?'

Of course, Peter had been locked up overnight once, for drunken driving. There'd been shit on the floor and he'd been threatened by a man who had fortunately been even more inebriated than Peter and couldn't follow through. 'I didn't really mean … I don't know what to do. What should a responsible parent do when their nominally adult son is out of control?'

Peter sighed. 'My mother is still saying that about me and I'm in my fifties.'

'This isn't a joke.' She couldn't stop herself, tears spilt down her cheeks. 'Max is exactly the age when young men go psychotic or commit suicide.'

'Oh darling, now why is it that parents always imagine the worst? If my mother's fears came true I would have been dead and buried ten times over.'

'The psychiatrist didn't take it lightly. He put the fear of God into me.'

'Not only psychiatrists do that. Look at you, your job. You're trained to find out what's gone wrong, not what's right.'

'That's not true! Where did you get that idea?'

'My GP. Whenever I go see him, he always wants to stick his fingers into me, to see if he can find some lump or bump.'

Carol had to laugh. 'How can doctors be sure everything's fine if we haven't checked out whether there's a problem?'

'I rest my case.'

Some kernel in her could not assume Max was okay. A tight knot of regret kept her awake and tossing at night, trying to find a comfortable position for her restless, troubled mind. She would struggle out of bed in the mornings, exhausted, and force herself to go to work, trying to focus while patients went through their lists of complaints.

'It's been six months since he died,' Edna Ogilvy sobbed, 'and I can't get my life back together again. I miss him so much. Everything feels … empty, meaningless.'

She kept blowing her nose and then wiping her eyes with her snotty hanky. At this rate she would add conjunctivitis to her other emotional and physical problems but this wasn't the time to point that out. 'We used to do everything together. Everything! The years I had with him were the best of my life. Fourteen! Now I've no one to cook for and I don't feel like eating by myself. I even miss his snoring at night and the way he used to wake me up in the morning with little kisses.'

'Losing a husband after years of marriage can be one of the hardest things to come to terms with,' Carol sympathised.

Edna's eyes widened; then her brows came down. 'I've never been married, Dr Trehorne. I'm talking about my dog.'

After work, Carol drove to the beach. She left her shoes in the car, hurried across the rough tar and over the railway crossing to where her soles could feel the crunch and silk of the sand. At the sea's edge, the water flushed and bubbled soothingly over her feet. She strolled along, trying to remember what Katy had told her about staying present and how that can help – opening her senses to the roar and suck of the waves, the squabble and waddle of gulls, the cool and vivid shifts of blue in the ocean, the mill and snuffle of dogs.

An adolescent couple walked past, each harboured inside the arm of the other. The boy, in a t-shirt with sawn-off sleeves and a cap worn backwards, had a lightness in his step as he jived along. He glanced happily at the girl whose bright kikoi and bikini top made her look like she'd stepped out of an advert for travel to an exotic island. They were joined by sharing a set of earpieces.

She's pretending, Carol thought. She doesn't really like him, or his taste in music.

A group of women friends laughed and shrieked as they sauntered along, strappy sandals swinging from their hands. An elderly woman in a pink dress ran by stiffly on bandy legs, accompanied by a small boy who was determined to keep up with her.

A large Alsatian bounded towards her, tail wagging. As a child she had been pushed over and bitten by a neighbour's dog; immediately she tensed up, lifting her hands to remove them from the possibility of sharp teeth. The animal kept coming and shoved his germ-infested nose into her groin. Carol twisted her torso away from the invasion of the snout. 'Bugger off!' she hissed, flapping and scowling, looking around for an owner, someone to take responsibility. The dog cocked his head, then trotted off, losing interest, joining a couple up ahead who were deep in conversation; the woman bending briefly to caress the animal's head.

Other than a bald man sprinting past in his Lycra skins, she was the only one by herself. Mostly she enjoyed being alone but today she would have liked company. Anyone. Max. Even Jack, just for a walk. But with Jack, one thing always turned into another. His presence was like the sea, making her lose her footing and sweeping her along. No, she wouldn't be stepping into Jack's current again if he ever reappeared.

She took out her cell phone, rang Katy. It went immediately

onto voicemail. Busy, busy Katy. It was Wednesday, so Peter was at his pottery class.

Carol rolled up her long pants and waded through the brown stream running from the wetlands across the sand and into the sea. Her eyes turned towards the dunes near the railway line. This specific location had a scene embedded in it that was on permanent replay, one that she was unable either to delete or alter. How she wished she could wander past, unconcerned and innocent, seeing only the undulation of the dunes topped with a sparse straggle of vygies and grasses, with the brown water meandering past below. She always felt compelled to stop and find something, an offering of sorrow, also of gratitude, and place it at the site. At the approximate site, as the shape of the dunes had shifted in the intervening years.

She found a brittle twist of dry kelp and a flat stone that felt pleasantly oily to the rub of her thumb as she held its shape in her palm, warm from the sun, like smooth skin. She pushed her feet into the soft sand, one step at a time, until she stood before the rise of the dunes. A small square of blue lay discarded next to a tuft of grasses; it was torn packaging that had housed a condom, used. Life carrying on at the site of death. She carefully placed the pebble and kelp on the sand, and spent a moment deciding on the arrangement, how the kelp might be positioned so that it would speak to the stone. Heavy, heavy, the memory still weighed in her. 'Oh, Daniel.'

If she felt this bad, how was it for Max?

She'd forgotten to tell Dr Ndlovu.

'You need a holiday.' Peter squeezed a small quarter of lemon into his tomato juice and added a dash of Worcestershire sauce. He had been on the wagon again for over a year. 'When last did you take leave?'

'September.'

'That wasn't a holiday! You stayed at home and kept your cell phone on. Your patients still had you at their beck and call, day and night.'

Truth was, Carol didn't know what to do with leave. Work

was her anchor. 'Okay, I'll take off if you come away with me. Greece, or Mexico.' She knew she was safe.

'You know I can't fly.'

'Do you really want to die having never set foot in an airplane? Or on a different continent? The world's a big place, Peter. We could go to the Royal Albert Hall to see Lang Lang, or New York City to hear Lou Reed.'

'Lou's dead.'

'Well, you know what I mean. Someone terrific.'

'I'm hyperventilating just thinking about it.'

'From fear, or excitement? You have your wires crossed. You've mistaken excitement for anxiety.'

'I came here to talk about your problems, not mine. Other people's problems are much easier to solve.' Peter shifted the vase of irises he'd brought her until it stood centred on the coffee table.

'I'll give you a big dose of Phenergan. Knock you right out at the start of the flight. Put you in an aisle seat. If you come round you can pretend you're driving along on a bus and that we've never even left the ground.'

'Scotch works better than antihistamines but you wouldn't allow that.'

'Oh Peter, life is so short, why do we spend it stressing out so much of the time? It cuts across the lovely time we could be having. Most of my patients are worrying themselves into their own graves.'

'It's a rev. Feeling afraid is better than feeling dead. Or bored.'

'I'm afraid for Max, that's nothing to do with avoiding boredom.'

'You sure? I think you're bored.'

'I'm not bored! My life is full and interesting. Interesting enough. For God's sake! I just care about what happens to my son.'

'If you care about Max, leave him alone. He'll stop running away from you if you stop chasing after him.'

'I'm not chasing him. It's *normal* for a mother to want to know how her child is doing.'

'You're too much. Some parents are too little but you, you're way too much.'

'Well that's fucking unhelpful. How can I be who I'm not?'

Peter went to the door and lit a cigarette, standing with one foot inside and one outside, imagining that the smoke would choose the outdoors. 'Take up pottery,' he suggested, picking at a flake of paint peeling off the door frame.

'Pottery! What's that got to do with it?'

'Take your mind off Max, put it into something of your own.'

'Why pottery, of all things?'

'It's soothing, making something from the earth. You could come to my class, Wednesday evenings, try it out.'

Carol shook her head. 'Don't have the time.'

After Peter had left, Carol sat in the kitchen and poured herself a large glass of cold white wine. How could Peter say she was too much? She always felt as though she had not given Max enough.

Bored! How dare he. It was Peter who was bored and projecting it onto her.

The wine was delicious. It flushed into her chest, made her head feel lighter. The edges of her mind were blurring in a pleasant way. She didn't know how anyone could live without alcohol.

8.

The next day during lunch her cell phone rang. Katy. 'Have you seen the interview with Max?'

'Where?'

'In the latest *Art Africa* magazine.'

Carol's heart sank. It was no use pretending she had seen it. 'Actually, no. No, I don't think so.'

'I'll bring it over tomorrow evening. What time do you finish work?'

Carol couldn't wait that long. She made it down to the bookshop and back in time for her 2:30 patient. She only had enough time to see Max's self-immolation piece on the cover, entitled: *Burning Man*. The interview was the main feature. It would have to wait until she was through with her patients for the afternoon.

A young man was waiting in the procedure room. 'Doctor, I have a headache and a feeling of water running down the left side of my chest. Down here.' He showed her, pressing his fingers into her rib cage right next to her breast. 'My mother says I might be having a heart attack. Am I having a heart attack?' His eyes searched hers anxiously, trying to read his future.

Her job frequently boiled down to reassuring people that they were fine when they thought they were dying. Why was it that people imagined all kinds of life-threatening diseases? Carol wondered as she glanced at the ECG which she'd known would be normal. The worried well. Why, she wondered, do we use our imaginations in such pointless ways?

Why hadn't her son informed her that he was being interviewed for the art journal? Was this the piece written by that awful journalist at the hospital? It was humiliating to find out from other people.

After work she took the back roads home, barely stopping at the stop streets, breaking the speed limit. She ran in, poured herself a whisky, sat on the sofa and opened the mag to see what her son was prepared to tell the world in print but not say face to face to his own mother.

BURNING MAN: TREHORNE TAKES OUR SKINS OFF

Performance artist Max Trehorne fuses Hollywood stunts, political protest, xenophobic attacks, chemical warfare and climate change in his work. Zolani Mangcu *interviews.*

ZM: Your art follows the tradition of practitioners like Steven Cohen, who make provocative visual statements in public spaces about vulnerability, risk, prejudice and death.

MT: Yeah, Cohen's work has been an influence. Also Biswas, Stelarc, Blaine. And Acord.

ZM: Acord?

MT: James Acord. He was this awesome American sculptor and performance artist, the only private individual who managed – after years of wading through bureaucracy – to get a licence to own and handle radioactive material. He had this huge pile of paperwork, all the forms and red tape he'd had to endure to get the licence. He actually put all that in one of his pieces, the paper trail showing the performance necessary to get inside the cloak of security and secrecy in the nuclear industry. Life as art. He's dead now. Weird thing is he didn't die of cancer. Committed suicide in his sixties.

ZM: As Acord worked with radioactivity, you work with fire?

MT: Radioactivity and fire are two natural elements that humans harness. They give us heat and light but we also use them for things like warfare and protest. I'm using various beliefs and materials as tools, sliding along the interface between life and death, sort of like a rock climber. I'm interested in how we generate beliefs, literally create them, then use these beliefs to create other stuff, out of our surroundings. Either making life on our planet better, or else making death.

I need to point out here that I'm talking about all life, not only our neurotic, entitled, selfish preoccupation with human existence.

ZM: The body is central to your work.

MT: The body is central to all performance art.

ZM: Of course, but you aren't merely sitting around on a pedestal in a gallery picking your nose. You're risking your very existence.

MT: You know, performance art began as a reaction, an objection to the disgusting culture where great artworks are bought up by a few wealthy dudes to put on their dining room walls to impress people. The worth of those paintings – and sculptures too, of course – had nothing to do with the millions of bucks paid for them. It's a disgrace. They are lost to society. Government-run art galleries can't compete, they don't have the bucks. But no rich prick can own performance art and it's shown in public spaces, so absolutely anyone can view it, even if they're poor and have never been into a gallery. I want to throw up questions about who owns an artwork – but in this case the work is the body, the body is the canvas, or sculpture. Who owns the artist? Whose life is it, the one Max Trehorne happens to be living now? It's a question I have to answer but not only me. It's for all of us. What is my life about? What do I serve? Money? God? Power? Perfection? Truth? We're all going to die anyway, so I have to ask myself: what am I prepared to die for? As an axiom, what am I prepared to live for?

ZM: What are you prepared to live for, to die for?

MT: Ha! That is a work in progress, it is the central question that each of my performances tries to answer. Answer in part. Bite-sized chunks.

ZM: You ended up in hospital because of *Burning Man*. I'm going to ask you a really embarrassing question now but aren't you afraid of dying?

MT: (*Laughs*) This isn't about me. Working at the edge of death is risky but at least I'm engaging voluntarily, unlike most people. Society claims to be afraid of death but that's obviously not true. We love death, we're obsessed by it, we love to watch it in any form – on television, in the news and in movies – we slow down at accidents, we want to read about it in *You* magazine, we go and gawk at death in *Body Worlds*. Crime fiction sells better than any other genre, death sells newspapers. We couldn't get enough of those images of planes flying again and again into buildings. What are our addictions but slow suicide? Smoking, alcohol, food, never mind heroin. Isn't it crazy, that you can kill yourself with food? What is environmental degradation but our compulsion to destroy the source of life, to poison the food we eat, the water we drink? What are extreme sports and mid-winter polar expeditions but our need to live as closely to death as possible? The heat-repellent gel I used in *Burning Man* merely represents ambivalence.

ZM: Well, the images of *Burning Man* have gone viral. Your work is all over the net.

MT: I aim to make potent art, which necessarily includes spectacle. Movies and novels are becoming more and more gruesome. People want more violence, more blood, bigger explosions and car crashes to get their adrenalin going. Ironically, it's adrenalin that has the potential to wake us up, that might make us get out of our cinema seats and recliner chairs and take action.

ZM: Already there's a backlash, people worried that you might spark copycat performances by people who don't know what they are doing.

MT: That's ridiculous. I'm the copycat. I'm using cultural and political forms of suicide and murder that already exist and have for centuries. Also self-harm, which includes harming our planet, our life source. I'm performing these cultural and political forms of death to draw attention to the way we live, or don't live and the ways in which we die, or kill, but don't understand that's what we're doing.

ZM: Does *Burning Man* specifically reference Tibet? Do you have a political stance on China?

MT: Any thoughtful work of art should spark multiple associations, so yes, the protest staged by Buddhist monks is one of the cornerstones of the piece. Not many people are aware that over thirty monks self-immolated last year. They haven't given up after fifty-four years of brutal occupation. The culture is still saying no and trying to draw world attention to their situation. To answer your question, I don't aim to make propaganda that has one finger wagging in one direction only. Buddhists are not the only people who set themselves alight, Mozambicans in South Africa are not the only ones who are burnt alive. The practice, if I may call it that, goes way back, further back than Joan of Arc. Burning is a way of taking the skin off, showing what lies beneath any culture that encodes these atrocities, punishments and rituals. Fire is a particular form, it brings up ideas of the alchemical crucible. Acord was interested in how transmutation, central to alchemy, was applicable to science and art, the mysterious transformation of elemental materials in both radioactive decay and in creating a sculpture. He was a very moral man, who was not interested in wealth but in his own transformation. The true alchemists, he said, knew that the real lead was in their own hearts and only through the purity of the fire of motivation could they transform that lead into gold. Going the other way, it is also worth noting that when we burn, when any living thing burns, we are reduced to ash. That's all there is. Ash. You are ash, I am ash. My worst enemy, the person I love best, they are just ash.

ZM: Aren't you going to get some flak for not drawing a distinction between criminal xenophobic murder and legitimate political protest?

MT: Both acts are fuelled by desperation and rage. Both acts highlight the body, what can be done to it, in the name of something else.

ZM: So what can we expect next? Should we keep the fire extinguishers handy?

MT: Call in the whole fire department, dude! There are going to be some big events but they will involve other elements. (*Laughs*) Seriously, the real question should be: what should we expect of ourselves? We're all performers, whether we know it or not. From the time we're little kids, our parents teach us to behave in certain ways. What is that but a tight, collective performance? Society is a rigorous teacher and we tend to stick to the script, the paint-by-numbers and stay-inside-the-line rules. Even if we rebel, we usually do it in formulaic ways. What would our performances look like if we discovered who we really are, if we returned to our original choreography, the one we were born with before society interfered? That would be awesome, don't you think?

Carol closed the magazine. Confusion swelled in her chest. Her son was being acknowledged, his work was attracting attention, he was developing his career. He was being provocative, making people think. She should be proud of him.

She looked out of the window at the evening sky. The clouds were riding uniformly towards the west over the wetlands as if propelled by an invisible conveyor belt towards the apricot smear of the setting sun. Flocks of pied swallows were interleaving with clusters of weaver birds – the swarm and flare of airborne life asserting itself upon the evening. A commotion was starting up in the reeds as crowds of birds set up hierarchies and places to sleep, or as they checked in with each other after a day of foraging.

She'd always loved the early evening ritual of the birds. It soothed her by taking her out of herself. It was a reminder – life continues and flourishes without human beings, even despite them. There was something immensely reassuring in that.

But tonight she was filled with grief at the impermanence of the people and places she loved, by how little impact she had on things that mattered most to her. Her beloved son was on a self-destructive course – fire engines, he'd joked! – and all in the name of caring about the world.

The latest Delilah Bezuidenhout was on the table where she'd left it the other evening. She picked it up, found her place and dived in. She had only read nine pages but she knew that soon she'd be sucked along, racing through bloody hotel rooms with body parts in hat boxes and village weddings where the bride is late and no one worries until it gets dark, and then she's discovered hanging by her satin sash from the elevated blade of the forklift truck belonging to the groom.

9.

She'd almost given up, after ringing the buzzer three times, when Max's voice crackled through the speaker. 'Hi?'

'Hello, darling, I was passing and I thought –'

'Come on up.' She was pleased there was no hint of annoyance or ambivalence in his voice.

She climbed the stairs to the second floor and found him waiting at the front door of his horrid little flat. His hair was growing and he was starting a beard; perhaps the facial burn had made it painful to shave. 'Nice beard,' she smiled, rubbing her palm against her son's surprisingly soft pelt. Max wrapped his arms around her and kissed the top of her head, his little ritual since he'd grown tall enough to do so. It was affectionate; also a reminder.

'Come in.' He looked at the flat white box she was carrying. 'Ooh, is that what I think it is?'

Little ways to keep the door to her son's heart open. Carol stepped inside and into the kitchen and tried to find space for the milk tart in the clutter on the counter. 'I got it at that place down the road. It's still warm from the oven.'

He put the kettle on. 'Lucky I was at home.'

'Yes, well, you're hard to get hold of.'

'Things have been hectic.'

'Is Hedley here?'

'Nah, he's away on some photo assignment.'

A sink full of unwashed plates and cutlery. Carol forced her gaze away. It fell upon two dead flies and a cobweb in the corner of the windowsill. She had to restrain herself from hunting around for a hand broom and pan. 'What're you up to?' Trying for light.

'Same old. Doing my corrupt bit for society. Yesterday I had to fix up an Edwardian mansion in the Cotswolds.' Max worked for an online estate agency in the UK. His job was to touch up photographs of crumbling homes that were for sale to make them look more attractive before they were uploaded onto the website. The pay wasn't great but it dealt with the bills in the way art didn't.

His eyebrows had almost grown back. 'Let's see?' she said, gesturing towards his belly.

Max pulled up his t-shirt. Several large white blemishes with central scabs. 'Almost healed. Isn't the body awesome?'

'How's your chest?' He hadn't coughed once since she'd arrived.

'Still on that pump thing but it's a lot better.'

She still sometimes felt a wave of painfully pleasurable astonishment that this living being had arrived in the world through her body. 'I saw your interview,' she ventured.

'Which one?'

'There are others? You didn't tell me –'

'Ma, you've got that tone,' he warned, in a tone of his own.

What tone? She was doing her best, couldn't he see?

'In *Art Africa*.'

He threw two teabags into two mugs with exaggerated force and poured boiling water onto them. The late afternoon light coming through the kitchen window caught his temple and cheek, and the curve of his upper lip with its light scrub of beard. He was exquisite to her, an Adonis. He was the kind of man she would have been attracted to when she was a young woman. She wanted to file this exact picture: her son bending forward slightly over the mugs, squeezing the teabags between forefinger and teaspoon; but already he had turned and the moment had gone and her memory would fail her as it had with all the other moments throughout Max's young life where she had watched him with amazement – this child who had something to do with her, her lucky mistake, her precious error. Where had the traces of all that huge, mundane, revolving wheel of mothering life gone? She was left with this, only this.

Now he seemed annoyed. 'So?' Max gave her one of his intense, challenging looks as he handed her the mug.

'Well done. It was a good interview.'

'Yeah, well, it's always a compromise. The artwork should speak for itself and then you have to go and explain it.'

'I suppose it's a hard balance, creating a work that stands alone. People are always interested in the story behind the story.'

'Yeah but then they try to pin my work onto something in my past, you know, make it about me.'

A smudge of pink on the drinking edge of her mug. Lipstick. Carol wiped it off with her thumb, turned the mug around and drank gingerly from the other side. 'You still seeing Tamsyn?' she asked, not wanting to embark on the real reason she was here, not yet. She was also hoping there was a different woman in his life.

'On and off.' Max's tone discouraged further questions. He picked a knife out of the sink and wiped it clean with a washing-up cloth that needed a wash itself

'You'd know by now whether it was going to work.'

Max stopped hacking two wedges out of the round of milk tart and stared at her, the knife in his hand smeared with light yellow custard. He looked sexy and dangerous, like a chef in one of those cooking programmes. 'You haven't bothered to get to know Tamsyn. She's a real survivor and I happen to admire her.'

He slid the knife under one of the pieces and offered it to her. It was so fresh it was threatening to crumble.

'Can I have a plate?'

Max opened the cupboard a little too brusquely and pulled a plate out with a clatter. She'd annoyed him again.

Carol went through to the lounge with her tea and tart, feeling like a cumbersome old drudge.

The room was a mess, and sombre despite the bright afternoon sun because the apartment faced straight into the back of another block. She reached for the grubby switch on the wall and the bulb hanging on a wire from the middle of the ceiling lit up with intense light. Rolls of paper lay stacked in one corner, boxes in another, old takeaway food packaging littered the coffee table. A trestle table, loaded with pencils, crayons, more paper. A laptop, with a screensaver of a severed head bouncing around the screen, leaving splashes of blood each time it collided with an edge. It was a photograph of Max's head.

'Max!'

'Isn't it great? I'm getting lots of orders. You want one for your computer at work? Send me a mug shot. I won't charge you.'

'You did that?'

'Yep.'

'Sometimes I think your mission in life is to upset your mother.'

'It's working?' Max had the grace to smile. 'Then I can retire,'

Also on the table was a large unfinished drawing, in pastel, a take-off of Blake's painting of God, with his divided beard, looking down on the earth. In this version, the earth was replaced by a large and scored medicinal tablet. Propped up in a corner of the room was a round placard, mounted on a pole. Concentric circles were painted on it, like a dart board with a central bull's eye. A string of tiny Christmas lights was affixed to the placard in the shape of the peace sign.

'What's this?'

'A prop.' An answer like a door closing.

Jack's old guitar that he'd given Max was standing against the wall, one string snapped and hanging slack onto the floor.

A poster that she'd not seen before, of a man with a beatific face – was it Martin Luther King? Yes it was; underneath was a quote, attributed to him: '… *there are some things in our society, some things in our world, to which we should never be adjusted.*'

Next to it was a large drawing that she recognised as one of Max's from art school: the crucified Christ, tied with His arms above His head to an enormous Coke bottle. Affixed to the other wall was a poster, torn in one corner, of a painting by Hieronymus Bosch, with its torture and mayhem. A blue yoga mat with curled edges lay on the parquet floor. Two skateboards, a beach towel, a bookcase made of planks and bricks, stacked with art books and newspapers.

Carol wanted to sit down. She had to move a mound of clothing to one side to make space on the sofa. She immediately started sneezing and had to fish in her bag for a tissue. Max sat down cross-legged opposite her on the yoga mat.

He gestured vaguely at the mess. 'As I said, things have been hectic.'

'Is Rosie still coming on Thursdays?' She could almost see the germs crawling through the dust.

'Nah, can't afford her right now.'

The silence stiffened. It's not my business anymore, she reprimanded herself. 'You've taken up yoga?'

'What's with the inquisition?'

'I'm asking about your life, Max, just catching up. I noticed the mat.'

'Meditation. It helps me prepare.'

For what? she wanted to know. She might as well go straight to the point. 'Are you … planning another … performance?'

Max took a large bite of milk tart. A few crumbs caught in the beard at the side of his mouth. He chewed, swallowed. Then he sighed, shrugged. 'At some point.' Wiped his mouth with the back of his hand.

It was unbearable. 'What are you going to do? What now? Max I hope …'

'Ma, I can't talk to you about my work.'

'Why ever not?'

Max tilted his head. 'Think of it as a generation thing. *Your* mother didn't understand you either.'

'Of course I understand you!'

'Obviously not.'

'Maybe … maybe I know something about you that you don't.'

'Jeez, really?'

'Well, I am your mother.'

'So let me into the picture.' He pushed the last of the tart into his mouth and leaned back on his outstretched arms, daring her.

'You're someone who wouldn't hurt a fly.'

'I don't hurt flies. Flies are not the problem. We are in agreement.'

'You hurt yourself! You hurt me.'

'You also put your mother through hell when you were young.'

'Oh, please, you can't compare this … this is completely different –'

'Every generation is different, so?'

'I wasn't trying to … to … kill myself!'

'Weren't you?'

'Of course not.'

'What about the heavy smoking, the drugs?'

'That's ridiculous, you can't kill yourself –'

'When you rode with your crazy drunk boyfriend on his bike over Ou Kaapse Weg and nearly crashed? And those times you went jogging at midnight, at Varsity, just because you weren't going to let any murderer or rapist stop you doing whatever you liked, whenever you liked?'

She should never have told him about her youthful escapades. 'Well that was stupid, I know that now and the whole point of telling you all those stories was so *you* don't have to be. Look, Max, don't misunderstand me, you're doing amazing work and getting recognised for it but it doesn't have to be so … so extreme.'

'Give me some credit Ma. I've actually spent a long time thinking about these things, it's way more complex. Taking risks, stupid ones, even calculated ones, when we get into trouble, you know, when we get really close to death, as close as possible, I reckon it's because it makes us feel alive. Extreme sports, endurance artists for example. Everywhere, people are trying to go deeper, higher. Look at David Blaine, training himself to do crazy things like hold his breath underwater. He got to over seventeen minutes. Seventeen minutes! You'd be lucky to get to two! What for? He's chasing death. He's had liver failure, kidney failure, breaking records, doing stuff like being locked up in a suspended box for over sixty hours. How about that old dude, Ranulph Fiennes, trying to lead the first expedition across the Arctic in deep winter? Even with all his financial backing, he couldn't be sure they'd pull him out before he froze to death.'

'They're crazy, that's not what I want for you!'

'What do you want for me Ma? I'm not a two-and-a-half kids and a picket fence kind of person. I'm never going to work a nine-to-five and then go home and read cheap crime novels.

'Say I was the best freediver in the world, or base jumper, or the fastest downhill skier, you'd feel different, you'd be damn proud of me.'

'I *am* proud of you. I'm also sick with worry!' How on earth had the conversation got to be about downhill skiing?

'I'm working in the same territory as the athletes only in art instead of sport and that's a hundred times better because it's not only about skill. Art has something to say. It shows the world, look, this is who we are. This is what we're doing to the world, to ourselves. I'm a serious artist, Ma, you'd better get used to it.'

'What if your next stunt goes wrong? Like last time, only worse?' She should stop now, but the words kept coming. 'Besides the fact you could … *die*,' she could barely say the word, 'do you ever stop to think about all the resources you waste, the people you put out? Ambulances, hospitals, medication … there are people who really need these things. When did you become so selfish, Max, so self-absorbed?'

'Fuck it, Ma, that's part of the performance.' Max stood up, started pacing. 'This is *exactly* why I promised myself not to speak to you about this.' He stopped and turned to her. 'I'm working on holy ground, trying to evoke what's sacred where those who've been here before – your generation, your parents' generation –' he cut across the air with his hand to underline his point, 'have spoiled and wasted. D'you really think politicians who declare war, or even those people – your patients – who smoke and drink and drug themselves to death, consider the resources they waste?'

'I don't care about politicians!'

'You should, they're messing up the world.'

'I care about you, Max, putting yourself in extreme danger on purpose, knowing full well what you're doing, it's not natural –'

'It's an old practice, an ancient one, so it must be natural. People have been killing themselves in protest –'

'Suicide's a taboo for very good reason.'

'… and killing other people to prove some point, for a hell of a long time.'

'There is absolutely no point worth proving if –'

'Listen to *me*, just *listen* for a change, if you care about who I am *at all*.'

'I'm your mother, Max, I gave you life, it's a precious thing, not to be squandered. I'm also a doctor, I know something about consequence.'

Max threw up his hands in defeat. 'This is so fucking point-less, you're a fucking doctor and you don't even know how to listen. You're only here to batter me with your arguments until I agree with you.' He turned and left the room; she was afraid that he was going to storm out of the flat but she heard the toilet seat go up and the stream of his urine drilling into the bowl.

Of course she knew how to listen! All day, every day, that's what she did. It was hard, though, to be quiet in the face of what her son was saying.

The space that lay between them was awful to her – cold, impenetrable, a void in the place where, when he was a young child, there had been a carefully constructed refuge for them both. Waste and rubble now lay at her feet. She wanted to run to him, to beg and plead. She knew she had to force herself to sit on her emotional hands, pretend that she was all right.

Max came back into the room but stayed standing, as though waiting for her to go. Had he washed his hands? It was too late now to bring him up properly.

'I'm … sorry. I'm listening. I promise.' Carol's eyes were pricking, her throat had two sharp dowels driven in on either side but she would stopper herself up.

Max sat on the yoga mat, then lay down and closed his eyes. From one of the adjacent flats came the sound of a TV going on; muffled talking, canned laughter. A siren started up, piercing the hum of traffic, then it moved off somewhere; danger and alarm crouched on every street corner.

Carol began to think Max'd forgotten she was there, or had fallen asleep, when he started speaking. 'I only have one life, Carol, and one body.' He opened his eyes, turning his intense gaze on her. 'This. Is. It.' He splayed his arms and opened his hands, to demonstrate. 'With it comes a fuck-load of responsibility. To the rest of life, to the whole earth. Actually, although you are not going to like this, d'you know what's the best thing that I can do for our magnificent planet and for all the non-human species we wipe out every single day because of our abundantly grotesque ignorance? The very best thing I can do? Commit suicide.' He sliced a hand across his throat in a melodramatic gesture but his eyes were two calm pools.

'Don't worry, I'm not going to top myself,' Max continued, 'not on purpose, but I am going to spend the gift of my life in a considered way. I really don't care if I live one more year, or until I'm a hundred. What matters is that I make good use of this strange thing of bodily life that most of us inhabit with such disregard, such boredom and waste, such perversion.'

Max studied the ceiling for a moment. He gave a deep breath, pushed himself up in a long, graceful gesture, came over and flopped down on the sofa next to her. He put an arm around her shoulders, gave her a brief squeeze. 'You know, arguments don't persuade anyone. Take what's happening right here, between you and me, for example, or politics, shit, politics is riddled with lies, power plays, corrupt agendas. Art is the only honest way forward, the only way I can apply myself. Forget worrying Carol, I intend staying alive, even while I'm taking on difficult stuff around death.' He sighed, slipped his hand into his pants and scratched his balls. 'Trust me. I am on a trajectory that started long ago. I can't stop now, even if I wanted to. The thing is, the thing you need to get your head around, is that I don't want to stop, it's not an option.'

Carol found her stifled voice. It squeaked out. 'I love you, Max.'

Max snorted, removed his arm. 'Yeah. Love. I'm not sure there're many people who have a fucking clue what that means.'

10.

The hill went on and on, relentless. Carol's heart was galloping around in her chest way too fast, crashing into her struggling lungs. Her face was about to burst and her thighs were painful jelly. She had to stop.

'I can't,' she gasped, bending and resting her hands on her knees so her flailing lungs could catch up. 'I'm about … to … have a heart attack,' she shouted after her disappearing friend.

Katy turned around, jogged back down and pulled up next to Carol. 'Nonsense.' She kept running on the spot, her ponytail swinging and flicking with each trot. 'You only start to get fit when you feel the pain.'

'I'm not … into pain,' Carol panted. 'Gimme morphine.' She was sick to death of Katy's trim little body bouncing up and down alongside her rather more flabby one. Katy's figure, together with what Carol thought of as her 'young hair' – dyed and streaked a variegated blonde – allowed her to pass as a thirty-year-old at a distance. When one came up close, the lines that were caught in the skin around her neck and at the corners of her eyes were a surprising contrast.

'Exercise is the best stress reliever. Better than Valium. Scientifically proven, you were the one who told me that, years ago. C'mon gal, you can do it.'

'Why have I … only got … irritating friends?'

'I'm not as irritating as Peter,' objected Katy, punching the air with quick fists like a boxer in training. 'I hope he's not going to get drunk at your birthday party. He's either falling all over the place, or he's neurotically straightening place mats.'

'He's not … drinking anymore. Besides, I'm not having a party.' Carol declared.

Katy frowned. 'What do you mean, no party? You have to have one.'

'No I don't.'

'But it's your big five-oh!'

'So?'

'Ritual is important. We're marking time, celebrating milestones.'

'I'm just treading water.'

'You're depressed, that's all. It's been a hell of a year.' Katy had stopped running on the spot and was looking at her strangely.

'What?'

'Come on! Let's go, we're nearly at the top. Exercise is good for menopausal mood swings too. Gets the circulation going, scrapes all your inner thinking tube linings clean.' Why did Katy insist on saying ridiculous things like that when she *knew* Carol was a doctor? 'You don't want to end up like your mother did,' Katy continued. 'Now *that* would give you something to get depressed about.'

That got to Carol, although many years of playing tennis hadn't saved her mother from the creeping tendrils of dementia. Carol gathered up her muscles into a slow jog, hoping that the memory of yesterday's overindulgent slice of velvet cake with butter icing would kick in and motivate her butt uphill. The world was trundling, trundling past, as she jogged through it. It was all about pushing through, pushing, pushing. Through to what? At what cost? Her left Achilles heel was burning. It was probably about to snap.

'What's up?' Katy worried. 'Did I say something wrong?'

Carol shook her head and pointed at her lungs, using unfitness as an excuse not to talk, not wanting to admit to her despondency. So instead she had to listen to the latest episode of Katy's family saga. Her youngest daughter had recently married a Muslim and had converted. Thing was, he already had a wife. Jessica, now renamed Ilhaam, was the second. There might be more to come.

Katy had been characteristically undiplomatic, announcing

66

her extreme disapproval to both of them before the wedding and then was mortified when she had not been invited. Now her daughter was pregnant with her first grandchild and not speaking to her.

'Who could have predicted this?' The more upset Katy became, the faster she ran. 'Jessica had everything going for her, everything! Brains, talent, a liberal upbringing, looks, and now she's thrown her life away on some … some patriarchal maniac, some flipping religious bullshit!' Carol was struggling to keep up, her heart roaring like a waterfall in her head. 'When our kids were babies the biggest problem was how to get them to shut up so we could watch *The Bold and the Beautiful* and how much medication we could shove down them to knock them out for the night without killing them. Who'd have thought things could get worse, that they'd turn into these wilful monsters. Ilhaam! For Christ's sake! She told me it means intuition, but her bloody intuition has gone straight out the window.'

They had at last reached level ground and were approaching a bench that overlooked the sea. Carol made it to the seat and collapsed. 'Come on, Katy, Max and Jessica … they aren't monsters.'

Katy settled her pretty bottom down next to her friend and was about to respond when something out in the bay caught her eye. 'Oh, look!' A scrape of cloud drew attention to the vivid blue expanse of sky; the far mountains were blurred with summer haze. A helicopter bit its way through the air. A regatta was underway in the distance, flocks of white sails driven across the water by wind, chasing victory. But Katy was pointing to something else – the sea near the harbour entrance where a large black shape had heaved itself up out the water and was crashing back down, breaking the surface open with a white slash. The last of the migrating whales, saying goodbye before returning south.

Carol never tired of watching them. It was a highlight of this time of the year. 'She has a baby with her!' Underwater, a smaller dark shape was following alongside the great bulk of the mother. Like the birds, these great cycles of nature helped to put human travail into perspective and allowed her terror to shrink into something more manageable.

'You think whales have problems with their young?' mused Katy. She tucked her chin in and put on a ponderous, whale-type voice. '"No my little tadpole, you'll mate with that no-good bum whale from the wrong side of Antarctica over my dead body. He'll drag the family name down." Or, "You absolutely cannot go to that beach party tonight with Eddie. I know his type. He'll leave you high and dry."' In a high voice, '"But Ma-a-a, he spouts all the right stuff!"'

Carol laughed, then sniffed and wiped her nose on the bottom of her t-shirt. 'What is one supposed to do? How can a parent stand by and watch the person they love best make all the wrong decisions?'

'You're asking me? Flipping hell, girl. To think, I used to have the answers for everything. Maybe we should phone Oprah. What would she say, d'you think?' In an exaggerated Oprah-voice: 'We all made problematic choices when we were young and yet not all of them turned out wrong.'

'Some do turn out wrong, very tragically wrong. How can we tell when to worry and when to relax?'

'I blame Jack for the situation you're in with Max.'

'You were always so critical of him.'

'Come on, girlfriend! There was a lot to be critical of.'

'A complicated man,' Carol had to admit, also wanting to defend how lovely he had been. 'I wonder where he is now, if he's still hanging off a cliff somewhere.' She remembered the worry when Jack and Max had gone off to the mountain and were late coming home and the relief when they arrived, sweaty and dirty with scrapes and sunburn. The sounds of the two of them sitting on the stoep sorting out their gear, karabiners clinking, the slap of rope. How Jack would share his beer with Max, only fourteen, fifteen, at the time. Their talk of routes, traverses and planning their next adventure. 'He was also very good with Max, Katy. Brought him back in more ways than one. Maybe you've forgotten how Max disappeared inside himself for a while and sometimes literally went walkabout after Daniel died. Goodness, how do we survive these things, as parents? Learning to rock climb gave Max a big adrenalin rush, plugged him back into life again. Maybe the best we can do as parents is to hold on to our hats.'

'Darling, I don't even *own* a hat, precisely because living directly in the path of the Cape Town South Easter, a hat needs holding on to. I can't possibly devote my hands to that because they're already full of tissues and antidepressants and a cell phone that's on permanent redial for my therapist, all because of my bloody kids. I'd only just recovered from Frank's cancer scare and Martin's drug-induced hallucination, when my daughter marries a religious nut who makes her cover her beautiful hair.

'I'd like to believe that everything will work out in the end but how can it? Odds are Jessica will eventually fall out of that crazy condition we call "love", the scales will fall from her eyes, she'll get the hell in with her husband and his concurrent wives and get divorced, with all the pain and drama that involves but it'll be too late for the next generation who'll already be all fucked up. How do you explain it? She had a perfect childhood.'

Carol thought back on Jessica's excessively controlled home environment and decided to say nothing.

Her friend stood up. 'C'mon, let's finish this damn run and go get a hit of caffeine.'

Carol got back onto her legs, her Achilles tendon twinge-ing. 'Only as far as the next steps down. I have my health to consider.'

Katy was getting back into her stride. 'The bottom line is that it's all a fuck-up.' She swung her arms widely, to include the entire world. 'All of it. If you start from that premise, you can have no expectations. You have to accept that that's the way things are. Then, if anything gets better, it's a bonus.'

11.

As Carol walked out of her consulting room, two small boys came running and shrieking down the passage. 'You can't run in here,' she told them, stepping into their path to bar their way. 'There are sick people in the clinic. You might knock someone down.'

'Stephan! Jordy!' A burly man in police uniform came striding after them. 'If you boys are naughty, this doctor here is going to give you a big injection.'

'Good morning Ernie.' Carol shook his hand. 'Please don't say things like that,' she appealed. 'Those comments make children scared of us, which makes our job much harder.' As she led them into her room, she contemplated how people used to control their children with warnings of God's all-seeing eye or of burning in hell but nowadays they threatened them with the doctor's needle. Were God and hell no longer so scary, or is medicine the new religion?

'What's the problem?' she asked the father, trying to ignore the children as they ran and rolled around on the circular pattern on the carpet like two untrained, clumsy puppies.

'Stephan's got sinus. He's been very sick since Tuesday.'

'We all have sinuses,' Carol explained. 'Are you talking about hay fever, meaning allergy? Or infection perhaps?'

Ernie stared at her, puzzled. 'You're the doctor.'

Carol pulled a slow breath into her lungs and tried again. 'Does he have a fever? What colour is his snot?'

Very-sick Stephan grabbed the back of her chair, spread his feet on the swivel mechanism at the base, then leaned back as though on a windsurfer, giving her a violent jerk. His brother was busy opening the drawers of her metal cabinet and fiddling with her containers of cotton wool with his grubby fingers. 'Please stop that you two. Come and sit down,' she told them sternly. 'There are dangerous things in this room that could hurt you. Besides, these are my things. I don't come into your bedroom and take your stuff without asking.'

The older boy, Stephan, stopped jerking her chair and stared at her, impressed by this thought but Jordy, oblivious, had pulled her weighing scale out from under the examination couch and was jumping up and down on it, delighted to discover that this caused a crunching sound as the dial swung wildly.

Carol stood and grabbed his arm. 'I said, stop that!' Jordy looked up with hard, belligerent eyes and stuck his tongue out at her. The appendage was a bizarre shade of blue, dyed by some chemical colourant that was probably contributing to his bad behaviour.

The father began to laugh. 'He's such a little terror.'

'You know what?' Carol decided, bending over the kid, her fingers still clenched around his arm, 'I lied to your Dad. There *is* a big injection in my drawer that I keep for children like you, the ones who don't behave.' Jordy's eyes widened.

Stephan was at the basin turning both taps on hard and pumping gouts of pink hand disinfectant out of the liquid soap mechanism. 'I'm a good boy,' he announced proudly, washing his hands. 'Can I have a sweetie?'

Carol's next appointment was a home visit. She was relieved to escape the surgery, still simmering with anger and shame about the way she'd handled the two children. They probably had ADHD. Combined with ineffectual parenting, it would set them up for a very difficult life. The practice of family medicine, her lecturer used to say, is filled with countless missed opportunities beyond the dispensing of tablets. She had failed yet again in her work, in her insight about parenting and parents. By extrapolation, she must have failed in her own mothering. Both jobs – doctoring and mothering – were too hard for ordinary mortals. The consequences were enormous when one got it wrong.

One day she'd open a coffee shop. Then all she'd have to deal with were problems like milk going sour.

She parked outside a small suburban house surrounded by an overgrown garden. Hilda still lived in her own home at the age of ninety-one. Until a few years ago she'd led an independent life after the death of her husband, gardening, playing tennis, painting botanical specimens. Then she'd taken a tumble over an uneven brick in a path and had broken her hip. The operation had been a success but she'd been left slow and a little confused after the surgery. Micro-vascular infarcts, no doubt. The fall had also damaged her confidence and Carol knew from experience that confidence is not as easy to restore as a hip.

'She won't eat,' the carer informed her as she let her into the house. 'Just sips of fluid. Stubborn old bat. Refused to come and see you at the surgery. I took a sample of urine to the chemist but it was clear.'

'Good thinking. Any other symptoms?' Carol asked. 'Cough? Constipation? Does she have a fever?'

Jenny shook her head. 'She tells me she's not sleeping well at night, then she nods off during the day. I think she's depressed.'

Carol went through to the bedroom and found Hilda sitting on a faded upholstered armchair in the dappled sun that filtered through her window. Outside in an alcove shaded by a wild olive tree, stood a bird bath, glistening with specks of light. 'You've just missed them,' Hilda said, looking up. Her eyes, blue and excited as a child's, shone out of a face full of drapes and folds of soft skin.

'Who?'

'The sunbirds and the witogies. They were right here, in the water, giving me a most splendid display. Look!' She gestured towards the ceiling where prisms, reflected off the water, shimmered like a light show. 'It's always like this, this time of the day in summer.'

Carol sat down next to her and took her hand, all bone and mottled skin. 'You're an inspiration, Hilda. I should spend more time quietly sitting and watching the birds in my garden.'

'Well, there comes a time that's all you're good for.'

'Jenny tells me you're not eating.'

'I told her not to bother you.' Hilda picked at a thread on her skirt. Her hand had a tremor Carol hadn't noticed before.

'It's not a bother. You're one of my favourite patients, but don't tell the others.' This raised a small smile. 'Are you nauseous? Or feeling ill in any way?'

Hilda looked at her long and hard. 'I'm not sick, Carol. I'm just finished with all this. We are not meant to live so long. Sorry to say, but you medics have not done the world a favour by keeping the old going. It's enough now.'

'Jenny thinks you're depressed.'

Hilda lifted her hand and swept any ideas of Jenny's away. 'I'm not depressed, only weary. So very weary. Now, if you were kind, you would give me a little something to help me go.'

'You know I can't –'

'Oh, I know, I know. But you've got to promise me.'

'What's that?'

'Not to put up drips, force feed me. That sort of thing.'

'You have a living will in your folder and of course I'll honour that. You still have a lot of life in you, Hilda, don't give up yet. Besides, you can't waste that new hip.'

Hilda sighed, exhausted. 'My dear girl,' she said, 'you have absolutely no idea.'

The home visit to Hilda took Carol back to the awful last years of her mother's life, when she had been trapped, not by her body, but by her failing mind. Carol had made it her duty to visit her once a week for years before she died. On occasion she'd phone Max to try to persuade him to accompany her, reminding him how good his grandmother had been to him when he was a baby. Max had always refused, saying it was pointless, except for the time his voice was thick and hoarse with flu.

'I'll come,' he'd said.

'But you're sick.'

'It'll be my last gift to her. I'll give her a whopping great kiss and hope she gets pneumonia and that the doctors don't go and treat her with antibiotics like last time, so she can finally escape.'

'Max!'

'It would be the kindest thing, to let her go.' It was true but she couldn't say it out loud. 'Maybe she can be in one of my performance pieces, what d'you think, Ma? Have her sit dribbling and in nappies inside walls built of all the tons of medicines that have kept her going over all the years. We've cured everything, now there's only Alzheimer's left to die from.'

'Don't be obscene.'

'She might enjoy a little outing, being the centre of attention. If the piece is successful, she'd be famous. My wonderful, famous Gran. Way to go. She deserves it.'

'She'd be terrified. It would be horrible. Don't other people's feelings matter to you at all?'

Silence. 'You still there?'

'Yeah, sorry, I just had a WhatsApp.'

Visiting her mother had been an ordeal for fifteen years – parking in the bleak parking lot outside the ugly building, making her way through security and up the ramp to frail care on the first floor with its smell of disinfectant and urine and the questionable stains on the synthetic blue carpet tiles. Then the bell she'd had to ring to be allowed through the second gate, installed to prevent confused inmates from wandering off. The run-down hospital atmosphere, with old-style grey-metal medicine trolleys, linoleum flooring, enamel paint and institution-type furniture labelled in permanent ink.

Save me from coming to this end, she'd pray sometimes, in case there existed a spirit who was both genial and listening and who was capable of acting against misfortune. She was almost the age her mother was when she'd lost her marbles, a terrifying thought, but at least there were options for care of sorts for people who could no longer look after themselves. Carol was grateful that she hadn't had to look after her disintegrating mother. A mere hundred years ago, instead of being a doctor, she would probably have been at home all day doing just that.

She'd walk through the lounge past some of the addled aged who had been propped up in their wheelchairs and lined up in front of the blaring television, mostly looking into their laps, some out of the window.

Paula would usually be sitting in her room as she'd start moaning and shrieking if she were parked in the lounge. Carol had been worried about the level of care, so she'd paid for nurse aides to tend to her mother and to keep her company. Liesbet, or Fozia or Lindiwe would be helping her on the commode, or doing her hair or cutting the old woman's horny toenails with some large industrial-looking clippers.

Paula would look up with annoyance. 'What the hell are you doing here, Elsie?' she'd demand. Carol's mother still hadn't stopped quarrelling with her long-deceased sister. 'Haven't you upset us all enough already?'

Carol had never been sure of what to say. Play along with the delusion, or keep trying, pointlessly, to correct her? 'I've come to see what you've been up to, Mother.' She would insert little fragments of reality.

'I don't know how you could have married him.'

Carol had had a vague recollection of her aunt Elsie who had run off with Paula's best friend's husband.

'I didn't ever marry,' Carol would remind her, patiently. 'I'm the one you were cross with for *not* getting married, remember?'

'Well it's never too late, is it?'

'You got someone in mind, Mum? For yourself?' Having more or less the same conversation every time was better than silence.

Paula would widen her watery eyes in shock. 'I'm already married! Don't you remember Barry?' Where to go from there. Every time Carol reminded her mother that her husband was dead and had died eight years ago, Paula re-experienced the grief and distress as though for the first time.

'Where is Barry?' Paula agitated. 'Where has he gone?' She hunched her shoulders and showed Carol the hopeless palms of her hands.

Carol would feel sorry for her mother but she could not touch her. She had been unable to take Paula's hands and cradle them in her own as a daughter should. 'He's gone to town, Mum,' she'd tell her. 'He'll be back later.'

'Oh.' Paula would nod, relieved. 'Town.'

There would be a brief respite, until Paula would again start looking for her husband, fretting, forgetting that he was permanently in town. Town had become a metaphor for the afterlife, it was an explanation for everything. Not that Carol's father was ever interested in shopping. He was far happier in his veggie garden than in a supermarket or a mall. Yet Paula hadn't argued with this unlikely explanation. It was the one thing she could fully accept.

Years after his death, her husband had still been her anchor, her attachment to place, time and meaning. Without him she had drifted through the days, anxious, puzzled, raging.

Every now and then Paula would become tearful. 'I want to go home,' Paula would plead, like a small child. 'Why won't you take me home?' The flaps of her lips would continue to move wordlessly, then she would begin to sob, her breath ratcheting in and out of her chest, snagging on strings of phlegm.

Liesbet would put her hand gently on the old woman's knee. 'You want to go home to Our Lord in Heaven, don't you, my darling?'

Carol hadn't had the heart to point out that her mother had been an atheist her whole life. But everything else about Paula had altered, so perhaps she had developed some vision of an afterlife, or perhaps a beforelife out of which she had been born and to which she could return.

Paula had remained distressed and anxious despite medication until she died. Max was right, thought Carol. We allow abortion yet refuse to assist people who want to die to do so. Instead we invest fortunes in things like the huge and expensive placenta of frail care to force the miserable elderly to survive. Perhaps it was because once a person had recognisable quirks and tics of character, it was harder to justify ending their lives, even when personality had disintegrated.

That was the hardest thing about dementia – it wiped out familiar traits and left an increasingly unrecognisable shell. The sickening thing was that Carol could hardly remember who her mother had been before her illness, as though this impostor had managed to delete all past versions of herself.

She would sit with her for about ten minutes before she couldn't stand it anymore. Paula would begin to doze off, her head thrown back against the headrest, her jaw dropped wide open, as if she was offering her few remaining, stained teeth to a dentist for examination.

12.

Carol was exhausted. She'd treated a woman who burnt herself when she threw boiling water at a spider, and a child had vomited on her shoes when she held his tongue down with a spatula to look at his throat. She'd had to break news of invasive cancer to a young mother, and had admitted a young man to hospital who was otherwise healthy but was so depressed he had tried to kill himself by drinking Jik.

All she wanted to do was to go home, pour herself a stiff drink and slide into bed with the new Delilah Bezuidenhout crime novel Katy had lent her, the third in the series. Switch off from the day.

The protagonist was a clairvoyant named Clara Cunningham who was consulted by a Siamese cat breeder whose husband had gone missing. The voices who were Clara's guides had told her the man was being held in a warehouse – or they might have said a whorehouse. Clara couldn't quite make out the voices and they refused to repeat themselves. She stuck to warehouse for the sake of the cat breeder who had offered her a huge amount of money to find him. Clara needed a hip replacement so she had to take it on. She decided to make a number of forays into the industrial area and the red light district, but first she stopped off at her GP to get her ears syringed.

As Carol entered her home and hung up her bag and jacket on the coat rack at the door, she was seized by the feeling that she was not alone. She stood with her back to the wall and listened, her heart racing, getting ready to run back outside. A muffled sound, right inside the room. Suddenly human jack-in-the-boxes were jumping up from behind the sofa and the kitchen counter. 'Happy Birthday!' they shouted, then burst into the traditional song. Max and Katy, Zubeida and Trevor from work, Katy's husband Frank, and her neighbour Pat. Peter must be here, she could hear him on his keyboard, providing a jazzed up soundtrack of 'Happy Birthday to You' medleyed with what sounded like 'Here Comes The Bride'.

'My birthday's only tomorrow!' Carol protested. She spotted Tamsyn standing in the kitchen in a slashed black outfit. She'd thought Max had broken up with her.

'We wanted to surprise you.' Katy came up and handed her a glass of bubbly. 'We knew you'd probably go into hiding tomorrow.'

Carol looked round at her friends and her son as they toasted her. She was grateful, relieved and furious all at the same time.

Katy was doing her thing of organising everyone into their seats round the table. Leave me alone, Carol wanted to object as she allowed herself to be directed into the seat at the head of the table.

The pop of a cork, followed by a loud expletive from Frank. His hand shot to his brow where the cork had ricocheted.

'For God's sake, don't waste it!' Peter shouted, lifting out of his chair as a fountain of champagne spilt out onto the table. Max grabbed the bottle and put his mouth over the opening. Bubbles started coming out of his nose. Trevor stood over Frank in doctor mode, applying a serviette to the cut above Frank's left eyebrow.

'Not too bad,' Katy decided.

'There's Steri-Strip and plasters in my bathroom cupboard,' Carol informed Trevor. He and Frank went through to sort it out. 'That's how your life can change in a moment,' Carol grimaced.

'Meaning?' asked Katy.

'Could have lost his eye.'

'Well, he didn't. Isn't that brilliant. Now we don't have to dwell on it.'

'My sister was hit by a car last year and now she's in a wheelchair,' Pat was busy dabbing at the wet patch on the tablecloth with a dish towel.

Katy was getting her look. This was not how she'd planned the evening.

'It could happen to anyone,' Pat persisted. She stopped dabbing and snapped her fingers to illustrate. 'Just like that.'

'Um, well, she *was* riding a *motorbike*,' Katy underlined.

Peter was staring dolefully into his glass. 'Someone dropped a piece of salad in my water.'

'Salad!' Katy leaned and peered. 'We're not even having salad.'

'Bad enough being on the wagon without having additional lettuce forced on me,' he complained.

'It's mint, Peter, mint!' Katy pointed out. 'Fresh from the garden. All the best restaurants put mint in their water. Drink up! It's good for your prostrate.'

'Prostate,' Carol corrected. 'Prostrate is when you're drunk and you keel over face down or when you abase yourself in front of a deity.'

'Well, I don't suffer from either of those afflictions,' Peter drawled, brushing something off the tablecloth, 'so in my case it must be prostate.'

'Please, Peter, do we really have to hear about your glands at table?' Trevor snorted.

'Katy started it.'

'Okay guys, that's enough!' Katy decided. 'We're here for something other than Peter's water problems.'

'Remind me, what are we doing here?' Peter popped the mint into his mouth. 'I came here under the impression that this was a specialist panel devoted to my health care.'

Trevor came back into the room with Frank, his brow sporting a plaster. Carol knew what was expected, so she got to her feet and raised her glass. 'I want to ... thank you. All of you. Only, I'm not sure what for.' Peter leaned back in his chair and folded his arms. 'Oh dear, that sounds ungrateful, I'm sorry. Let me start again.' A muscle was interfering with her throat, contracting without her permission. 'I'm fifty years old. Nearly fifty.'

'Welcome. Best years of one's life, the fifties.' Peter offered.

'I'm sure we're all hungry, so I'll keep this short.'

'Take your time!' Trevor chipped in. 'We've got all night.'

'Well, it doesn't feel like I've got a lot of time, so I'll talk fast. I've been trying to ignore the fact of fifty. It feels so … enormous. But you, my friends, haven't let me. Ignore it, that is. In fact tonight you've shoved my face right in it. Forced me to celebrate something I feel extremely ambivalent about.' She was speaking from the ache stuck in her belly which seemed to have swallowed the world of niceties. 'None of you are old enough to tell me what's coming next – yes, I know some of you are older than I am but still, I maintain, you are not old *enough*!'

'Oh for God's sake! Have another drink.' Frank grabbed the bottle by the neck as though trying to get revenge by strangling it. He decanted more of the frothing liquid into Carol's glass. Frank raised his drink and aimed a look at Carol. 'Life is what you make of it!'

You should have told that to my mother, she wanted to throw back at him but she'd already said too much.

'You've made a good life, Carol.' Trevor, coming to her rescue.

Now wasn't the time to get all maudlin. She had to get herself jollied up somehow. Her job tonight was to make her friends feel good about the trouble they had gone to. 'I want to thank you,' she pressed on, 'for being there when I needed to inflict my dramas on you, for dragging me uphill in running shoes, for reminding me that life is bigger and better than I can ever imagine all by myself.' It wasn't what she wanted to say, not at all. She wanted the evening to be over and done with, so she could go to bed and stay there until she'd cried herself out and could think straight.

What was wrong with her? Maybe she needed antidepressants.

'I wish us all well on the road ahead. Thank you,' she wound down feebly, waving her glass, 'for coming tonight and making my life so special.'

After dinner Katy got everyone arranged in the lounge while Max set up his laptop and a projector. Peter took a painting down off the wall – the one of Kraken that Max had done at school when he was only fourteen, working from a photograph. Her son switched the projector on and there was an image of a baby laughing a two-toothed laugh as she swayed to one side in her pram, a photograph of herself that she hadn't seen in years. A soundtrack started up, one of her favourite songs: 'What a Wonderful World'.

She sat and looked back over the length of her life: the baby in the floppy blue hat propped up on a mound of sand at the beach; another of her being held up proudly by her young attractive mother – oh, now her dead mother, who should have been sitting next to her; then the toddler struggling to wield a croquet mallet by a handle longer than she was tall; the young girl posing self-consciously beside a fish pond; one of her bending to stroke Smoky, her cat, looking up at the camera from under her fringe; the shy child wearing her school uniform for the first time, smiling tightly, not yet knowing how to fake happiness convincingly; one from the party where she'd dressed up as Tinkerbell in that horrid prickly tutu; the school play where she'd been given a singing part as a scullery maid; the class photos and the snaps on hockey tour to Pietermaritzburg, also to Port Elizabeth; and goodness, a picture of her sitting on the couch at home with Martin, her first awkward boyfriend. A matric dance photo, as the two of them had come through the arch of crepe paper flowers, Martin looking adoringly at her, she, not trusting his devotion, looking away. Swimming in the Olifants River with Chippy and Hal from medical school, and sitting round a table at a farm on the wine route with Paul and Andy and Stacey, and photos of herself with Jeremy – dancing at the medical residence ball, then at the beach and at parties with their arms around each other, in love, imagining they loved each other. Photos of her graduation and of her trip overseas, even of Paris: but none of Max's father Neil. She had destroyed those on her return to South Africa, first stabbing them repeatedly with the sharp tip of a pair of scissors, then cutting them up into tiny pieces and flushing them down the toilet. That was before she'd discovered that Neil had left a tiny piece of himself behind inside her, stuck to her uterine wall.

Then a photo of Max on her lap as a baby, chubby and dribbling, reaching up to her face, her wide-eyed, exhausted stare. Another of her and Max in the Cederberg on a school camp, standing in slices of sunlight in the Wolfberg cracks; another time camping in Hermanus – or was it Kleinmond? – with Katy and Jessica, the two of them sitting with their backs to the night round a fire roasting marshmallows. Standing on a ladder, smiling down at the camera, roller in hand, painting a wall in this very house soon after she'd bought it. Oh God, one of her running down the beach with Kraken splashing in the shallows beside her. None of her with Jack. She didn't have any photographs of Jack, he'd deprived her of that, always avoiding cameras, even mirrors.

She saw the whole slide show through a mesh of heartache. Who was she, after all, after all this? What had she been? What had happened, that her path had gone this way instead of that, mostly accidentally, repeatedly so, until the direction of her life had hardened into this precise shape and she had lost all the other possibilities of who and where she might have been. It was astonishing how she'd ended up in this corner, not a bad one as corners go, but still that feeling of being trapped in a particular life, in this room with these exact people.

Didn't that happen to everyone?

Even now Katy was snapping away with her camera, fixing these very moments so that the images could live independently of her in electronic storage and in photo albums along with all the other depictions of the plot points of her life, to be retrieved for her eightieth birthday party, and again at her wake, then for her grandchildren, long after her physical self had returned to the earth.

Later, after most people had gone home, she ended up outside drinking tea. Peter was sitting on the other wrought-iron chair and Max and Tamsyn on the bench below the window. The sky was wiped across with stars, like bright droplets on a windscreen. The luminous pool of the moon, a sliver short of full, had long since risen and was riding the sky. They sat in silence a while, Carol stealing sidelong glances at Tamsyn who appeared to have less metal embedded in her face. She had been very quiet all evening but she was often like that. It was horrible that her son was intimate with someone she hardly knew. She should make more of an effort.

'What a soundscape,' Peter murmured.

The wind had dropped and Carol could hear the soothing shush of the sea in the distance. From the trees at the bend in the road came the low fluted notes of an owl hooting. Again, hooting. Frogs were popping and chirping down near the vlei.

The scrape and flare of a match. Tamsyn's face, bending towards the flame, looked softer, almost beautiful, as she lit a cigarette. 'I wish I was a frog,' she said, tossing her head back and blowing smoke.

'A frog!' Peter exclaimed, amused.

'Then you know what you're supposed to do, you know, without knowing.'

'You're talking about instinct.' Max sounded irritated.

'It's more than instinct,' insisted Tamsyn. 'It's like, being in tune. Like Peter said, out there in the vlei, everything's in tune, it all comes together.'

They sat, listening to high staccato sounds playing over long low waves. 'You feeling out of tune?' Peter asked her gently. 'You have an extraordinary voice.'

'She sings in a band,' Max revealed, 'called Identity Theft.'

'You've heard them?' Carol asked Peter.

'No, Tamsyn was standing right next to me when we sang Happy Birthday.'

Max leaned to one side in his seat and released a trumpeting fart.

'Oh, for goodness' sake, Max!' Carol snapped.

'B flat major,' he announced. 'I, for one, am totally in tune with nature.'

'Thanks for that contribution,' laughed Peter.

Tamsyn giggled. 'It's his favourite note, especially in bed,'

Spare me the details, Carol thought.

Max forced a burp. 'The body,' he declared, 'is an amazing instrument.'

'All I can hear from my flat in the city at night is traffic and neighbours fighting,' Peter said, 'and the odd siren.'

'There's a big siren going off inside me at the moment.' Carol wanted a cigarette but she wasn't going to ask Tamsyn, not in front of Max.

'A siren!' exclaimed her son. 'Pay attention to that. Could be a big arty fart coming.'

Carol smiled, despite herself. 'Seriously, how did you cope with it, Peter?'

'What?'

'Turning fifty. We went to the Mount Nelson for high tea, remember? God-awful place.'

Peter pulled his sleeves down against the slight chill of the night air. 'With my genes and my condition, all of my conditions, I don't expect to last very long, so I suppose I felt grateful. I'm still grateful that I've made it this far.'

'How are you?' She sometimes forgot what he'd been through; his drinking bouts had overshadowed his other ailments. Although they were mostly connected, even enmeshed. The chromosomal weft of addiction and cholesterol providing the foundation for the warp of HIV, gout and heart disease.

'Well, as you can see.' He spread his arms as though he was opening up the book of his body for her to read. 'Sober, no chest pain, my cholesterol is down, my blood sugar is normal. My colon is chugging along and my prostate is perky despite going into retirement *and* my CD4 count is over 800. I'm working out at the gym most days. I don't think I've ever been fitter.' A flare as he too lit a cigarette.

'That's good news, Peter. Pity about the tar and nicotine.'

'You *know* I always get sick when I stop smoking.'

Carol shook her head with resignation. 'Logic is the most astonishing thing.'

'When last did you have a check up, Ma?' Max kicked a sandal off and put his foot in Carol's lap, his code for a massage. His feet looked clean enough, so she obliged, rolling the pads of his toes under her thumbs, stretching his toe joints, grateful for any opportunity to touch her son.

'You know very well that medical facts don't apply to me. I'm the doctor, the one the other side of the consulting room table.' What the hell, she thought and reached an arm towards Peter. 'Give me a drag.' She took Peter's cigarette out of his mouth, pincering it between her thumb and index finger, brought it to her mouth and sucked hard. Exhaled. 'Anyway, Max, I thought your position was "Save The Planet – Die Young".'

'Your mother's onto you,' Tamsyn observed.

Max wasn't listening. 'I've got this idea for a performance, where I'm hooked up to a bank of machines that screen for health issues, continuously displaying, or spewing out graphs and numbers and beeps, while I trash myself with booze and smokes and drugs. Can I borrow your gadgets from work? Heart monitors? ECG machines? What do you call it – that blowing tube that tests your lungs?' When Max was ill as a child, Carol would take him with her to the practice and put him into the bed in the procedure room. Often enough she would find Max out of bed and experimenting with the medical equipment under Zubeida's encouraging eye.

'Carol!' Peter was indignant. 'Are you serious? You don't have check-ups?'

'Look, I don't have a family history of colon or breast cancer. I don't smoke or drink excessively, I exercise a bit and I'm not indulging in sex, so …' She shrugged.

'Make an appointment with my doctor, Harry Holdin,' Peter admonished. 'He's very thorough.'

'It's past midnight and officially my birthday so stop pestering me. While we're on the subject, don't ever *ever* give me a surprise birthday party again.'

'Why? Didn't you have fun?' Peter sounded hurt. 'I thought you were enjoying yourself.'

'Of course I was.' She pushed her son's foot off her lap. It was time for all of them to go home. 'But you know very well I prefer to know what's going to happen next.'

'Not even frogs know that,' remarked Max.

13.

'Here's a little gift for the summer holidays to remind you of our amazing new product.' The young pharmaceutical company representative pushed a large carrier bag emblazoned with the DynaPharm logo towards Carol. Inside was a transparent plastic holder containing a folded blue item. The label explained that it was a self-inflating lilo. The accompanying card said: *DynaPharm products always come out on top.*

Carol stared at it. She usually gave the pharma bribes to the poor via Pumi, but unlike the Weber braai, the umbrellas, the insulated mugs and the blankets, a lilo wasn't exactly something that could be put to good use in the township. Yet those who have very little are inventive – perhaps the lilo was sturdy enough to be used as an inflatable mattress.

'Thank you.' Carol smeared the last of the wasabi paste onto her maki with a chopstick, topped it with two flakes of pickled ginger, dunked it in the little dish of soya sauce and placed it on her tongue. The delicious burn and salt as the wrapped fish morsel went down overrode the discomfort of her conscience. The system was bigger than her moral queasiness would ever be.

'Please remember DynaPharm when you next prescribe,' the rep pleaded. 'You know, times have been really tough for me lately what with divorce. Please, write on the script "no substitution". You only want ethical medicines for your patients, right?'

The next patient was starting on the details about how he put his back out when Carol was called to the procedure room. A young girl of about ten had been carried in by her father, with a short history of confusion, drowsiness and vomiting and was lying on the emergency trolley.

'Glove up!' Carol reminded her staff, concerned that they were dealing with a severe form of meningitis. Before Zubeida had checked her blood pressure, temperature and blood sugar, Carol had revised the diagnosis from the child's sighing breathing and the sickly sweet smell of her breath. No fever, no neck stiffness, pupils equal and reactive, Glasgow Coma Scale of 8. It had to be a diabetic ketoacidosis.

'She been thirsty lately?' she asked the father as she hung a vacuolitre up on the drip stand and ran the fluid through the tubing.

'Very thirsty but you know, it's summer and she's very fond of Coke.'

Carol tightened a tourniquet around the child's upper arm and started searching for a vein with some difficulty. The girl was dehydrated.

The father, hovering anxiously. 'Will she be okay, doctor?'

'Off the scale,' Zubeida read out from the glucometer. The high blood sugar reading confirmed her suspicion.

'Seventy years ago she would have died,' Carol explained to the father, pushing the cannula into his daughter's vein. 'Ten units, please sister. Nowadays we can treat her.' Zubeida passed her the syringe and she pushed half the contents into the girl's arm and half into the drip bag. 'She should be okay. It's a miracle, really. We're very lucky to be living in this age.'

Two weeks later Max was admitted to an Intensive Care Unit after taking an overdose.

Carol swung through the ICU doors and located her son lying supine on the bed near the window. Max was on a ventilator, his eyes closed, an ET tube rammed into his nose and down his trachea and secured with tape. His chest was rising and falling, rising, falling to the rhythmic shush of the machine. A drip fed fluids into a vein in his arm. A nasogastric tube drained his stomach into a bag hanging next to his bed and urine collected in another.

Carol tried to piece the story together from what the doctor on duty had gleaned from the paramedics. They had got their information from a cameraman at the scene. It appeared that Max had taken huge quantities of medication in a mall.

Hedley. Bloody Hedley. Carol didn't have his cell number and Max's cell wasn't on him. She couldn't remember Hedley's surname. Smith, or Smit?

The sister had handed her a large plastic bag containing the clothes Max was wearing when he was brought in. She opened it briefly. A priest's cassock, reeking of vomit.

The physician, Dr Abbass, had gone through the effects of the medicines with Carol as though she were a layperson. The anti-histamines, antispasmodics, cough syrups and sleeping tablets would knock him out for some time. He'd had to intubate Max to protect his airway in case he vomited while he was unconscious and to deliver oxygen. Other effects would be heartburn from the anti-inflammatories and constipation from codeine and calcium, both of which were easily remedied. The only drug of major concern was paracetamol. Carol knew it could induce liver and kidney failure if you took it in high enough doses.

She recalled sitting in a lecture in her fourth year where the pharmacologist had spelt this fact out. 'These young kids have a break-up of a relationship, or some other traumatic event,' he'd explained, 'and if they don't have the ego strength to handle it, they sometimes take whatever they find in the medicine cabinet on an impulse. Many over-the-counter medications contain paracetamol which is otherwise an effective and innocuous drug. But when someone takes it in large quantities as a suicide attempt and then realises a day or so afterwards that pop songs are wrong and it is possible to live without someone who has made you miserable and you decide that you no longer want to kill yourself, it's too late. Your kidneys and liver have already started failing and you die three days later.'

Max had been admitted early enough to have his stomach washed out and to have dialysis to extract paracetamol from his blood. Dr Abbass put his hand briefly on Carol's shoulder. 'You need to have a good talk to your son,' he said.

Time marched on with every ventilated breath. Carol wanted

to be there when Max woke but that would take a while. So she went to find Hedley.

At Max and Hedley's flat she pushed the buzzer repeatedly but no one answered. Where was the fucker while his friend lay dying? She drove back to the hospital.

The next morning, Max was still unconscious. Katy phoned to alert Carol that the story was featured on the front page of the paper.

Carol took the stairs down to the cafeteria and found the article in the column at the bottom of the front page, the one that was usually reserved for whacky and ridiculous items. There was a small indistinct photograph of an unconscious man being carried away on a stretcher through a crowd of onlookers.

Suicide Artist: Are Pills Killing Us?

Performance artist Max Trehorne again shocked the art world with another public suicide attempt. In October he set himself alight; yesterday he put himself on display in an unoccupied shop next to an art gallery in Lakeside Mall and proceeded to consume vast quantities of over-the-counter medication as a protest against Big Pharma. Trehorne is in hospital in a stable condition. His manager, Hedley Anderson, released the artist's press statement. 'HOLY TABLET: In performance: Coming down from the Mount of Misinformation, trying to find the PILL that will finally cure me of this profit-driven LIFE. CREATE MORE ILLNESSES, EAT MORE MEDICINES, MAKE MORE PROFIT! I die so that Big Pharma can live.' His performance has been uploaded to YouTube, where it has had more than 60 000 hits in less than 24 hours.

Carol ordered a coffee, got out her iPad and Googled YouTube, Max Trehorne, Holy Tablet.

Hers was hit number 83 071. There were two other clips alongside tagged with Max's name: *Burning Man* and one called *Food/Fast*, uploaded two years back, one she had never heard of before.

She clicked on *Holy Tablet*. Max, dressed in the black cassock, was sitting ceremonially at a table in the shop window under display lights. A hymnal chant was playing – whether this was part of the performance, or whether it had been added afterwards as a sound track to the clip, she wasn't sure.

The partitions behind Max were covered with posters advertising medication – sexy young women in virginal white promoting vaginal douches, paunchy middle-aged men gripping their graphically inflamed bellies in an agony of indigestion, adolescents posing in before and after shots, their faces initially bubbling with acne then rendered clear-skinned.

The hour and minute hands on the large clock positioned behind Max's head had been speeded up and were moving faster and faster as one watched. On the table in front of Max was a large collection of medicines, a jug of water, a ceremonial pewter wine glass, a burette and some test tubes in racks, and several sticks of incense burning. He opened each package slowly, extracting the cards of tablets with their neat rows, pushing the pills out of their blister packaging, decanting capsules out of bottles, opening sachets and pouring powder into the wine glass, then adding water.

He was totally focused on his task, handling and measuring the medicines with enormous care, as though they were precious materials used in scientific experiments requiring exactitude, or religious artefacts, or talismans. He counted them into piles as though they represented wealth and created patterns on the table out of clusters of colours and shapes, as if intent on inventing or deciphering a code. An alarm went off that sounded like an ambulance siren, activated by the hour hand reaching ten. In response, Max held up a tablet as if it was a communion wafer, mouthing a silent prayer, then placed it ceremonially onto his tongue. He took up the goblet and drank the tablet down. The alarm subsided and stopped. As the clock speeded up and reached four, the same occurred – the siren, the sacred taking in of medicine; this was repeated at two and then again at ten. As the clock hands got faster and faster and the intervals between each ceremonial dose of medication got shorter, Max began to gobble the medicine. Trying to keep up with the time frame of taking medication every eight hours, with an increasingly faster clock, he started ripping open boxes, stuffing medicine down. The slow ceremony was becoming an act of greed, or desperation. The siren alarm began to merge into a long hollow howl.

A screen had lit up to his right, displaying a slide show of graphs of the escalating profit margins of pharmaceutical companies across the world, interspersed with newspaper headlines about fraudulent research findings and promotions funded by the industry.

The camera panned across to the crowd that had gathered outside the shop window; some were laughing, pointing, commenting to each other, thinking this was comedy; others looked bemused or puzzled; some merely glanced and walked on.

After a while, Max's responses started slowing down; he appeared disoriented, confused. A security guard tried to open the door to the shop and found it locked; others came running with more keys. By this time Max was randomly drinking down pills and potions, half-leaning on the table; then his head rolled back, his body swaying in his chair. He slumped forward and began to heave, then to vomit onto the table, a slurry of brown flecked with a multitude of coloured specks. The crowd murmured with disgust as he slid to one side, smearing the disgorged contents of his stomach; he tried to right himself, then lost his grip on the table and went down, collapsing with a rush onto the floor, where he banged his head. He lay there, skew and crumpled, amongst discarded packaging and vomit, not moving.

The guards, in the meantime, had managed to break the door down; someone stepped in front of the camera and the clip stopped, abruptly.

14.

Dr Ndlovu looked down at his notes, lacing his fingers together, as though he was about to pray. Pulled them apart, slotted them together again. 'Does Max abuse substances?' he asked. He'd had his glasses frames fixed, which was surely a good sign.

'No. No, I wouldn't call it abuse. I'm sure he has the odd recreational … joint.' Again she found herself censoring information – that she had, on occasion, spent a hilarious evening smoking dope with her son.

'Tell me more about Max, why you think he took an overdose.'

Max was right, she didn't understand him. Yet she had to pass on what she knew, as she'd been taught at medical school. Extract the clues, nail down the facts, the planks one could walk on over the void of not knowing. Carol had been trained in observation and interpretation – putting together the patient's story, family and work history, the physical findings and the laboratory results, working like a detective to accurately assess the culprit causing the disturbance. Once that was done, one could intervene to restore order and normality, in other words, health. She'd had almost no postgrad training in psychiatry yet she was aware that when it came to disorders of the mind, the boundaries between normality and illness were a lot more blurred than with those of the body.

She did not believe that Max's thinking was sick. They'd had an enjoyable breakfast together just last weekend. He had appeared quite upbeat, talking about how things were going at work and about a friend's exhibition opening. He'd even agreed to go with her to the theatre the following week.

'Is there any history of mental illness in the family?'

'No,' she said. That wasn't accurate. Her grandfather had drowned in uncertain circumstances, either by falling overboard when drunk or committing suicide by throwing himself into the ocean. Had she ever told Max? Oral histories are easily forgotten or stuffed away in a cupboard, unlike genetic threads that imprint on character all the way down the family tree.

And Max's father's family? Her recollection of Neil was hazy and she could remember nothing about his relatives, if he had told her anything at all.

They had met in Paris, of all places. He was an American postgrad anthropology student with abundant hair tied up in a Samurai knot and large leather sandals. Carol was a recently qualified doctor, unsure which career direction to take. She was also on the rebound from a relationship with a surgical registrar who thought that problems, like tumours, could be easily excised. Carol had attempted to follow his logic and remove her deficiencies. But when a friend of hers had seen him coming out of a hospital linen cupboard with a nurse, Carol was not convinced by his explanation that he had been helping her make the patients' beds.

She tried to move on from heartache by travelling as far away from the break-up as possible, her home reduced to a brown backpack. An interesting-looking stranger struck up a conversation with her on the Metro in Paris, then asked her out for lunch. Instead of a restaurant, he took her to a supermarket where he purchased bread, cheese and a bottle of cheap Italian wine. Then he walked with her along the River Seine to a park, where they encamped on a stretch of lawn next to a sign announcing in French that the grass was forbidden.

Neil took out his penknife and opened the bottle with the corkscrew attachment and they drank straight from the bottle as though from the bountiful teat of heaven, and tore chunks of baguette off with their teeth and bit into the cheese, creating a delicious mix of flavours. It was so exotic, so Bohemian, definitely the sort of thing Carol's parents would disapprove of – as did the park attendant, a burly man in uniform who hurled long French sentences at them and chased them off towards the gate. Half-drunk and laughing, Carol took Neil back to her pension and snuck him upstairs and sat with him on the bed and poured her life out in between gulps of wine from a bottle that was empty too soon, whereupon Neil pushed her gently down onto the creaky wooden bed and consoled her so vigorously the condom broke.

The concierge, despite her hearing impairment, had found out that Carol's room had another inhabitant and there was more French shouting until, fearing eviction and in a dizzy post-coitus fug, Carol agreed to pay for Neil as well.

Suddenly, wonderfully, laughter and pleasure were part of her life again and a sense of belonging; also, strangely, of terrible longing even when he was right beside her, walking hand in hand along the Champs-Elysées or through the Latin Quarter. Even when they were in bed together Carol yearned for him, her body a tinderbox waiting for his match. He told her he'd been studying in Paris for the past two years; he seemed to know everything: how to get into the Pompidou Centre for nothing, where to eat cheaply, the best second-hand bookshops, where to find free poetry readings and the best rooftop nighttime view of the Eiffel Tower.

One morning when he was supposedly at lectures, Carol walked past a patisserie that he had taken her to on a number of occasions, an expensive place where she always ended up paying because he was a student. Glancing towards the window to check whether the wind had done a bad hair job on her, she saw his distinctive red jacket angled over a table on the other side of the glass. Excited to see him so unexpectedly, half thinking she was mistaken, she entered the shop. He was leaning towards a young woman whose magnificent head of auburn hair cascaded in shaken curls about her face. Neil was holding her hands in his on the table top. His dark, earnest face was filled with the deep compassion that Carol thought he reserved especially for her. The woman, who looked like she'd stepped out of a foreign movie, was also leaning forward towards him as though magnetised; her lips were slightly open with admiration and – Carol recognised the flushed look – lust. As the woman spoke, she started to weep long streaks of mascara down the undulation of her cheeks. Neil extracted a serviette from a holder, wrapped it around his index finger and, with excessive care, gently wiped her face, giving her two black eyes. Then he lifted his beautiful behind right off the seat in order to lean still further across the table; he tilted his head and kissed her, full on the mouth; the soft underbelly of his jaw, where his tongue was rooted, started working. In full view.

Carol stood and watched, horrified, mesmerised, as Neil's mouth sucked onto, then socketed deeply into his companion's. The auburn woman's eyes slid closed.

The consequent scene resulted in yet more shouting, some of it in French from the patisserie owner, and another ejection. Their argument continued on the cracked pavement outside, where it became evident that the movie star was not new on the scene; in fact, the redhead revealed that she considered Carol to be the usurper and that this was not the first time; there had been others.

The grey sky broke and it started to rain. The awning outside the café was very narrow and, what with the large pot plants, there was not enough space for the three of them to shelter under it. Somehow, Carol found herself left out in the rain. Cold water was hitting her skin, spitting in her face, stinging her until she came to her senses. She understood: the man was a serial consoler, moving through the romantic city like a metal detector, his apparatus beeping whenever it came across the broken-hearted.

Dr Ndlovu was waiting for a reply. Had he said something?

'Sorry?'

'Has your son shown any signs of depression, or anxiety lately? Loss of appetite, or insomnia in the past few months?'

'No, but I don't see him that often. You need to talk to his flatmate.'

Dr Ndlovu consulted his notes. 'Hedley Anderson?'

Anderson, that was it. 'Yes, Hedley. He's played a part in all this. Calls himself Max's manager.'

'Tell me about Max's childhood, anything you didn't remember last time we spoke. Any aggression? Signs of depression?'

There was that incident when Max put his fist through a laminated door while they were on holiday in Paternoster. He had not only crashed a hole into the wood, he had broken a metacarpal bone in his hand.

That adolescent change in his behaviour, the outbursts, the sullen withdrawals, had come after Daniel had suffocated to death and Max himself had only just escaped the same fate. The psychologist he saw at the time – that she had forced him to see – said he was suffering from survivor guilt. Her miraculously-saved son was upset that he had not died alongside his best friend.

What Carol knew about that time was muddled up with what she'd imagined into the gaps until it all felt as real as a recollection. Recently she'd seen a documentary on oceanic pollution, depicting the huge clogged vortex of plastic accumulating in the Pacific Gyre and it had felt like a manifestation of the way she'd felt at the time – the toxic waste, the irreversibility, the horror, the asphyxiating congestion. It had sat in her chest, in her dreams. She'd often woken up gasping.

Max had refused to speak about it to anyone. Except for the police, at the time, and that one session with the therapist.

Dr Ndlovu listened carefully, jotting it all down.

15.

That afternoon Max and Daniel had gone down to the beach, eager to carry on with a project that they'd kept secret from their parents. At their age they should have known better was the unhelpful thought that kept intruding into Carol's mind for months afterwards.

When the phone rang, Carol was in consultation with Yolanda, a sobbing adolescent schoolgirl. Yolanda had found out that her boyfriend had made her mother pregnant, so this was not the time to be taking calls. She had ignored the phone, which was the signal for Naledi not to disturb her.

What could she say to this young woman? She knew the mother, a manipulative person who sought out any available man to cling to. She was also her patient. Carol had even seen the mother flirt with patients in the waiting room.

'It's a terrible betrayal,' Carol sympathised, 'from people close to you.' She wished she could ring up the mother, tell her to come down to the practice so she could smack her, hard. 'But sometimes good can come of bad things,' she offered. It was too soon to say something like that, it sounded stupid. 'Can you go and live with your father until you decide what to do?' Although the father didn't sound as though he was much better. 'It might be helpful to get a bit of space from your Mum.'

'I want to kill her!' Yolanda raged, reaching for another tissue.

Sometimes Carol didn't know whether she should take the threats she heard in her consulting room seriously. 'I can imagine how you feel,' she said, about to point out that the boyfriend could have said no, when she was interrupted by a knock at the door.

Naledi's worried and apologetic face. 'Sorry. It's Max. He's at the hospital. The doctor wants to talk to you.'

'What's happened?'

'An accident. Apparently he's all right. I don't know anything else.'

Carol felt the tear of fear. 'Take the doctor's number. I'll phone back in five.' She closed the door and turned to Yolanda, her breathing constricted.

Yolanda was still pulling tissues out of the box and depositing sodden ones into the wastepaper basket, oblivious. Carol had to bring this consultation to an end.

'I suggest you and your Mum make an appointment to see me,' she turned to her screen and consulted her diary, 'first thing tomorrow. Can you do that?' She started writing out a sick note. 'In the meantime, where are you going to stay?'

'My aunt,' Yolanda decided. 'I'll go and stay with my aunt.'

'He's so lucky to be alive,' the enthusiastic young ER doctor informed her as he took her through to her son's bed. 'We need to observe him for an hour or two. Make sure his Sats don't drop.' He pulled the curtain aside for Carol to enter, then bolted off to the patient who was groaning in the next bed.

Max was lying on a trolley, his face turned to the wall. His skin and clothing salted with sand, his hair thick with it.

Carol took Max's hand in hers, cradled it. It was cold, despite the blanket. 'Could we have another blanket here please?' she called to a nurse.

'I'm fine, please Mum.' Max's voice was croaky, his eyes were rimmed with red.

Carol put her hand on her son's forehead and carefully brushed the sand out of his hair. The grains fell in crisp little showers onto the linen saver. His face was elongating out of childhood, becoming more defined, the growing bones beneath his skin sculpting his features into that of a man.

She didn't know what to do other than to stand next to him watching the miracle of his chest rising and falling with each breath.

'I'm so sorry, my darling.' The doctor had told her that a tunnel Max and Daniel were excavating into the dune had collapsed. Max had been dug out in time by a man who happened to be passing and saw the event. The doctor had had to give Max a tranquilliser when he'd told him Daniel had suffocated.

Max wouldn't look at her. 'I want to go home,' he managed.

Back at the house Max spent ages in the shower. Carol didn't tell him to hurry up, that he was wasting water and electricity. She leaned her ear against the cool painted door but could hear nothing except the hiss and pelt of spray. She was afraid of his silence. He was closing himself away from her, from her ability to comfort him.

Later that evening she had forced herself to phone Daniel's parents, whom she didn't know very well. Decent people, but that was not enough to protect anyone against the injustice of premature death. The father had answered the phone and had thanked her for her condolences in a curt, tight way, then asked about Max, how he was doing.

What to say? 'He's doing okay, only he misses ... so very terrible –'

Guilt and shock pursued her through the following days. One of the places it ambushed her was in the supermarket aisle. She was walking along, pushing her shopping trolley next to a bank of fridges comparing chicken prices, when suddenly she felt ill to the marrow, winded, as though her legs might give in.

She stopped and steadied herself, holding tightly on to the shopping trolley handle, trying to recall why she should be feeling this way. Then, like a bucket of crushed ice, it dropped on her: Daniel's death by burial and her son's revival out of the belly of the earth.

16.

Dr Ndlovu handed her a box of tissues. Carol wasn't against crying but she didn't like to do it herself and certainly not in front of a junior colleague.

She pulled another tissue out and blew her nose. 'That was such a difficult time.'

The psychiatrist had put down his pen. His face seemed to have softened; in fact he was starting to look benign, even kind. 'Are you all right to go on?'

She hesitated, then nodded. Talking about what had happened had released a clamp that had been obstructing something in her innards.

'What do you think about the idea of survivor guilt? In Max's case?' he asked. Was Dr Ndlovu asking her as a colleague, or as a mother?

Carol shook her head, reached for another tissue. 'I don't know.'

'It's not uncommon. It used to be a separate diagnosis in the DSM but recently it's been redefined as a significant symptom in post-traumatic stress disorder. Do you know whether he's had other symptoms of PTSD, flashbacks, nightmares, irritability?'

'He had nightmares straight after the accident, I would hear him yell and I'd come running into his room. He would get irritated. After days of him sitting at his computer playing games, I persuaded him away for a weekend to a place along the coast for a change of scenery, hoping that would help. On the second day he put his fist through the door during a disagreement and we had to come home for an X-ray.'

The degree of violence in her child had shocked her, how his face had darkened at some minor thing she'd said, how quickly his rage had spilled. He'd released his arm as though it was under some central pressure, sending his fist crashing into the wood. The crack of the laminate and perhaps the bone as it snapped. 'That's when I took him to see the psychologist, but she must have said something that annoyed him. He refused to go to the next visit, said he was fine.'

Thinking back, Carol was amazed she hadn't insisted that Max continue to see the therapist. Perhaps if he'd got proper help then, none of this would have happened. But there had been Jack; Jack had entered their lives at that point and he'd had a way with her son, a father figure. 'After all this time, could Max still have PTSD? It is treatable, right?'

'There's a lot that can be done for most psychiatric disorders to help patients manage better, if they are willing.'

'Max isn't willing –' How to get someone in trouble to accept help? It was something she was confronted with every day as a doctor.

'Max has found a way to manage his feelings in a specific and risky way,' observed Dr Ndlovu. 'There's an adrenalin rush when people put themselves in danger. Did this obsession with risk only start when he went to art school?'

'No. He always got a kick out of speed on his skateboard. After the accident he did some crazy things.'

Carol kept Max home for a while after Daniel's death. She'd phoned the school and had taken a week off work, imagining that the two of them could go out and do things together.

The evening she brought him home from the hospital, the phone rang. A journalist from the morning paper introduced himself. He wanted to ask a few questions and asked whether he could interview Max. Carol had told him what she knew, thinking it could help to prevent other similar accidents. She told the reporter that Max was sleeping and could not speak to the press and no, they couldn't come round to take photographs, he was not in a fit state. Then the local community paper phoned, also wanting the story, pressing her for details. By the time *You* magazine was on the line, she told them to get lost.

Max stayed shut up in his room the next morning, playing loud hectic music. Under the circumstances she let it go. She was about to do the washing up when the front door opened. Pumi. Of course, it was a Tuesday. Carol explained why the two of them were at home.

'Sorry,' Pumi said. 'It's not right. Daniel.' She shook her head. 'So young.' Carol realised that she must have met Max's friend after school. Her tear glands were pricking again, so she made some excuse and headed towards her bedroom. She found herself hovering around in the passage outside Max's room, wanting to knock.

'Leave him,' Pumi advised, as she took the vacuum cleaner out of the cupboard. 'He will come out when he is ready.'

What if she was wrong? Carol had three patients whose sons had killed themselves in the past couple of years, two by hanging. None of the parents had seen it coming. If one saw it coming, would that prevent it from happening? She was a scientist. She must try to think like a scientist.

There must be theories, strategies, advice available somewhere. The library, for example, and the internet. She realised that when she'd counselled the bereaved in her rooms, she really hadn't had a clue.

Pumi started the vacuum cleaner. Carol was shocked by the racket it made. A couple of weeks back she had dashed into a shop to get a replacement for the one that had broken and had grabbed a model that was on sale without trying it out. Carol stood in the passage, feeling battered by heavy punk metal grunge garage – whatever Max's music was called – on the one side and a shrieking appliance on the other. Pumi was grinding the cleaning attachment of the machine to and fro over the lounge carpet, yet it wasn't even managing to pick up a blade of grass stuck to the weave. She should take the damn thing back.

Carol went to her bedroom, pulled open a bedside drawer and scrabbled around until she found some earplugs, but shoving them in her ears bottled in and amplified her thoughts.

The vacuum cleaner, she decided, was a metaphor for her life. Ineffectual, pathetic. Much bluster with little result. The fact was, she had not been paying attention. More haste, less speed – her father's critical voice boomed in her ear. Followed shortly afterwards by another of his infuriating sayings: Come on girl, there's no time to be lost. She hung paralysed between the poles of her father's contradictions.

Carol closed her bedroom door and took out the earplugs. Found herself in the en suite bathroom, holding a sponge and household cleaner. She bent over and started scrubbing the bath to get her damn father to shut up. He was what happened whenever she was at home with time on her hands.

Her work phone rang. Heidi Fraser's elderly father had been hovering on the brink for a few months and she'd just found him dead in his chair. Carol was about to explain that she was on leave and that Heidi should get hold of whoever was on call, when she decided she might as well go down to their home, which was only a few blocks away, and sort out the death certificate.

By the time she arrived, the undertakers were there. The ninety-two year old was cold, his pupils fixed and dilated. She put her forefinger on his eyelids and pulled them gently closed, covering his eyes. Some doctor had done exactly that to Daniel the day before.

After she'd completed the death certificate and cremation forms and the undertaker had taken the body, Carol spent half an hour having tea with the family, commiserating and reminiscing. They had clearly not yet heard about what had happened to her son and to Daniel. She didn't dare bring it up, tears were so close. She drove home slowly, stopping to buy the morning paper.

Max was still in his room behind a closed door, playing video games by the sound of things.

'I took him his favourite,' Pumi said. A chocolate milk-shake, no doubt.

The article was on the second page. The reporter had several details wrong, including Max's age and even the spelling of Daniel's surname. The accompanying photograph of the collapsed tunnel had two blurred photos of the boys as inserts. Carol recognised them as being from the class photograph a year back.

There was also mention of the man who had dug Max out. John Stone was running through the dunes down to the beach with his dog when he saw the boys excavating and witnessed the collapse of the tunnel. 'I was yelling for backup as I dug,' he told the reporter. 'The first boy started breathing quickly enough once I'd got him out and blown a few puffs into him but the other one, it took too long.' Death boiled down to chance. Where one was sitting when a roof caved in or how fast a man could dig you out.

She could phone the paper, get his number.

Pumi came over and leaned on the counter, taking it in. 'You have another chance. My son, he passed away in grade four.'

'I didn't know.' Carol realised that she hardly knew this woman who cleaned the most intimate corners of her home. 'So sorry Pumi. What happened?'

'Before I came to this house, to work for you. Six years ago.' She shook her head. 'I was working for another lady. My son was in the Eastern Cape, with my mother and sister. A snake bit him, while he was looking for firewood.' The whites of her eyes reddened. 'If I kept him here, in Cape Town, if I kept him …' She put a hand inside the neckline of her dress, pulled a hanky out and blew her nose. 'I would still have my Zolani.'

Carol put the kettle on. What to say? 'I'm so sorry.' A parent never recovered from losing a child. Snake bite, in this age. That shouldn't happen anymore. Pumi tucked the hanky back inside her bra, next to breasts that had once fed her son.

Another chance; what did that mean, practically? Life with Max had become a functional thing – laundry, shopping, cooking, homework, bedtime. Where did one start? Maybe she should take him away for a few days, along the coast. Without other distractions, perhaps they could have a proper conversation.

Max's bedroom door opened; Carol quickly folded the newspaper and put it in a kitchen drawer. Not now, not yet. She would show him when it wasn't all so raw.

'Let's go for a walk,' she suggested the next morning when he emerged around ten o'clock for breakfast. They would have to avoid the beach, and head for the mountain.

'No thanks,' Max said, fiddling with the scrambled egg on toast she had made him. She was glad to see him downing the banana and berry smoothie. She popped out to the shop; when she returned, he'd gone out. On the kitchen counter was a message on the back of an envelope written in his awkward scrawl. 'Back later. Need some fresh air.' That was a dig at her, always going on about fresh air when he was holed up in his room playing computer games. Nothing about where he was going which was absolutely against her rules.

This was crazy, she'd taken off work to be with him and now she was at home alone, twiddling her thumbs. A restlessness seized her that wouldn't let her sit quietly or read. The gardener had been recently, so she directed her energy towards the cupboards in the lounge where everything she had no use for was stored. She'd been avoiding them for years. Black bags and ruthlessness, that's what was required. Out with clutter. No stopping to consider yet again whether this torch, that second-hand piece of string or those sunglasses with one arm missing might come in useful at some point. Out, out! Start again, clear, clean, so she could breathe and think straight.

Come 3 p.m., Max was not yet home. It was unlike him to be out alone for so long, unless he was with a friend, but his friends would only be coming out of school now. She rang him, heard his cell go off in his room. She went into his bedroom to check for any clue as to where he might have gone.

His backpack wasn't where he usually left it at the bottom of the cupboard. His skateboard was gone.

Carol waited another half an hour, then started phoning his friends' homes. No, Max wasn't there. No, sorry. Not there either. He's not come home? Blanks everywhere. Reassurance from one parent that it was still early in the afternoon. Offers from another to help look for him. Carol refused, despite her mounting concern. It was probably fine. How could he do this to her?

She drove down to the beach, parked and ran down to the sand, half-expecting him to be sitting somewhere amongst the dunes, perhaps at the site of the accident. She took off her shoes and crossed the stream, went round the back of the dunes and came across the collapsed excavation. It was out of sight of the main beach. A miracle that anyone had been passing at that exact time and had noticed the boys in trouble. Who was this man who had dug her son out? She must find him, thank him. How did he feel, that he had saved one, been too late for the other? According to the paper, he had put his mouth over her son's and breathed life into him.

She climbed to the top of the dune and scanned the beach. No Max.

Carol went back to the car and drove past the wide pavement next to the road as it sloped down towards the beach. Max and Daniel would sometimes race each other there and her heart leapt at the sight of a boy on a skateboard with his cap on backwards. It wasn't her son.

It was almost 5 p.m. Should she go to the police? It was still a few hours before dark; they would probably laugh at her concern.

Maybe he was already at home? She phoned his cell, no reply. Drove to the other end of the beach, to the swimming area; still no Max. To the skateboarding park in the school grounds but there were only a couple of Max's friends messing about and they hadn't seen him.

Back at home she made herself a cup of tea and considered the options. Could he have gone to Daniel's parents? She should phone to check but she couldn't face them again. She had a live boy to worry about when he was late; their boy was never coming home again.

She poured herself a large glass of white wine and started on the cupboards in the study.

By 6:30 she couldn't take it anymore. She was trying to find the telephone directory to look up a number for the police when the front door opened and Max came in. He was absolutely filthy, his clothes and skin smeared with mud. His skateboard was under an arm. He dropped it in a corner.

'Hi, Ma,' he said, as though nothing was wrong. He looked better, as though a spark had found its way back into him.

'Where the hell have you been?' Carol burst into tears.

A clasp in Max's face closed. He shrugged. 'On the mountain. I'm going to take a shower, okay? Save the drama for later.'

'He'd been to the caves,' Carol told Dr Ndlovu. 'The mountains behind our home are riddled with apertures and caverns, some of them safe and straightforward but some are very dangerous. I've never gone myself, it's not my thing, I can't bear confined spaces. I do know that you can get lost, if you don't know what you are doing. You can fall down a crevice, you can die. He'd been a couple of times with Daniel and his father who was a member of the speleological society and super safety conscious. This time Max had gone alone and the torch battery had given out. He had to feel his way back to the entrance.'

Max had explained this casually over dinner as though he'd simply missed a train and had had to walk home. Carol could barely speak she was so horrified by what could have happened to him.

'There isn't a problem, Ma,' he'd pointed out, coldly, reasonably, through a mouthful of potato. 'Here I am, I'm fine. *You're* the one with the problem.'

'If there's one thing you need to learn, my boy,' yelled Carol, 'it's to take responsibility. I'm not the bloody problem! You're the one who put yourself at risk, yet again! Why are you doing this? You've put me through an exceedingly stressful day.' She couldn't believe her ears. She was shouting at her beloved son. 'Oh Max! You were damn lucky today, you need to realise that. The other day, at the dunes, you were also terribly, terribly lucky. If you keep doing risky things, one day your luck will run out. You have to promise me not to be so stupid!'

It was too late, she had said all the wrong things. He stared at her as though she was the enemy. 'It was fun,' he said, picking the olives out of his salad with fingers that still had black rims of cave dirt under the nails, and placing them onto her plate. 'But you wouldn't understand about fun.'

17.

Dr Ndlovu looked in his diary. 'Would you come to have a session with Max before he is discharged?'

Carol nodded. 'Good idea.' She was sure Dr Ndlovu would shore up her position.

'I'll give you a ring then, once I've spoken to Max.' Dr Ndlovu rose, indicating that the interview was over. But Carol wasn't ready to leave.

'Are you ... do you have a moment?'

Dr Ndlovu glanced at his watch. 'All right.'

'Thank you. I wanted to ask, what do you think about dreams?'

He resumed his seat. 'There are several theories. One is that they are random events in the brain which help the mind to rest and recharge. Like when you defragment the hard drive of your computer. Another is that dreams assist memory in some way that is linked to metaphor. The latest finding is that dreaming involves the area of the brain devoted to searching. What we are searching for is still under debate.'

'What's *your* opinion?'

Dr Ndlovu shifted in his seat. 'Some branches of psychiatric thought don't dismiss ancient belief systems. Many ancient cultures across the world view dreams as a coded language through which the collective unconscious, or the ancestors, communicate with us. They believe dreams can be messages of encouragement or can contain guidance or even warnings and prophesies. Mainstream psychiatry regards these theories as unscientific. At this juncture. Why do you ask?'

'The night before Max did this stunt I dreamt about him. It was a very powerful experience and the feeling of the dream has not let me go.' Carol scanned Dr Ndlovu's face. 'I don't know whether it is relevant.'

'Would you like to tell me?' Hard to say whether he was merely being polite or if he was genuinely interested.

She hesitated. 'Dreams are a bit like emotions, aren't they? Scientists avoid them, because they are so … nebulous, subjective, so *illogical*.'

Dr Ndlovu twitched his cheeks into something close to a smile. 'It is changing. We now have ways to study emotions and we know that the emotional systems are crucial for psychological development and for learning. In other words, for survival.'

'You think that maybe that's true of dreams?'

'I do, but don't tell anyone.' There was definitely a smile playing at his lips.

Carol took a breath. 'I was walking along some cliffs next to the sea. It was a clear blue day, warm and relaxing. Then I saw an airplane high in the sky, a huge passenger plane. I realised, to my horror, that Max was the pilot and that he didn't know how to fly planes. He started doing tricks, aerobatic stunts, loop-the-loop, things like that. I didn't know whether he was doing it on purpose or whether he was out of control. The plane was full of people and I knew he was going to kill not only himself but everyone else on the plane. I was rigid with fear, not knowing what to do. I was absolutely powerless. It felt absolutely dreadful to stand there, impotent in the face of this disaster.

'Suddenly the plane tilted and went into a downward spiral, completely out of control. Just before it crashed into the sea, something shot loose from the plane and I realised that Max had managed to eject himself from the cockpit. A parachute unravelled above him and snapped open. His body jerked on the end of the strings, slowed down and floated towards the sea. Below him, the plane smashed into the water and disappeared.

'The next thing, Max came walking up from the coast. He was unhurt, strong, confident. He strode straight past without looking at me. I went after him, wanting to talk to him but he came to a high fence made of barbed wire, jumped over it in one stride and carried on without hesitating or looking back.

I stood there, unable to scale the fence myself, watching him tramp away across the fields, getting smaller and smaller until I couldn't see him anymore. I realised he wanted people to think he had died in the plane crash.

'Also, I knew that it would take ten years.'

'Ten years?'

'Before he came back.'

Dr Ndlovu nodded and folded his hands over his abdomen. 'What do you make of that?' he asked.

'I don't know. It was both terrible and reassuring. Can you trust a dream, what it appears to mean? How symbolic are dreams, or how literal? Can they help in any way, can they give us practical information?'

'These are important and profound questions,' Dr Ndlovu replied. 'They are worth asking. We don't have the answers yet. You must understand that I work in a department that for the most part is fairly hostile to the idea that dreams have meaning.' He hesitated a moment. 'My personal view is that it is arrogant to assume that the ways people have tried to understand the world before the advent of science is all superstitious nonsense. The Xhosa culture, as with all very old cultures, values the stories that arise in the night. The old way is to consult our dreams to help direct our actions.

'Your dream speaks to the heart of this matter. What it is trying to tell us is a question for poets, traditional healers, prophets. It is a mystery that we should not put too quick an interpretation on.'

'The ten years? Do you think it's a literal ten years?'

'We don't know. If dreams were easy we would have worked it all out by now. I'd say that the dream is optimistic, even if he doesn't turn around and acknowledge you or if he only comes back after ten years.'

Carol had an urge to rise, cross the room and squeeze in next to Dr Ndlovu on his wide government-issue chair, even to sit on his lap and ask him to put his large warm arms around her and to hold her, keep holding her tight, while she sobbed into his white-coated shoulder.

Instead, she held herself in her seat and wondered about this man, whether he was married and had kids, whether life had tripped him up yet, whether he ever felt desperate in the middle of the night. No wedding ring on his finger.

Dr Ndlovu glanced at his watch and stood. 'Thank you for trusting me with your dream. Excuse me, I must go. The ward calls.'

18.

Before going back to the ICU, Carol stopped off at the ladies' toilets. Once inside a cubicle, she flipped the lock. She was usually squeamish about public loos, spreading toilet paper on the seat before she sat, but today she didn't care. She sat straight down onto the toilet seat and released her bladder while letting tears flood her face. She wiped them away, kept wiping them with the back of her hand, then pulled a long streamer of toilet paper out of the dispenser and blew her nose. Tears kept coming, a wellspring rising out of the mess of emotion in her chest.

'You okay?' A concerned young voice from the other side of the partition.

Carol controlled her sobbing. 'Absolutely fine, thanks.'

'You sure?'

'Please, just leave me alone.'

Carol waited for the restroom door to bang closed behind the owner of the voice, then reached to pull out another length of paper. Next to the metal casing housing the stack of rolls was a line of graffiti scrawled in a slanty black koki: *Could you please fuck the sadness out of me.*

The futility of the idea, that sex could displace more sadness than it ultimately generated. Alone, she felt very alone, kept from everything she loved by barbed wire. She sobbed for all the intimate losses she had suffered over the years, a blunt pain inserting itself behind her ribs, brought on by the memory of how the taste and caress of another human being had been able to delay the terror of uncertainty for a while. Jeremy, during medical school and Jack, more recently, had been the loves of her life. There had been others but those were the two she'd hoped she could build a home with, a refuge. She had wanted to create something different from the way she'd been brought up, the staid convention that her parents had adhered to. That way of life had looked unattractive to her as a girl, in fact she had despised it, but it now looked fantastically and wonderfully stable.

A sad understanding came to her of the illusions she'd tended with such hope, how she'd imagined she would be able to make a particular kind of life for herself and her child, composing it out of sheer goodwill and willpower. It was too hard, being a single parent, particularly of a son, a human being filled to the brim with those mysterious Y chromosomes, who could walk off out of her life, away from the embrace of her breast and into another parallel and incomprehensible universe. If she'd known better, could she have avoided all this? Although she couldn't think of any of her friend's children who had turned out completely normal. Except, of course, for Pat's son Malcolm, who had a job at the bank and played cricket and had married the girl across the road who had given up her teaching job because she was pregnant with their first child. It wasn't normal to be so normal, something was bound to come along and upset the predictability those two had innocently, yet determinedly, engineered for themselves. Upsetting seemed to be the new normal.

Upset. Of course, that was what Max was aiming for, to tip up, trip up, our ideas of normal, ideas that were clearly completely mad. She flushed the toilet, unlocked the door, went to the basin and washed her hands. Stood in front of the mirror for a while, trying to restore her eyes.

Max didn't own the rights to performance art! a voice in her head pointed out. Anyone could do it. Maybe she could get through to him in his own language. She could parade around outside his flat in sackcloth and ashes, wailing and beating her chest. She could chain herself to the security gate and howl.

As she stepped out into the hospital corridor, the ground seemed to tilt and list. She put a hand against the wall. Vasovagal. Stress. Whatever. She had to get a grip on all of this somehow, in order to get through day-to-day life. She had never felt so out of control.

Hedley was at the bedside when she returned. He got up when he saw her, scraping the chair back. 'Afternoon, Mrs T. Good news! Max tried to pull that breathing tube thing out just now so the doctor came and took it out. Max is starting to wake up.' He looked over at Max whose eyes were still closed. 'I pinched him and he told me to fuck off.'

Carol felt a flush of relief. The oxygen saturation monitor showed that his levels were normal. Her son was going to be okay. Until next time. 'I don't know what to say to you, Hedley.'

'Hi there?'

'You know exactly what I mean.'

He offered her the chair but Carol wasn't about to sit and give him a height advantage. They stood and looked at each other over the chair. Hedley cracked first. 'Okay, Mrs T, look, I don't have kids but I reckon you must be a bit freaked out.'

This wasn't the place to tell Hedley what she thought of him. She beckoned him to follow her. There was an alcove outside the ICU with hospital chairs for relatives to wait their turn while visiting their loved ones. Even there she would have to keep her voice down and her language clean. A stooped and elderly man with a goatee was pacing the corridor, too distressed to sit, waiting for something, news of an operation perhaps?

Carol indicated to Hedley that he should sit opposite her. 'Look, I don't know whether you talked him into any of this but we have to damn well talk him out of it.' Hedley raised his eyebrows. 'You realise, he will actually manage to do it one of these days. Don't you? Don't you care that your friend will kill himself?'

'Of course I care, Mrs T. Why d'you reckon I'm right there when he does his performances? I'm not only recording his work, my job is also to pull him back if he goes too far.'

'That is blatantly not true! I saw the YouTube footage, how the security people had to break the door down to get to Max! Why was it locked?'

'That wasn't the plan! The dude didn't tell me! You should know your son by now. He gets these crazy ideas, many of which I also happen to think are very, very amazing. No one's going to stop him doing what he does. He's got the whole thing worked out. The Goodman Gallery's approached him. They want the videos of *Burning Man*, *Holy Tablet* and *Shoot The Messenger* to be on a group show next year.'

'The Goodman! In Cape Town?' One of the most prestigious galleries in the country.

'Yep. At the end of the year.' Hedley was beaming. 'Then the work will go to AARG.'

'AARG?'

'The Art Attack Remix Gallery. A new contemporary gallery in New York. Isn't that so amazingly cool? They want four pieces, so he has to complete *Shoot The Messenger* and one other he's planning.'

'What's *Shoot The Messenger*?' Pressure was building in Carol's neck.

'He's still got to work out how I get to video it without –' He saw the look on Carol's face. 'Sorry Mrs T, I've already said more than I should've.'

'Tell me!' Already her imagination was flashing scenes of Max putting himself in front of a firing squad.

Hedley shifted uncomfortably. 'Ask Max rather, but don't stress.'

Stupid oaf. 'Don't you tell me not to stress! What's wrong with you, that you're so okay with all this?'

'Because your son's going to make it big. He's applied for some artist's residencies in Europe, at Bellagio and some island off Germany. He's already uploaded his CV and artist's statement. I've got to finish editing *Holy Tablet* and get it off today, in time for the deadline.' Hedley fumbled his cell phone out of his pocket while he talked and checked the time. 'Got to go, Mrs T. Watch this space. You got a son who's going to the top and he's got something amazing to say. As long as I've known him he's lived on the edge. That's his space, that's his comfort zone, he doesn't give a flying fuck how freaked out that makes the rest of us, excuse my French. That's what he's aiming to do, spread alarm. As he would say, we're all alarmed and armed to the hilt but we're not alarmed enough.' Hedley's eyes were shining.

'You mean the art galleries are encouraging Max to put his life on the line?' Carol felt ill. 'It's unethical! Surely this is … it must be illegal?'

'There's no law against killing yourself or at least making a stab at it. Er, excuse the pun. Us humans, we're doing that most of the time anyway only we don't know it. Max is on a mission to show us. That's his subject matter, man. That's where you're at too as a doctor, hey? You see it every day. We're all on a humongous suicide mission, fucking up the earth too. The two of you, you're looking down the same tube from different ends.'

It was a shocking thought. Carol wanted to point out flaws in his argument but her mind was stuck in emotional quicksand.

'There is one thing you could do for Max. Be on his team. He needs a doctor on standby, you know, right there, when he does his performances.'

'Are you out of your …'

'Okay, okay, don't hassle. I got to mission.' He stood and a sliver of white belly streaked with dark hair winked at her from between his t-shirt and jeans. 'Max'll kill me if I don't get the video off.'

He turned to go, then remembered: 'Sorry to ask, Mrs T, but d'you think you could organise a script for me? For my acne meds?' Going by Carol's expression, he decided to drop it.

She watched him lope away, his outsized jeans creeping down his bum, the crotch halfway to his knees, the tattered ends of his pants scraping on the floor. 'I'm not a Mrs!' she shouted after him but he had already disappeared into the lift.

She went back into the ICU. Max had turned onto his side but was still sleeping, his long hair a mess on the pillow. His legs were pulled up, his hands curled under his chin, foetus-like, the sleeping position he had adopted since childhood. The exposed skin of his face and arms was so pale and his breathing was so shallow, that, if it wasn't for the regular beep and the skip of the line on the screen of the heart monitor, she would have thought he was dead. It was a matter of time before she was called to identify his body on a mortuary slab, shot through with bullets, or charred, or with life flushed out of it with a cocktail of chemicals. Not trusting the machines, she touched his arm to check with her own body, and felt the warmth of his life still in him.

He gave a small sigh at her touch but didn't wake.

Carol sat down to wait. She should have brought a book to distract her from the terror agitating inside her. Flipping through the newspaper, she finished the sudoku and word games quickly, then stared out of the window at impassive clouds drifting over a grey sky.

We all wanted to save the world when we were young, she thought, remembering her student involvement in the townships and ploughing her way through Marx and Gramsci.

She had the sudden notion that cutting his hair and shaving his beard off would change him back to kind, innocent compliance.

Or Jack. Maybe if she found Jack and told him what had happened he could help. The thought of him brought twists of anger and of longing to her gut. Bad idea, but she couldn't think of a better one.

19.

A week after Max had broken his hand, Carol was cutting his steak up for him when her work cell phone rang. Her son glanced up as she took the call and started rocking on the back legs of his chair, which always annoyed her.

'Dr Trehorne speaking.' Zubeida was right, she should switch it off when she was not on duty. She worried about not being available in case something happened to one of her patients.

'Um, is that Max's mother?'

'Yes, who is this please?' Another reporter, no doubt.

'Ah, it's Jack. Jack here.'

Jack. Carol flicked through her mind for a patient of that name. 'What can I do for you, Jack?'

'I'm calling to find out how your son's doing.' Some crank, who'd seen the article in the paper?

'Who are you, Jack?'

'Ah, I, um. I was there. When it happened.'

'Sorry, I'm confused. You mean you saw the accident?'

'I dug your son out and I wondered how he's –'

'Jack! I thought the person's name was John, the papers –'

'Well, yes, strictly speaking, my name, the name I was christened with, is John. That's the one I used, ah, for the papers.'

'Oh, John, I mean Jack, I've been wanting to get hold of you.'

'I don't mean to intrude –'

'No, no, you aren't, not at all. I didn't know how to get hold of you to thank you.'

Max: 'Who's that?' Pushing against the table top, rocking his chair.

'My son's right here, he's doing well. Max, this is the man who –'

'I, er, have his cap. The ambulance left his cap behind. Red. Arsenal. Your son's a soccer fan?'

'Oh, thank you. Where do you live?'

'I can drop it round.'

'Well, thanks so much. He's got your cap, Max, the man who saved you.'

'Well, I was in the right place, um, at the right time.'

'How about tomorrow? Come for tea, three p.m.? We're in Clovelly. Twelve Robins Road. Look out for the purple gate.'

'Let me speak to him.' Max grabbed the phone from her. 'The colour wasn't my idea. It's my mother, she likes purple.'

Carol surveyed her living room, trying to see it as if for the first time. Pumi only came once a week and the place was a mess – plates from lunch not yet washed up, Max's daypack and takkies abandoned in a corner, yesterday's paper open on the sofa.

The living room needed painting again, the wooden countertops in the open-plan kitchen needed resealing. She hated the Jetmaster fireplace, so angular, black and squat, like a monster alien virus beamed down into the heart of her home. The curtains simply had to go. What had she been thinking those years ago when she'd chosen the pink floral pattern on cream? It was so sentimental. Jack would get the wrong idea about her.

She liked the sound of Jack. The hesitant, warm voice, with a slight lisp, conferred humility on the owner. She imagined a studious, serious man, whose hairline was retreating slightly from intelligent temples. Strong hands connected to a shy heart. Hands that knew exactly what to do in a crisis.

Carol caught sight of herself in the mirror hanging near the door. Too hard, too fierce, with a frown furrow gashed into the skin between her eyebrows. Enough to put anyone off. She tried to soften her features, pulling up the corners of her mouth. Unconvincing.

It was ridiculous. The man was probably married.

'Max!' she yelled. 'Come and tidy up.' Her instruction was the first step in their habitual dance where Max had perfected the sidesteps and she would inevitably end up at the sink with her hands in soapy water, irritable with the knowledge that she had been manipulated yet again. Now with his fingers strapped, he had a good excuse. She was raising a patriarch, she worried as she rinsed the plates off, a man who expected the woman to do all the housework. 'Max!' she tried again. 'Come and put your stuff away.' No response.

At 3 p.m. sharp Max was out of his bedroom and on the sofa looking out of the living room window towards the gate. At eighteen minutes past three Jack had still not arrived.

Max came through to the kitchen and opened the fridge door. Stood staring at the contents. 'He isn't coming,' he said, with what sounded like a mix tureof disappointment and relief.

'Lucky he wasn't late when he saved you,' Carol remarked as she folded the dry washing.

'Ma-a! You can't be late *and* save someone!' They both went quiet, thinking of Daniel.

'Maybe he got lost. Maybe we should phone him,' Carol suggested, noting her own mixed feelings.

'You got his number?'

'It'll be on my phone. Close that fridge, you're letting all the cold air out. Come and help with your socks.' Why were there hardly ever matching pairs? 'Do you remember what he looks like?'

'Sort of. There were loads of people, all gawking.' He went silent for a moment, remembering. 'He had a funny lip and dark hair. A bit curly, I think. Dark brown.'

'A funny lip?'

'He had this scar.'

A gangster? 'Did you get to speak to him?'

'No. I was coughing too much. Then they put me into the ambulance.'

The buzzer went. Max ran to the intercom and pressed the button to open the gate. A massive black dog with a disproportionately huge head burst into their garden. A tall man at the other end of a lead was dragged into view behind the animal who came to a halt, sniffing round the bottom of a large terracotta pot containing a wild olive tree. The dog lifted his leg and released a long, splashing stream, wetting the red ceramic. The man looked up towards Max and Carol, who had rushed outside and were standing expectantly on the stoep, and half raised his hand in a shy greeting. He was muscular and tanned, with a wild mess of dark hair, slashes of grey at his temples. A scar ran from his upper lip into his right nostril, slightly distorting the contour of his mouth as though someone had pulled a thread in the cloth of his flesh. A prominent nose and brown eyes slightly hidden beneath emphatic eyebrows. An interesting rather than handsome face.

The dog was roaming around at the end of the leash, snout down, sniffing like an olfactory vacuum cleaner. Then he galumphed off the path, jerking at his owner, his large paws crushing the pennyroyal that had come into bloom. Jack came towards them, half-smiling, or was he scowling? Perhaps not, perhaps the lip made it seem so.

Carol went down the steps, trying to convert her wide-eyed, clenched-shouldered horror about the dog into an enthusiastic, relaxed, wide-eyed greeting. 'You must be Jack! Hello, I'm Carol and –'

'What a great dog!' Max was holding his uninjured hand out for the animal to sniff, then was patting it and putting his arms around the creature. He had always wanted a dog but Carol had a thing about the way they rolled in shit and, unlike cats, didn't clean their bums and then sat down on the carpet with their wormy, E coli-infested anuses right up against the weave.

'Um, hi.' Jack grabbed her hand, squeezed the blood out of her fingers and let it go. The skin of his palm was surprisingly rough. He turned to Max. 'Hi buddy.'

'Careful, Max,' Carol worried, 'he doesn't know you, he might bite.'

'Oh, I don't bite!' Jack exclaimed; Max glanced up at him, his face breaking open with laughter, his eyes alive. 'Kraken won't either,' Jack reassured Carol. 'He's a very gentle giant.' He looked around. 'Any cats?' he asked.

'No.'

'Oh, good. He's scared of cats.'

'No, really?' Max, astonished.

Jack flashed a smile. 'Nah, just kidding.' He glanced at Carol. 'Dogs?'

'No dogs either.'

'Do you mind if I take him off the leash?' He was already bending over the dog to release him.

Of course she minded. 'It's fine,' she said.

'Kraken? Isn't that a sea monster?' Max asked.

'Yep, he loves the beach. He chases after ships, especially navy vessels.'

'Really?'

Jack gave a snort. 'Never managed to catch one though.'

Max realised he'd been caught again and giggled. 'What make is he?' Max ran his hand down the dog's back.

'He's a cross between a Land Rover and a Rolls-Royce,' he said, 'with a bit of Great Dane thrown in.'

Excited by the attention, the dog was wagging his tail so much his hindquarters swung from side to side. He lifted his head and barked enthusiastically, great bites of sound, as though trying to contribute to the conversation. Turning his head towards her son, he opened his vast and sloppy jaws, stuck out a walloping great steak of a tongue and licked him on the cheek. Carol wrestled with herself to overcome her disgust, realising that it was the first time since the accident that she had heard Max laughing.

'What happened to your hand?'

Max's face darkened.

'He had an accident while we were away for the weekend,' Carol explained. 'Knocked it and broke the bone.' That's what she was saying to people to save Max's feelings, to save her own.

She invited Jack inside. The dog, of course, had to come too, bringing dirt and faeces and fur into her home. She wanted to protest about allergies, infections; she was sure dogs could pass on terrible diseases to humans, tapeworm, perhaps?

That tail. Any moment now, Aunt Josephine's antique

porcelain vase would be swept off the top of the bookcase or her father's crystal decanter would crash into splinters on the floor. Carol's smile had turned to sparkling ice.

'Sit!' Jack ordered and thank goodness, Kraken not only sat but collapsed down onto the kelim in the centre of the floor, his tail thumping. Bang, bang, bang.

Max sat next to him and continued to fondle the loose flaps of his ears. 'He's as big as a horse!' he exclaimed.

'Well, as big as a pony, maybe.' Jack sat down in the middle of the sofa, legs akimbo, his hands clasped behind his head. 'Good thing he's a strong boy. He helped dig you out.'

'Really?' Max's face opened with awe.

'Yep, he's a great digger. You should see the garden where I stay. When I saw the dune cave in with your foot still sticking out, um, I didn't have to say a thing. As soon as I started digging, he did too.'

Max turned to Carol, his eyes glowing. 'That's why I had scratches on my legs! It was Kraken!'

'What a wonderful animal,' Carol conceded in a thin voice, staring at his jaws. They were like the chomping compacting mechanism at the back of rubbish trucks. It wasn't the animal's fault that he was a dog. 'He must have some St Bernard in him,' she offered, trying to whip up enthusiasm. His pink slab of tongue was draped over a rim of potentially lethal teeth and dangling over the slack black mouth edge; it slid in and out slightly in time with his whole-body panting, like a metronome. There were probably fleas hopping off and infesting her home right now. She forced her attention onto Jack. 'Tea? Coffee?'

'Coffee please.'

She went through to the kitchen and put the kettle on. Jack looked like a nice enough person at first glance but even a psychopath wouldn't walk past a suffocating child. Then she castigated herself for her paranoia, her suspicious mind, her lack of gratitude.

'Here's your cap,' she heard Jack say.

'Thanks a lot. You got children?' Max asked.

'Nope.'

'Why not?'

Jack was quiet a moment as though sifting through possible replies. 'I reckon … well, there are already too many of us.'

'Too many?'

'Well, yes.'

'How do you know?'

Good question, thought Carol.

Silence. Then Jack replied, 'Well, um, in nature, in the way of nature, populations are kept in check by famine and predators. Infections, ah, things like that. But humans have found ways to exterminate most of the things that are a threat to our lives.'

'What's exterminate?'

'Get rid of. So we live too long and there are too many of us. We get out of balance with the other animals and plants and things. We take up too much space, use up too many resources. That causes problems.'

This is so inappropriate, Carol worried, as she spooned coffee into the plunger. He's talking to a child who has lost his best friend.

'My contribution,' continued Jack, 'to life, is not to make babies.'

Didn't stop you having a dog, thought Carol. Too many damn dogs in the world. Besides, that's not the real reason, she decided. It's your bloody birth defect. You're making up this whole long story to justify your inability to get it together with a woman.

'Why did you have me, Ma?'

Good God, she had no idea that sex education would start with this tangent. She absolutely could not admit that the condom broke. 'Because … I love you.'

'You didn't know me before you had me, so how could you love me?'

'I just did. That's how it was. Sometimes love is what makes things happen.'

These were things she hardly discussed with anyone, certainly not in front of strangers. Carefully carrying the mugs through to the lounge, she skirted the mound of moulting dog in the middle of the room and came to stand beside Jack. As she leaned over and stretched her arm to set down his mug of coffee – strong, black and sweet – in front of him, she was aware of their sudden proximity, of the musk sweat smell of him, not unpleasant, and the slightly skittish way he held, even withheld, his otherwise full and able body.

He's someone who's been hurt, Carol thought, someone who understands how it feels to be unwanted. She straightened up, feeling a pressure in her chest of wanting to explain that he needn't be afraid, not of her. Jack looked up quickly, a guarded look; embarrassed, she went to sit opposite and ran her fingers through her hair, pushing it off her forehead. Was she attractive? Enough? 'What do you do, Jack?'

'I … um, repair computers.'

'Really?'

'Wow Ma, Jack can fix your laptop!' Max bent his knees to gather his legs into his arms and rocked enthusiastically on the fulcrum of his bum.

Carol's screen had been freezing and she had to constantly restart. Messages popped up containing incomprehensible warnings. The computer man had failed to arrive as arranged and then had not been contactable.

'Would you? Take a look?' He didn't come with references but she owed him. She couldn't help it: when she looked at Jack, her eyes automatically slid down to where his upper lip had been sewed closed, no doubt as well as the plastic surgeon could manage given what he'd had to work with; nevertheless the job looked unfinished. She wondered whether Jack had ever let anyone close enough to kiss him, put their whole lips against that scar and kiss him better.

Jack appeared disconcerted. 'Ah … I'm quite busy at the moment –'

By the time he left, he had Carol's laptop with him and they had an excuse to see him again.

20.

As Carol made her way to the psychiatry department, she wondered whether she should bring the subject of Jack up with Max in Dr Ndlovu's presence. Could Katy be right? That Jack's example those years ago had set her son on this track? The way Jack had left must have done damage, too.

Max was already sitting outside Dr Ndlovu's office door. Hedley was next to him with his video camera equipment. 'What are you doing here?' Carol demanded.

'Good morning Mrs T!' Hedley had shaved his beard off and his pale cheeks had surprisingly cherubic dimples.

'Cool it, Ma! You can be so rude.'

'Well, sorry, I didn't mean to be, I'm surprised, that's all. Just trying to get some information where there's a lot missing.'

Dr Ndlovu's door opened. He blinked at them through his heavy lenses. 'Do come in.'

Max stood, inserted his hands in the back pockets of his jeans, pushing his chest out. 'Dr Ndlovu, would you mind if my friend Hedley films our interview?'

The psychiatrist looked from Max to Hedley to Carol.

'I mind!' Carol's face heated up.

'Sorry, Max,' said Dr Ndlovu. 'In that case I can't agree to it. All parties must be comfortable with something like that.'

'What is your problem?!' Her own son, turning on her. Other people were staring. 'You always have to have things your way.'

'If you think about it Max,' interjected Dr Ndlovu quietly, 'we might well get round to discussing sensitive and personal issues. If you record it, that material can be shown to anyone else. It isn't surprising that your mother is unwilling.'

'Who exactly is this session supposed to be about?'

'Come inside, so we can discuss this.' Dr Ndlovu gestured.

'Let him in!' A henna-haired, middle-aged woman in a colourful robe shouted. 'He deserves a place in the Kingdom of Heaven.'

'Hallelujah!' Max called out, smiling at her. He put his palms together and bowed towards the patient in a confusingly Buddhist gesture. He turned back to the doctor. 'My mother is not required to say a single thing. I thought we were meeting so I can explain my actions to her –'

Dr Ndlovu looked at Carol. 'You all right with that? As a place to start?'

Max was glaring at her, daring her. 'I don't want to be filmed,' she insisted. 'I am not a pawn in one of your art pieces.'

'You okay with being filmed?' Max asked Dr Ndlovu.

He hesitated. 'It's very unusual … but … all right, if it is important to you –'

Max turned to Hedley. 'It could be quite cool, to have this disembodied mother, as a voice in the background.'

'Come in then.' Dr Ndlovu led them into his office.

'It was ghastly. I don't know my child any more. He was deliberately provocative, a damn impenetrable wall.'

'What happened?' Peter was sitting next to her on a bench overlooking the wetlands with the evening sky spreading like fire above them.

'Max wouldn't take it seriously. He turned the whole session into performance. He lay down on Dr Ndlovu's desk and closed his eyes and started a kind of incantation, something about him being a sacrificial lamb, that he was carrying the burden of the sins of the world yet the world had turned on him, turned him into the problem. He sounded psychotic, I didn't know whether to be afraid or embarrassed, he was going on and on about how he'd been very sick and through his sickness he'd been called into service, that his calling would help to cure him but that even if the cure killed him, he wasn't sure it was enough to remedy the world, alleviate its own death, or madness, something like that, I can't remember all of it.

'Hedley filmed the whole thing, so no doubt you will be able to see it on the internet. Poor Dr Ndlovu just stood there, not knowing what to do. I was thinking, why doesn't he call security in, get this maniac off his papers? He stood and listened as though Max was a bloody orator, or a prophet. He actually showed him respect!'

'That's amazing.'

'No it's not! Max pushes things too far, he's inappropriate. He was being disrespectful to me, wasting my time and Dr Ndlovu's, so why does he deserve respect back? The very crisis in the world that Max is trying to stare down is caused by lack of consideration for others. The Great Performance Artist is missing his own point!'

'Maybe the best way to help is to listen respectfully, no matter what else is going on. You can't get very far if you don't even do that.'

Carol stared at her friend, then looked away towards the birds fidgeting and chittering in the reeds. The stretch of water before them amplified the beauty of the sky. Her HIV-infected, alcoholic-in-recovery, struggling musician friend possessed an attitude she didn't share, not really, not when it really mattered, like with one's own flesh and blood. She was still left standing at that hurt locked gate, needing to turn her son around no matter what clever arguments he might construct, needing him to face towards her and away from the cliff and the mystical pull of death.

After Max had left, Dr Ndlovu had assured her that he was not psychotic. But, as she knew from interactions with self-destructive patients in her own consulting room, psychosis was not the only way people lost touch with reality.

She felt the warm pressure of Peter's hand on her knee. 'I bet before you had one that you thought having a child would be easy.'

'*Not* having a child wouldn't have been easy for me either, so that is a remarkably unhelpful comment.'

'I'm sorry.'

'I want to ask him, what is wrong with you? But the task

of life seems to be to stop yourself from saying all the spot-on things you've always wanted to say for fear of alienating, or interfering, or dominating your child, or doing all those damaging things the psychology books are brim full of.' She stood. 'There's another clip of Max's that I stumbled across the other day, another performance on YouTube that he never told me about. Will you come and watch it with me? I'm scared of what I might see.'

They started strolling back. She was grateful for the comfort when he put his arm around her shoulders. To see them together, they could easily be mistaken for a couple. If Peter wasn't gay and HIV positive and terrible with money and a struggling musician, if he preferred Joni Mitchell to Bach and wasn't neurotic about things being straight and symmetrical, if he could get over his fear of dentists and flying, she could marry him and live happily ever after.

Back at home, she got out her laptop and sat next to Peter on the sofa. She went online and checked for Max's clip. *Food/Fast*. Steeling herself, she clicked on play.

A younger Max was slouching in an armchair in a studio – was it at art school? – watching television. On the screen, a hearty chef was doing a cooking demonstration with close-ups of the food he was preparing. He was whipping cream into stiff little peaks, grating slabs of dark chocolate, lowering cuts of meat into sizzling pans. To Max's left, a conveyor belt emerged from behind a curtained-off area bearing all manner of foodstuffs, delivering them to a coffee table in front of him – fruit, packets of nuts, cooldrink, ice cream, popcorn. Items of food kept on coming from under the curtain and kept arriving at the table. Max's eyes hardly left the screen as he reached for the items – chips, roasted chicken drumsticks, bars of chocolate, polystyrene plates of sushi, fish fingers, burgers, bananas and then ate them, kept eating, crumbs and sauce dripping down his fingers and chin onto his t-shirt.

Behind him, back to back, was an elderly man, thin, in torn clothes, who was rummaging through a rubbish bin, looking for scraps of food. As Max finished a portion, he would throw the packaging or peels over his shoulder, aiming approximately for the bin, while keeping his eyes on the cooking programme. As the packaging fell into, or next to the bin, or even onto him, the man would grab it hungrily and start to lick it, trying to extract the smallest discarded morsel.

The cooking programme started speeding up, jumping around and looping; at the same time the conveyor belt began to run faster. Max was tearing packets open, not even stopping to check what they contained. He was shoving food into his mouth, chewing faster and faster, struggling to swallow it down – he was clearly full, yet the food kept coming. The table was becoming clogged with unopened edibles, packages were falling off the edge, food and sauces were spilling onto the floor. Max – his mouth bulging, gorged and nauseous, bits of food dropping from his lips – gave a couple of heaves then bent over to the side, stuck a finger down his throat and vomited; as he righted himself, his eyes locked back onto the cooking programme. He took a paper serviette from his lap, wiped his mouth and resumed eating.

The beggar continued to scratch in the bin.

A slide filled the screen:

A third of the food produced and bought is thrown into the bin or otherwise wasted. Half of our population is obese. The other half is starving.

Then the credits rolled.

Peter sat back. 'I was going to invite you out for a meal but after seeing that I don't exactly feel up to it.'

'I'll fix us something.'

'It's amazing how we all know this stuff, intellectually, but experiencing it on a visceral level really gets through.'

'Yep.' Carol was forced to admit. 'It's very ... raw.' As Carol opened her fridge the abundance inside seemed grotesque. There were definitely items in there that she would chuck because they were past use by date. 'I'm sure he hasn't got his facts right,' she said. 'It can't be a third, surely. He needs to get his facts right.'

'The fact is that we waste enormous amounts of food in the face of poverty. Why quibble about exact percentages? If I were a farmer, I would be furious.'

'Should art be about trying to change things? Doesn't that make it propaganda rather than art?'

'Art has always played an important role in holding up a mirror to show us who we are. Images are more powerful than facts. Advertisers and dictators know that.'

'Could you stomach an omelette?'

'Yes, thanks, but hang on a minute, follow the argument through. You think *Guernica* was propaganda?'

'*Guernica* was a protest against war, wasn't it? I don't see that Picasso's efforts have made any difference to the amount of aggression in the world.' Carol smacked an egg open, glooped it into a bowl.

'That painting travelled the world. It raised awareness about the Spanish Civil War. I'm sure that put pressure on Franco.'

'Has a work of art ever changed your bad behaviour?' She took up a whisk and beat the eggs with more vigour than necessary.

Peter laughed. '*Calvin and Hobbes* made me rethink my relationship with my father.'

'Seriously,' Carol insisted. Peter pulled out his cigarettes and lit up. He inhaled and blew some smoke rings towards the ceiling, watching them wobble open as they rose. 'See, you can't think of anything.'

'I was lucky enough to see one of Rothko's canvases once. I'd seen his work before of course, in books and had hardly bothered to look, they'd appeared so nondescript. But when I found myself in front of one of his actual paintings, I fell into great yet simple beauty that required deep attention. I sat in front of that painting for the whole afternoon. At first I had to fight the feeling that I must rush round and see the rest of the exhibition, or I would miss out. We were leaving Joburg the next day, so it was my only chance. The experience made me understand the power of slowing down, and what taking your time can bring to one simple, single thing.' He took a deep breath, remembering.

'That taught me something very valuable.'

'I'm talking about something practical, Peter, like giving up smoking. Is there any painting in the world that could induce you to chuck those disgusting Benson and Hedges? Or a sculpture that could stop Katy from bullying her awful husband? Never mind the grander projects of better laws and more thoughtful decisions made in government. Saving the planet, etcetera.'

'Katy's husband loves being bullied.'

'Ha! Maybe.'

'Playing Brahms makes me forget nicotine for a while.'

'Admit it, I've got a point. You know as well as I do that Max risking his life is not about to affect anything. If Max stuck to demonstrations like this one we've seen, about eating too much while people are starving, that would be fine.'

'Max understands what he's doing, it's not mindless, that's something to hold onto.'

'Does he?'

'We all have to live with ourselves, our choices.' Peter looked sad and old. 'We must all be able to go to sleep at night, at peace with our consciences.'

'I'm having a hell of a time trying to sleep and it has nothing to do with my conscience.'

That was a whopping great lie. Max's behaviour and her regrets about bad parenting had entangled her nights.

The omelette was sticking to the pan. She had to attack it with the egg flip to get it off, and now it looked more like scrambled egg. Carol's eyes were watery with thoughts of ruin. Stop being such a drama queen, she scolded herself. The damn stuff will end up tasting more or less the same.

21.

Soon Max was spending most afternoons after school at Jack's place. He lived a few kilometres from Carol's home on the Fish Hoek side of the vlei. Although Max could easily have walked home at suppertime, Carol would usually collect him on the way back from work.

The first time she fetched Max she was surprised to find she was quite nervous. She pulled up across the road from Jack's address. The apartments he lived in were stacked like building blocks – a top row with jutting balconies plonked on top of a bottom row that opened onto small boxed-in gardens. The residents in the top row had probably had a glimpse of the sea beyond the dunes before the shopping centre had erupted on Main Road; now the entire block looked directly onto the tarred, cemented and littered landscape of chain-store commerce.

Once through the security gate, she found Jack's flat on the ground floor at one end. Max opened the door, his face shining. 'Come look, Ma!' She stepped into a room which was originally an open-plan kitchen/lounge but was now a mayhem of surfaces cluttered with computers and computer parts and saturated with the smell of wet dog. Leads tangled their way across the dingy carpet, screensavers swayed and bounced across several screens around the room, complicated motherboard and wire innards stuck out of gutted metal box frames. Against the closest wall hung a rack of backpacks, loops of rope and bunches of small metal contraptions. Coffee mugs containing curdled liquids stood discarded on various surfaces. A guitar leaned against a wall. A net of cobwebs hung in one corner of the room.

At least this horror show was evidence that Jack didn't have a woman in his life. There was no way she could survive in this unholy, unhealthy mess. Jack, silhouetted against grimy French windows, was hauling his tall frame up from a dilapidated office chair where he was busy with some operation involving wires. A loud bark from outside and the monster bounded in, tail slapping, tongue flapping happily. In one movement he shoved his way past Jack and thrust his snout into Carol's crotch as though attracted by a magnet.

Carol cringed.

'Hello Ogre!' Carol gushed merrily, attempting to clench her legs closed while ineffectually trying to push the hound's head away without coming into contact with snot and saliva.

'Kraken, come here,' commanded Jack. 'Sit!' Kraken disengaged his snout and stared at Jack, wagging his tail. 'Tea? Coffee?'

'Come see, Ma.' Max sat down at a desk in front of a laptop and waved her over but Kraken was in the way, still lavishing his slobbery attention on her. 'Jack's given me a program you can draw with.'

'Sit, Kraken, you beast!' Jack's voice firmed up. The dog reluctantly obeyed his owner. 'Or perhaps you'd like some wine?' he suggested.

She glanced at her watch and hesitated. It was only 4:30. 'Max, have you done your homework?'

'Yes, Ma, I have, look here –'

'Isn't that my laptop?'

'Jack's fixed it and he's put this program on –'

'I don't want games on my computer.'

'It's not a game, it's a proper program, for professionals, it lets you draw and paint ... Look what I made.' On the screen was a cartoon of a boy riding a dog. Max and Kraken, down to the long tail and square head.

'He's got something.' Jack, behind her. The drawing was skilful. 'Here.' He handed her a mug of wine. 'Sorry about the vessel. I'm right out of cut crystal.'

'Thank you, that's very kind, I mean, the program ... You sure he's not disturbing you? Hanging out here?'

Jack shook his head. 'He's good company.' He raised his

mug. 'Besides, as you can see, I'm already very disturbed.' He smiled his scarred smile.

Carol clinked her mug against his and laughed. She thought Jack was joking.

After that, Max spent many afternoons with Jack, learning about computers or playing with Kraken, or else they were up the mountain together. Jack knew the local caves well and he was also a rock climber, which thrilled Max.

There was a solid aspect to Jack, a core that Carol felt she could trust. Something that Max could hold on to.

Her home was starting to feel like home again; her concern that she could not possibly be both mother and father to an adolescent boy was resolved. She sat on her veranda on one Sunday afternoon, when Max and Jack had gone climbing at Silvermine. For the first time in ages, Carol felt relaxed. She allowed herself a few tears of relief and a sad happiness. Being a single parent was too hard, it had made her too tough. She should soften up, she mused, be less resilient or at least chuck the habitual pretence at resilience. She should become more vulnerable and let the mad vicissitudes of life in. It was impossible, anyway, to keep them out, so one might as well take them on as a project.

It was almost a decade since anyone had put their compassionate, passionate arms around her, years since she had really been held other than the impersonal hugs everyone seemed to give out to anyone else at the drop of a hat. She missed the intimate embrace of being desired and of desiring, of being filled with the overt, tumescent evidence that a man actually liked her enough to get really close and personal. On occasion, sometimes in ridiculously inappropriate places like supermarkets or coffee shops and for no apparent reason, she would suddenly feel breathless with ardour. Her whole pelvis would ignite without warning, responding to some inner cue while waiting for some arbitrary person to weigh a bag of onions or bring her a cappuccino. Out of the blue she would be run through with want, the drive to engage with another person in the exquisite physical wrestle, the strange and complicatedly simple act of assisting one another towards the secret peak with its extreme pleasure, fulfilment, relief. She still had some hormones left and now and then they would scream around her body, rocking her boat, making her scan the lonely seas anxiously for possible docks.

Was she doomed to be on her own for the rest of her life? What was that – around forty more long years, going by the longevity of her maternal relatives? Was this the end of the relationship road? Where on earth were the men?

It was not as though she worked all on her own in an office or was self-employed in a business that required her to be closeted up at home. She worked right in the middle of one of the great corridors of life: in clinical medicine, which was a transit lounge where human beings were forced to spend some time. She had met a huge number of people, kept meeting them all the time and many of them were men. Men who were in pain, depressed and anxious men, men with abscesses and piles, concussion and chainsaw accidents. Men who had stomach ulcers from binges and stress, athletes who limped in with inflamed tendons, boozers hobbling with gout, men sweating or gasping with chest pain or kidney stones; men with broken fingers, eczema, palpitations and allergies.

She was practised at placing her left hand reassuringly on their shoulders while she pressed her stethoscope to their chests, listening to the timbre of their hearts and the shush of their lungs; she would gently examine their painful testicles with gloved hands and bend over their split, hurt foreheads to stitch them carefully back into their skins, or probe their cramping abdomens with her inquiring fingers. Up close she'd get, but never personal.

Yet very few of them had appealed to her. Why was that? Was there something wrong with her? Granted, many of the men were already in relationships; some – going by the gonorrhoeal discharges and HIV test results – were in too many. There were also those who did not appear to be involved or who were even frankly available and she had hardly felt a flutter in their company. True, these males she came across in the course of her work were not exactly at their best, displaying their weaknesses before her discerning eye, instead of the usual opening move of presenting their strengths and disguising their problems. Also true was that she was bound by a professional oath to regard her patients as patients and not as prospective partners, an oath that required her to straighten up her curves and refrain from lowering her eyes suggestively during a consultation. Still, the question worried at her ragged thoughts: was she too adept at finding fault? Peter had once said that she expected too much. Well how much was too much? How much was too little? One had to have some kind of benchmark to live by.

Love me, love my dog, was the horrible thought that came to her.

The more she saw of Kraken, the more she had to admit that he was a beautiful, enthusiastic, gentle animal. If only he were more contained, fixed inside a photograph, for example, that they could hang on the wall, or somehow restrained from physical contact and making a mess, behind bars perhaps, if only she didn't have to deal with the hot hair, steamy breath, the hard wound body, the invasion of snouts and fleas and shit. Could she learn to love dogs? To love men? Were they the same thing?

The evening began to sing; lurid colours spilt and washed through the sky.

The fact was, Jack had not touched her, not once in the two months since he'd first come round, not other than a handshake. Had she imagined that, on occasion, there had been something like a spark between them?

Perhaps he was gay. That would explain a lot. She would introduce him to Peter to be assessed by Peter's gaydar. What if the two of them hit it off?

That was the moment she managed to acknowledge that she wanted Jack for herself. She wanted to kiss the imperfect lip that had covered her son's mouth and had breathed life back into him; she wanted to be brought back to life.

She would invite him to come in that very evening when he brought Max home. She'd make a special supper. Something quick but delicious, like a paella with a garden salad. Bring out the bottle of Diemersfontein she'd been saving for a special occasion. Light candles, put on Satie. She would praise Kraken, telling him what a good dog he was, then bestow a hearty pat on the animal's head, timing it for when Jack was looking. Or on the dog's rump? Which was safer, she worried, to avoid slobber? She would make it clear, without being pushy, that she was interested. Available. Enough that he would get it but not so much that he wouldn't be able to politely ignore the invitation if he wasn't interested. Not so much that he would drop Max and disappear.

That was them, at the gate. Carol leapt to her feet, her heart interfering with her breathing. The gate opened, Max entered, then he turned and waved. The sound of a car heading off. Jack hadn't even come in to greet her. He must have intuited the extent of her want across the full length of her front garden and had turned and fled.

Max came up the steps with his daypack. Scraped knees, filthy, sweaty, glowing. 'I climbed a grade 15 pitch,' he announced proudly.

'Good for you, darling.' She should ask what a grade 15 was but the other question was more pressing. 'Where's Jack?'

Max shrugged. 'Gone home.' He threw his backpack inside the front door.

'Take your shoes off before you –' Carol called after him but it too late. Max had left a trail of sand and dried mud on the floor behind him.

22.

Carol and Jack were walking up the mountain overlooking the sea, with Kraken and Max up ahead. The walk was Jack's suggestion after he had come round the previous day to give Max a guitar lesson.

The two of them had gone into the garden and had sat on the bench near the kitchen window. Carol could hear Jack strumming 'Blowin' In The Wind' as she prepared lunch. He had a lovely, gravelly singing voice and he played fairly well. The song brought back memories of End Conscription Campaign evenings and smoking dope around the fire in that student digs with Jeremy and his friends. A good thought-provoking song. Then Max's slow-fingered attempts at finding the chords, stringing them together with the words – lyrics she was glad her son was coming across in this way and at his age.

Jack had suggested they walk up the mountain together the following day. He was making an effort to include her.

The day had dawned still and light and they had set off early.

'I don't know whether I've said thank you properly,' Carol ventured. 'Not only for your quick response on the beach.'

'No need.'

'You're so good with him.'

Jack shrugged. 'He's a great kid.'

'Interesting how well you get on with him when you don't have your own.'

He was silent a moment as he walked up the path ahead of her, his firm muscles working under the skin of his legs. 'Maybe I remember how hard it was, being a kid.'

'You had a hard time?'

'Sort of.' He wasn't going there.

'I wish I could do something … you know, for you. In return.'

'Lemon tart. You make a mean tart.'

'Right. Another life-saving lemon tart coming up.'

They continued on up the trail under a sky mottled with cloud. The sea spread out below, cold and blue-grey. Beyond the rocks, close in to the shoreline, dark clots of kelp rode the swell like surfers waiting for a wave.

How to reach him. Carol was tired of waiting for him to make a move. 'Have you ever been married?' she tried.

Jack shook his head. 'I'm not an optimist.'

'An optimist?'

'Most people are convinced they can do better than their parents. My folks … I wouldn't wish, ah, that kind of drama on anyone.'

'What happened with your parents?'

'My father was a gluten-intolerant, Presbyterian, alcoholic jazz trumpeter and, um, my mother was a teetotalling, pasta-addicted, Catholic opera singer.'

'Ha! Goodness. The perfect combination. How long did that last?'

'My mother didn't believe in divorce, she believed in opera. So she did the martyr thing, clutched her breast and sang Verdi at the top of her voice until my father drank himself to death.'

'Tough beginning, for you.'

Jack hesitated. 'I learnt to stay out of their way. My mother was embarrassed by me anyway.'

'Why?'

'Take one guess.' Jack turned on the path to face her, his scar a raw exclamation. 'She always said she wasn't but I knew. Even the way she told me it didn't matter, that I could grow a moustache when I was older.' He carried on walking. 'Fuck that.' Jack's voice had turned hard and rough, he had quickened his pace. 'My mother, with all her multiple deficiencies, thought my *face* was a problem! That I'd need to hide it behind some … some Omar Sharif fucking furze.'

Carol was out of breath, keeping up. There was a minefield here. 'That must have been very … difficult,' she gasped.

Jack laughed. 'It was the moustache that was difficult! It

142

doesn't grow there, you know, where the scar is, so it amplifies the whole damn, um, thing. That's life, huh?' He stopped suddenly, lifted a foot onto a rock and bent to tie his lace. 'And you? You ever been shackled by the promise implied by the perfect ring?'

'Marriage? Nah. Not because I'm a pessimist."

'So why no husband?'

'Because ... no one –' she might as well say it, 'ever wanted me. To marry me.' She yanked her water bottle out of the side pocket of Jack's backpack, clamped her mouth to the teat and sucked hard.

'Really?' Jack sounded surprised. 'You lucky woman.'

'You think it's unlucky to be loved?'

'Ah, don't confuse being wanted with being loved.'

Carol felt a flicker of irritation. 'I'm not. But they do overlap, you know, loving someone and wanting to be with them. To help them and to work things out. You learn something about love, living with someone.'

'You've lived with someone, long-term?'

'Yes. When I was a medical student.' Jack looked at her askance. 'Well, I suppose four years is not particularly long.'

'You're as resolutely single as I am.'

'It gets harder, doesn't it, once you've been on your own for a while.'

'What?'

'Harder to make the adjustments necessary to share your life with someone else. Everything is just the way you like it when you live alone. The furniture, what you eat, how you spend your time. Someone else would try to change that.' She was thinking of his flat.

'Do you, um, do flings?'

'No!' Was he inviting her? She laughed. 'Well, not in theory. I suppose Max is evidence to the contrary.'

'Hey!' Max up ahead, waving from the top of a rocky promontory. 'We're almost there.'

'Where?'

'You'll see.'

They followed the path up the ascent. Had the two of them contrived a picnic? Max and Kraken came bundu-bashing through to join the path, the dog pushing past Carol and up the incline like an adolescent with no manners. She arrived at a wall of rock, where the boy and the dog were waiting. The path seemed to have petered out. Graffiti, loud and incongruous, on the rock in a black script proclaimed: *Ray loves Jolene*.

'Did we take the wrong path?' asked Carol.

'Look!' Max pointed.

Partially obscured by a bush, at ground level, was an overhang beneath which was an aperture. An entrance to the underworld about a metre high. Her heart turned and ran at the very sight of the dark maw. *Boomslang Cave* was scratched onto the rock at the opening.

'Want to go in?' Jack asked. 'I have a couple of torches in my rucksack.'

Carol felt ambushed. She'd thought they were making allowances for her for a change, for what she liked to do, but instead these two had tricked her. 'Oooh, no thanks,' she smiled, trying to make light of it, 'I can't take confined spaces. Even the loos on planes give me palpitations.'

'Come and have a look, Ma.' Max was already crouched under the overhang with his headlamp on, the light shining and flashing like a third eye from the centre of his forehead. 'You'll see, it's not so bad.'

'Max, you know I can't –' Angry, now.

'You don't know till you've tried.' Max encouraged. 'We'll help you, you'll see, it's so cool. The cave goes right through the mountain. You crawl in here, then you get to this amazing cavern then you walk out the other side.'

'You two carry on. I'll go back down.'

'Aaah, please Ma!'

'No, Max!'

Jack was watching the exchange. He beckoned Max to come out. 'Next time, buddy.'

'But you said –'

Jack shook his head. 'Your mother's not going down the

mountain by herself. And you're not going in alone. Come Kraken.' He turned and started the descent.

Carol had another look at the cave entrance. The sight of the tunnel disappearing into a black void made her breath struggle in her throat.

She should do it. At the very least she should muster some character, get down on her hands and knees and go a little way in. She was spoiling their day. She was, at heart, a spoiler. They would never invite her to go anywhere with them again. She would be left on her own at home, a pathetic, scared, miserable old lady.

Max was staring at her reproachfully. Even after his burial, he had no fear of being under the earth. What was wrong with her? Life called for some attempts at bravery, some small effort towards exploring terrain outside one's comfort zone. Logically, in her stupid brain, she knew very well that no harm would come to her if she ventured into the cave. Thousands of people had crawled through that gap without a second thought.

Again, she looked at the opening, felt terror cling to her like a small animal. It was ridiculous, she scolded herself, she was standing on solid ground in a clearing in the fynbos, with sunbirds fussing in the protea bush nearby and with people she loved who were ready and willing to accompany her, talk her through, yet none of these comforts could overcome her horror of the open throat of the mountain.

'I'm sorry, Max.' Carol turned away from her son and his disappointment. 'You should've known. I just can't.' She followed Jack and Kraken down the path.

23.

'Bye, my darling.'

Max allowed her a brief hug but turned his face away when she tried to kiss him. As soon as her arms unwrapped themselves from his adolescent body, he slid into the back seat of the car and started talking to his school friend next to him.

'Thank you,' Carol said to the mother, a stumpy woman with blonde streaks in her black hair. 'This is so good for him, to get away.'

'It's a pleasure, really.' The woman, what was her name? Lesley. Lesley squeezed herself into the driver's seat, then smiled up through the half-opened window. 'Sorry you're not coming with us. Don't you worry about a thing and don't work too hard.'

Carol waved as the car drove off, then went back up to her house. She'd lied about being on call that weekend. She had other plans.

'I'm sorry. About last weekend.' Carol struck a match and lit the candles. It was such a still evening they had decided to sit outside.

'What?'

'My stupid fear of enclosed spaces. I feel such a fool.'

Jack shrugged. He had put some effort in for this evening and was wearing a crisp blue and white striped shirt instead of his usual scruffy t-shirt and old jacket. For once, he had not brought Kraken. 'We're all afraid of something,' he said, twisting open the bottle of wine he'd brought.

'So, what are you afraid of?' Carol wondered aloud. 'Cheers.' The red wine slid deliciously down.

'Hmmm.' Jack nibbled on an olive and threw the pip into the darkness. 'I'm afraid of … being afraid.'

Carol laughed. 'Surely fear is not only a bad thing. If you aren't afraid of something that could kill you, you could die. Like a snake, for example.'

'If you respect snakes, um and their habitat, you won't get bitten. Fearing snakes? That's just ignorance and it gets them killed, massacred. The whole web of life gets messed up.'

'Maybe … a fear of snakes and caves is really a fear of sex.'

Jack gave one of his rare full-bellied laughs. 'Okay, here's another one: I'm afraid of rubbish pop psychology.' He stared at her. 'You afraid of sex?'

'No. Nor, actually, of snakes. We get them here occasionally coming down off the mountain. I must admit, the first time I saw one round the back, I nearly had a heart attack. A huge Cape cobra and Max was only five. We called a snake handler who came and caught the creature without any fuss. He held it by the neck and got us to touch it. The feeling was amazing, quite different to what I expected. Silky, almost. Such a delicate patterning of colour.'

'There are still a surprising number of snakes on this mountain.' Jack nodded his head towards the dark bulk of Trappieskop behind the house. 'It shows, if you keep your head down and avoid people, it is possible to survive.'

His face in the warm light of the candles was a mix of strength or stubbornness in his brow and jawline, and soft weakness around the mouth, where his genes had dealt him that blow.

Jack glanced at her, his dark eyebrows gathered into a frown. He looked away, planting his elbow on the table, resting his chin in the palm of his hand, with his fingers covering his lips.

'Okay,' he said gruffly. 'I'm afraid of people staring.'

'Oh!' Carol immediately looked away. 'I'm sorry! I didn't mean to … I wasn't staring. Not in the way you mean. I was looking at you because I … like you. I like the way you look.'

Silence. She was too afraid to turn her gaze back towards him but she couldn't keep looking at the potted basil plants at the edge of the paved area for the rest of the evening. 'We all have something we can't stand about our appearance,' she consoled.

'What's yours?'

'Oh, I have a long list.'

'Give me the top three.'

Carol shook her head. 'They're too embarrassing.'

'They're well hidden.'

Carol took a deep breath. She could not bring herself to say anything about the marks that Max had stretched into her belly, but she wanted to respond bravely, so that Jack could also be vulnerable in her company. 'One of my breasts is bigger than the other because Max would only suck on one side, and my knees are fat and shapeless so I never wear shorts or a short skirt and I dash into the sea if I swim which is hardly ever, and my smile is full of fillings and crowns, and my flesh is starting to obey the law of gravity, so I'm full of sags and bags and wrinkles and my bum is too big, always has been and no one is ever going to love me again.'

Jack was laughing. 'My scar has just paled into insignificance. I had no idea you were such a freak show.'

The evening got colder after dinner so they went inside. Jack made coffee and carried their mugs through to the sitting room. He came to sit next to Carol on the sofa. Laid his hand on her thigh. The warm weight of a man's hand through the fabric of her skirt. The sweet ache started up, quick as a switch. Shyly, out of practice, she placed her palm on the back of his hand, his knuckles rough from rock climbing, her fingers sliding into the gaps between his. His breath, now audible.

She turned her face into the hollow at his shoulder, breathing the warm smell of him, her hand finding its way beneath his shirt, the skin of his back under her fingertips. Alight, her mouth searched out the wet warmth of his. The charge, like a slight shock, as his hand slipped up the inside of her leg, the tips of his curious fingers touching the gusset of her panties. She sank back onto the sofa under the pressure of his body, the hard knot of his sex insistent against her thigh, constrained by his jeans. Her leg at the wrong angle, something underneath her on the sofa digging into her back. The shallow, quick shush of his breath in her ear, his mouth on her neck, her fingers combed into the thick mess of his hair, her hand cupping his scalp, the weight of him on her chest as he struggled to open his fly with one hand.

Carol twisted her mouth away from his and exploded, laughing.

'What?' Jack jerked his head back, coming to a dead halt. He pulled away from her and sat up.

'Oh, it reminded me of being an adolescent, you know, grappling on the sofa.' She took hold of his arm and tried to pull him back to her. 'I had this sudden flashback, worrying that my parents would walk in on us.'

Jack resisted, stayed sitting upright, took a sip of his coffee. 'What's wrong?'

'Nothing.'

'Come then.' Carol tried again to pull him closer; instead, he stood.

'Need the toilet.'

The cold oozed back in as she waited. What had happened?

He returned from the bathroom, tucking his shirt into his jeans, not looking at her. Picked up his jersey. 'I'd better be on my way,' he said. 'Thanks for a nice evening.'

Carol realised she was still half-lying on the sofa, with her skirt up, her scant underwear showing. She shot upright, straightened herself. 'I'm sorry; did I do something wrong?'

'No, it's getting late.' It wasn't late, couldn't be past nine. 'Finish your coffee, at least.'

Jack stood there, unresponsive. Stone, true to his surname.

'I've done something. I'm sorry, I didn't mean –'

'It's fine, no problem.'

He went over to the front door where he struggled with the lock. 'Could you let me out please?'

Carol touched his shoulder at the gate as he left but still he wouldn't look at her. She stood and listened to his bakkie sputtering off down the road, then went back inside. The lemon tart. He hadn't even had a slice of her thank you gift. Bizarre bastard.

That was it, she was finished with men. In between sobs, she managed to cram in two helpings of lemon tart by washing it down with the rest of the bottle of wine.

A few days later, while Carol was chewing on a chicken sandwich and filling in chronic medication forms at work, her private cell phone rang.

It was Jack. 'Kraken and I are, um, going for a walk on the beach. Later. Five thirty. Want to come?'

As soon as Carol switched off, she dialled reception and told Naledi to cancel her late afternoon patients, she had an urgent house call.

He was waiting for her at the car park, Kraken revving at the end of his lead. 'Hi,' he said, as though nothing had happened.

'Hi there.' She started down the path to the beach. It was up to him to make an effort.

It was high tide and the soft sand was tough going. Once released, Kraken rushed into the sea, bounding along in the shallows and barking exuberantly, as though trying to chase the restless water and pin it down.

'You been well?' Carol offered coolly.

'What's with the formal shit?' Jack was laughing at her. 'I've seen the colour of your undies and you ask me whether I've been well?'

Carol stopped walking. 'You can't have everything your way, Jack.' He swivelled towards her. The loose curls of his hair were a dark copper in the glow of the evening. 'Why have you asked me to meet you here? You made it quite clear that what happened the other night was a mistake, on both our parts I might add, and now, when I'm civil to you, you laugh at me.' She started back towards her car, pain riveted into her chest. It was a stuff up. She had ruined everything for Max by even thinking she could get close to this man. She should have known better.

'Hey.' Jack, coming up by her side. 'Come sit a moment.' His tone was softer, pleading even. Carol hesitated, then followed him to a spot against a dune.

They sat in silence a while. The wind had died and the opaque grey slate of the sea blurred without seam into the iron grey of the sky. A string of birds beat their way through the air. Carol dug her fingers into the sand and closed her fist around a packed handful.

'Look.' Jack started. 'I need to … apologise.' Well, that was something. She could hear how hard it was for him to say that. 'I … I thought you were laughing. At me.'

Carol looked at Jack, at his bowed head, his hurt face. He looked away. 'Oh, Jack,' she melted, 'I would never – It was a misunderstanding. I –' She wanted to reach out, to hold him.

Kraken came galumphing and dog-slobbering up, kicking up sand and shaking a minor storm of sea water out of his thick coat. Carol leapt up, trying to escape the worst of it, laughing despite her horror. 'Kraken! You terrible animal!' she yelled. It was too late, she was wet, sprayed all over with dog germs and sand. She shuddered, then thought: what the hell, and gave up, running her hands down his wet pelt and scratching his neck to his tail-whumphing, huge-bodied, sloppy-jawed delight.

'Carol?'

'Yep?'

'D'you think, ah, we could go home?' Jack asked quietly. 'And carry on where we left off?'

Where was Max, Carol wondered. It was a Thursday, so he was at soccer practice. 'I'd like that,' Carol ventured, hoping this was not a further mistake. 'I'd like that very much.'

24.

It was seven years since Kraken had died and Jack had left. She'd thought she was over him, yet here he was, coming up again because of the things Max was doing. Jack had set up camp in her brain, smiling his scarred smile. Fact was, she still felt fondly towards him despite all that had happened.

'Jack,' she scolded her ceiling at two o'clock in the morning. 'Where are you? You stupid, fucking idiot. Why didn't you realise, why couldn't you see, you could have had it all?' Round and round, too tired to read, too awake to sleep, until her thoughts and her sheets were in knots and the alarm started shrieking and she was obliged to push herself up and get ready for work.

Had Jack cared at all about the two of them? Had he really been capable of caring about anyone else other than himself and his bloody dog?

'You okay?' Trevor asked at teatime.

'Fine, why?' Was her insomniac turmoil showing?

'You seem … distracted. You left a box of Tetavac out of the fridge yesterday.'

'Did I? Damn. I must have –'

'I know it must be hard for you, what with Max –'

'I'll re-order, replace them. For my account. Damn.'

'Maybe you need some time off?'

Carol managed a noncommittal grunt. 'No, I'm okay, thanks.'

Trevor started avoiding her, taking his tea slightly earlier or later. Or was she imagining this?

Neville Cupido was Carol's next patient. His family had been with the practice for over twenty years. He had put on weight since his last consultation.

'Good morning Neville. Have a seat.'

'Hi Doc.' He heaved himself into the chair and sat there sweating, short of breath from the walk down the passage, and bunched his cheeks into a smile. The rectangular shape of a box of cigarettes pushed out his shirt pocket.

'So how can I help you today?'

'Just came for my repeat prescription.'

Carol opened his folder. His chart, brought up to date by Zubeida in the procedure room, showed that his blood pressure was 176 / 105. His weight was 124 kilograms, an increase of eight kilograms in the past six months. His blood sugar was still in the normal range but that could go any time what with half his family dead or dying of diabetes.

She remembered him as an athletic youngster; now he was in such bad shape he was threatening to split his skin. With a wife and three small children he had a lot to live for.

'What's going on, Neville?'

'Doc?'

She tapped his file. 'Have you been taking your medication? Your blood pressure is way too high.'

'Ah, no, it ran out two weeks ago. Just jumped down out of the cupboard and ran out.' He hooted with laughter at his joke.

Carol gave a tight smile. 'Oh. Okay. So, please explain to me, what stopped you from coming in and getting a repeat script? *Before* your meds, um, ran out? This is not the first time.'

'I was busy, doctor. Rush jobs on at work, big contract to install twelve Jacuzzis in a new housing estate. Working ten hour days so the rich can relax.' Another laugh, inviting her to laugh with him, to laugh it all off.

'It's your own business, isn't it?'

'Yes. Built it up from scratch.'

'You've done well, but I'm worried about you. We've spoken about it before, putting your work before your health.'

He frowned. 'Hey Doc, the kids have to eat.'

'Are you aware that those working hours are illegal? Under the Basic Conditions of Employment Act?'

Neville snorted. 'Come on Doc, no ways you medics work the hours set down by some official. Those rules don't apply when there's a deadline.'

'Thanks for your concern about me, Neville, but we're talking about you for the moment. Think about those words: Dead. Line. I imagine you haven't got round to exercising either. Takeaways, you still eating takeaways? No time to cook, right?' Neville chuckled, nodding, like a naughty child. This inquisition was the wrong approach to a patient, it went contrary to everything Carol had been taught in family medicine but she couldn't help herself.

Carol checked the other observations in the folder. 'And your weight? What's happening there?' Her voice was edging higher.

'Well, you know how it is, Doc, over the festive season, with the family from up country visiting, it isn't possible …'

Some huge calamity that had been sitting like a tight fist in the centre of her chest began to expand. 'Tell me something, Neville. I'm really curious …'

'Yes, doctor?'

The ball was getting bigger and bigger, it was pushing against her restraints and she was too exhausted to stop it: 'Tell me: why the hell should I care about your health if you don't?' He stared at her, surprised. 'How long has this situation been going on? Years now, right?' She put her pen down. 'Well, I can't do this anymore – our little song and dance routine every few months – me giving you information about what you should be doing to *save your own life* and you completely *ignoring* me, I mean, we are talking about your *life* here, the thing which presumably is the most precious thing you have, do you understand me? Without which you are nothing, nothing! Gone! Buried and dead.

'Although, believe me, death is most certainly not the biggest problem that is likely to come your way seeing you insist on your appalling lifestyle! What you refuse to understand is that just around the corner are conditions that have your name on them, in bold, in enormous Gothic capitals, things like *disability*! And *immense suffering*! Not to mention the suffering you will also inflict on the people who love you, like losing a functional father and a breadwinner, your wife having to wipe your bum as well as her own every day for the rest of your miserable life if you have a stroke, or your children having to push you around in a wheelchair on oxygen, if you have a bad enough heart attack, or having to take you for dialysis twice a week if your kidneys pack up.

'To think, it all could have been avoided, only you didn't give a damn and you took your precious health and life for granted, didn't bother to take care of yourself, you know, we're talking about the *absolute basics here* – exercise every day, proper food and not too much of it, not smoking or drinking too much, all of which you do, or don't do. Whichever one is the wrong behaviour, blow me down, you do it! You should be afraid, very afraid, of what is going to happen to you in the relatively near future, yet nothing I say or do to try to motivate you to change your ways has any effect *at all*.'

Neville hadn't budged during the tirade. He sat staring at Carol with shock, as though his doctor had leaned over and smacked him.

'You know how that makes me feel? A failure. A fraud.' A mixture of grief and rage caught in Carol's throat. 'It makes me feel like giving up medicine, doing something else where people's lives aren't at stake, like knitting jerseys, or … or … selling manure. I *care* about my patients, it *horrifies* me to see what is happening to you, you're a young man and look at you!' Neville sat, stunned.

'Thing is, you don't really believe you will die and I don't blame you. You don't get to see much suffering or death, those who are dying get locked away in hospitals and bedrooms, out of sight, so the rest of us don't have to worry ourselves about consequences, we can carry on with our dreadful lives thinking we can behave in any way we like and it doesn't matter. But me? I see death and disability all the time, I'm a doctor and I know what happens to people like you.'

She leaned towards him. 'So, I have decided to change the way I do things around here. Not only concerning you, but also for the other third of the patients in my practice who expect me to worry about their well-being while they party themselves into an early grave or nursing home: unless you take your own well-being on as a priority, a *priority*! Do you hear me! I am not interested in having you as a patient any more. You can go elsewhere, where some other corrupt defunct doctor can make loads of money out of your self-inflicted misery, your self-destructive, self-deceiving, self-sabotaging project of slowly killing yourself.'

Carol sat back and pulled a desk drawer open so fast the contents rattled. She took a prescription pad out and spoke aloud as she wrote the words down: 'I, Neville Cupido, hereby declare that from today onwards I will take responsibility for the basics of my daily health care, including, but not restricted to, eating sensibly, losing weight, exercising, stopping smoking and taking my medication. This is in order to prevent further self-inflicted illness and accident, which is a huge burden on my body, my family, my financial situation and last, but not least, on my doctor's mental health.'

Carol turned to her patient and offered him the pen. 'So, Neville. Sign here, at the bottom or stop wasting my time.'

'You didn't!' Katy exclaimed over her cappuccino.

'I did. It was terrible, I couldn't stop myself. But you know what? He signed. Then he started crying and came out with it, that he had been abused as a child, an awful story. I felt so bad. That alone can mess up your body image. I apologised for shouting at him but he told me he was grateful. He understood that I really cared about him, and that I wasn't merely doing my job. For the first time ever we had a real conversation about his health.'

'Max would have been proud of you. What a performance!'

'Yes, well, I'm lucky it was that man. If I had lost it with someone else, they might have reported me to the Health Professions Council for unprofessional behaviour.'

'It's unprofessional to tell the truth?'

'It's the way I said it. Doctors are supposed to be endlessly kind and understanding. I still feel embarrassed. I went ape.'

Carol stuck her finger into the coffee cup to get the last of the foam. 'I think we actually managed to get somewhere. Let's see. His determination to change might last five minutes.'

'I should send Frank to you for a good lecture.'

'Why Frank? He's in good shape, isn't he?'

'Ye-es, well, only because I'm on at him! He's started running with me on weekends and I've got us on the low carb diet. Then a few nights ago I woke up and he wasn't in bed. I thought he'd gone for a pee but when he didn't come back I got this feeling that he was up to no good. So I got out of bed quietly, without switching the light on.'

'You snuck up on your husband?'

'Well, I was worried about internet porn, something like that. We haven't had sex for a while, which is unlike Frank, normally he's a stallion. Or an affair. I just knew something was going on, you know, maybe messaging some floozy from the office in the middle of the night.'

'So?'

'So I heard something downstairs and crept towards the sound as quietly as possible. It was Frank, in the pantry. I caught him red-handed, eating a whole packet of Zoo biscuits.'

'Zoo biscuits!'

'He was wolfing them down. It's beyond belief. Jeez, if you're going to break your diet and put your heart at risk, why would you do it with something as disgusting as Zoo biscuits?'

During the day Carol could keep herself busy and her attention elsewhere, but at night her thoughts kept veering towards the horror of her son's violence towards his own body. Clara Cunningham had managed to limp her way into an ambush at the Flame 'n Grill, but even her predicament couldn't keep Carol's attention. Her eyes read the same sentence again and again without comprehension while her mind scurried around with worry.

She invited Peter over for a meal. He watched hungrily as Carol dished up a steaming plate of curry and topped it with some fresh coriander.

'How are you, darling?'

'I'm exhausted all the time, my stomach is in a constant knot, I am having difficulty concentrating at work. I left a box of vaccines worth R800 out of the fridge the other day.'

'Good Lord. You are in a bad way.'

'I'm so alone in this.'

'What?'

'Max, of course! Parenting.' She glared at Peter. 'I deal with patients every day who are unconsciously destroying themselves. Some doctors seem to be able to handle it but I can't. I've come to think of our bodies as these beautiful vulnerable animals that have been entrusted to our care, yet we don't look after them. My patients are like people who have forgotten about the little creature that is dependent on them. My son, however, is like someone who is torturing his animal to death. I can't stand it. I can't even get *you* to talk to him.'

'What, exactly, do you think anyone can do or say?' Peter waved his fork over his food. 'Delicious, thank you.'

'Exercise your imagination for a moment, Peter. How will you feel if Max kills himself? Is there any part of you that might stop and think, Hell, I should have done something, intervened somehow?'

'Have you considered going into therapy?'

Carol stared at Peter, furious. The bugger was eating her food, as usual, and suggesting she was the one who had the problem. 'Jeez Peter! Me going into therapy won't stop Max from throwing himself off a building, or whatever he's planning to do next!'

'I still think you should trust your boy. It's not as though he is doing these things on his own in the wilderness. By the very nature of the work, he has to perform to an audience in high density situations, where there is medical help nearby.' He moved the salt and pepper grinders so that they lined up with the candle. 'Maybe that's what he needs, maybe that's what every child needs. His parent to trust him.'

'Did you expect your parents to trust you when you were trashing yourself with alcohol? Driving into trees and ending up in jail? Having drunken, unprotected sex with strangers?'

'Ah, they didn't exactly know about that last one.'

'For God's sake, Peter, that's really asking too much of the people who gave you life.'

'Look at me now. Wouldn't you say things have turned out fine?'

'Do you have no regrets? Do you never think, if only someone had intervened, got me to really look at what I was doing to myself, then I wouldn't be, for example, HIV positive?'

Peter smoothed the tablecloth down with the palm of his hand while he considered this. 'I have to say, no. It's something I've obviously thought about and no, I don't think so. How can you live life without making mistakes and then hopefully learning from them? Having HIV has made me more aware, more … humane. Less critical.' He pulled at some hairs in his beard. 'There was absolutely nothing my parents could have done to stop me, especially my parents. Nothing more than they did already, paying for rehab a few times. I was in the grip of something I had to work through, to find out who I am. This,' he gave a grand gesture towards his body, 'is who I am, in all its glory and deficiencies.' He cracked a poppadum between his lips. 'I'm truly sorry, Carol, that you're taking so much strain, but I'm not worried about Max. I really do think he'll be fine.'

25.

A crowd of about thirty people had gathered on the street corner outside the church. They were focused on what appeared to be a tall sculpture of a crucifix erected behind railings in the church grounds, facing Parliament. As Carol strode closer, she recognised what she already knew but could hardly believe: the body suspended high on the wooden cross was not made of marble or alabaster but of muscle, hair and bone. The person hanging from the cross was her son, naked in the cool air but for a loincloth.

Above him was a banner with the words: *Cross/Purpose*.

Max's head was hanging forward on his chest, his features obscured by his long, matted hair, which the wind was whipping erratically across his face. His whole body was visible above the crowd, his feet resting on a shelf nailed onto the vertical beam of the cross. Straps of cloth bound his ankles and wrists to the beams. An additional strap around Max's chest and under his arms looped over the topmost upright, providing some additional support for his body.

At least there was no blood, no metal nails.

She stood at the edge of the crowd, her heart thumping. As she watched, his loincloth darkened at his groin; urine trickled down his legs and dripped off the footrest onto the ground.

'Sies!' A woman nearby exclaimed, turning to her friend, laughing. 'He peed himself!' They had their cell phones out and were holding them up and taking pictures, no doubt posting them on Facebook.

'Blasphemer!' A man shouted. 'You should be ashamed of yourself after what Christ did for us.'

'This *is* the Christ!' another man proclaimed. 'He has come here to die to wash your filthy sins away.'

'He doesn't even wash his own knickers!' the young woman giggled.

'Los hom,' said an elderly woman standing near Carol. 'He's hanging there for love. He is love.'

'He's a bloody whitey!' a man yelled. 'He got nothing for us. Who do you think you are, pretending to be Jesus. Jesus was Palestinian! Palestinians are black!'

'If you're the Christ, get yourself off that jungle gym, man!'

'It wasn't only Jesus who got tortured! It's not only Christians who suffer. Look what he's saying, read the notices! If you can't read, just shut up!' This from an old man in a grubby oversized jacket.

Max shifted slightly, not responding to the taunts. He lifted himself, stretching stiffly within the restraints. His skin glowed in the late afternoon light against the shadows of the church behind him. He raised his head, his parched lips moving, muttering, as a madman's or as in prayer. The arcs of his ribs slid up and down under his skin with each laboured breath; whether the way he was breathing was for dramatic effect or not, Carol couldn't tell. According to the morning paper, he had been hanging there since the previous evening – almost twenty-four hours. He would be getting dehydrated – had no one tried to stop him, or take him down? The evening air was getting chilly. Could people die of exposure in March? He was out of reach unless one had a ladder.

Three large notice boards were positioned behind him. They each displayed a headline declaring a manifesto. Carol pushed through the crowd to get close enough to read the texts, then saw two women in light blue robes and veils kneeling on either side of the foot of the cross facing the heckling crowd and the Parliament buildings. They looked like the two biblical Marys as they bent their heads in prayer. The clothing of one of them was wet down one side and on the ground were a few crumpled cooldrink cans.

MANIFESTO I

We line the streets, strung up by poverty and illness, paralysed by hunger. You walk past us every day, refuse to take up the knife of compassion and cut us down. You think we deserve this punishment, that what Caesar does and says is right. We did not ask to be born. We do not ask for much.

Matthew 25: 35–40 "'For I was hungry and you gave Me something to eat; I was thirsty and you gave Me something to drink; I was a stranger and you invited Me in; naked and you clothed Me; I was sick and you visited Me; I was in prison and you came to Me." Then the righteous will answer Him, "Lord, when did we see You hungry and feed You, or thirsty and give You something to drink? And when did we see You a stranger and invite You in, or naked and clothe You? When did we see You sick, or in prison and come to You?" The King will answer and say to them, "Truly I say to you, to the extent that you did it to one of these brothers of Mine, even the least of them, you did it to Me."'

MANIFESTO II

Crucifixion is a form of slow and painful execution in which the victim is tied or nailed to a large wooden cross or tree and left to hang until dead. It was used for centuries as punishment by humiliation, torture and death and as a deterrent for witnesses. It is principally known from antiquity but remains in occasional use in some countries.

Surely not. Which countries? Public execution by hanging or the axe was bad enough, but this! Used for centuries! What was it about human beings, she wondered, that made them so cruel?

MANIFESTO III

A hunger strike is a method of non-violent resistance or pressure in which participants fast as an act of political protest or to provoke feelings of guilt in others, usually to achieve a specific goal such as a policy change. Most hunger strikers will take liquids but not solid food. It has been used as a means of protest for thousands of years across many cultures.
In the first three days, the body still uses energy from glucose.

Then the liver starts processing body fat. After three weeks the body mines the muscles and vital organs for energy, and the loss of bone marrow becomes life-threatening. There are examples of hunger strikers dying after 52 to 74 days.

Famous South African hunger strikes:

1966, 1981 and 1990: Robben Island prisoners protesting prison conditions.
1971: Rev. Bernie Wrankmore, protesting the death in detention of Imam Abdullah Haron.

She recalled adults talking about Reverend Wrankmore when she was little and how scathing her father had been about the protester's fast on Signal Hill, calling him a religious nut who was trying to attract attention, his tone implying that attracting attention was one of the worst behaviours. She couldn't remember how long the reverend had lasted, or if he had died. But he'd had some kind of shelter to sit in while he was on hunger strike and was not subjected to additional physical torture.

'Here's something to eat, you antichrist!' shouted a middle-aged woman. She hurled a yellow oblong object through the air, which hit Max on the chest. It fell to the ground – a mango pip, still wet and stringy. Some people laughed; Max let his head drop.

'Shame man!' another woman objected. 'Can't you read? It says in the Bible, be kind to the poor, so why do you throw things?'

'He's not poor! He's a fraud, a rich man trying to squeeze himself through Jesus's needle and into heaven. I bet his Merc is parked round the corner.'

The crowd shrieked with laughter.

Max lifted his head again, raised his eyes to the sky. 'Forgive us!' he shouted. 'We do not know what we are doing.'

'Yes, blasphemer, we can see you don't know what you're doing!'

'God won't forgive you!'

She should confront the crowd, explain to them that this was her son, he was a good man, he didn't deserve this abuse, but then she'd become part of the performance. Someone was watching her. It was Hedley, his video camera had been trained on her while she'd been looking up at her son on the cross – as though she was another Mary to this Jesus. '*Stop* that,' she shouted, lunging towards him, snatching at the lens.

Hedley stepped aside, carried on filming. A young man with his cap on backwards stepped between them, faced the video camera and started rapping. 'Shoot me rather, mister, c'mon you YouTube dude, aim right here, in my chest hair, I'm in training, I'm the chosen one, this God's son is aiming high, on his way to neon sights, to Hollywood with its dark soul and bright lights,' he rapped, using physical gestures to punctuate his phrasings.

'Excuse me,' Carol called through the railings to the praying women. She needed someone responsible, someone who would help. The church must have agreed to this, he was on church property. One of them looked up at her: a woman of about sixty with a face lined with years of difficulty. 'Sorry, excuse me but that's my son, he needs something to drink and eat, I need to get him …'

The woman nodded. 'Come,' she smiled. 'Come round and join us. You have a son who is a saint. Come and pray for him and for our people.'

Carol saw there was a way through to the enclosure from the steps leading up to the front door of the church. She realised that, once she was next to the women, she would be in the spotlight too and the crowd might start throwing things at her. 'I want to know, please, how can I get him something to eat and drink. I am a doctor, I'm afraid that he needs medical attention, we can't leave him there.'

The woman smiled benignly. 'There are many people in South Africa who need medical attention,' she said, 'and who do not have what they need to stay healthy or even alive. Food, clean water, sanitation. Don't worry Mama, we are looking after him. We offer him water and bread every four hours. That's his instruction and we are Christian people. Sometimes he takes it, sometimes he doesn't. He is very strong, your son. Is he really your son?'

'Yes, my only child.'

She nodded. 'I am praying for your son, for what he is doing. My son, my only son, died of HIV because of the government's policies,' she jabbed her finger towards Parliament, her tone tightening in anger, 'and we are poor and could not afford the medicines that could have saved him. We are suffering but no one sees us, no one hears us. The politicians, the rich, they don't want to look at us, they hide us in the townships, in the factories, in the rural areas. Your son is bringing the suffering of our people out into the streets where everyone can see and be shocked and afraid and say "This is how we treat the poor".'

'But these people,' Carol gestured to the crowd, 'most of them aren't sympathetic ...'

The woman shook her head. 'Some have brought food, some have prayed with us. You'll see, by the third day, God will reach down into all of their hearts. He will flick their eyes open with his finger. They will become quiet. Scales will fall from their eyes and ears and they will see and hear as if for the first time, as if they are born again, new into the Kingdom of Heaven.'

Carol saw a movement, at the church steps. Two more women in blue robes and veils were making their way into the enclosure. 'Oh,' the woman said, getting up stiffly off her knees. 'This is the next shift. I will be back tomorrow to look after your son, don't worry. Now I must go see to my grandchildren.'

The women exchanged silent greetings as they changed places. A thin young man dressed impressively, his priestly white robe stark against his dark skin, appeared behind them from inside the church and walked solemnly into the enclosure. From behind a buttress he brought out a ladder and leaned it against the side of the cross. He held it steady while one of the recent arrivals climbed carefully up it, somewhat hampered by her long blue robe and the plastic bottle with a straw inserted that she was holding in one hand. As she came within reach of Max's mouth, she stretched up and offered him a drink; he sipped a little, then shook his head. She took something out of a pocket and held up an energy bar to his lips but he turned his face away.

Carol made her way to the steps going into the church to intercept the man in the white robe as he came out of the enclosure. 'Excuse me, are you the priest in charge?'

He looked at her, startled, his Adam's apple jumping in his throat. 'Hah no, actually I'm an unemployed actor. A friend. Of the artist.'

Carol glanced at the new shift of women, now kneeling at the foot of the cross, their heads bowed over their hands in prayer. 'And – those women? Are they also actors?' Was the whole show, even the conversation she'd just had, all staged?

'They're volunteers from the church. I'm standing in for the priest who goes home in the evening.' He jigged a finger in his ear and stared at her. 'Can I help you?'

'It's your friend who needs help. Get him down! They might start throwing stones, he's so helpless …'

'Are you …'

'I'm Max's mother.'

'Aaah! You're the doctor! I'm Siseko.'

'Siseko, are you really okay with sitting around and watching this?'

Siseko frowned. 'We must be brave. Your son needs us to have courage.'

'*I* must be brave!'

'You know, in our culture, when a boy is even younger than Max, he must go through terrible difficulty to prove himself a man. He must go to the bush, be cut without anaesthetic. Sleep on the ground with only a blanket, in the cold. His mother must release him, so that he can go and meet his own death. He must look his death in the eye, until he understands. If he survives, he comes back a man. If he dies –' Siseko shrugged. 'Don't worry, Dr Trehorne, Max won't die. We're looking after him. To do these things is hard. Very hard, for everyone. Me too. It has to be like that. Otherwise it means nothing.'

'You mean –'

'Excuse me, let me explain. In your Western culture, you don't give boys a chance to show themselves, to prove themselves a man. Instead they do drugs, motorbikes. They look at their own death without understanding what it is, without understanding anything.'

Siseko smiled at her, kindly. 'Be proud of your son, what he is doing is a good thing.'

It was getting late; the first stars were pricking the sky near the horizon. The street lights came on, as well as a security light in the eaves of the church; the three notice boards too were lit. The crowd had begun to disperse. She looked around for Hedley, but he had gone. Carol could not think of going home. Her son had put himself in an extremely vulnerable position, tied up on a street corner in the middle of town with only two kneeling women and an actor to protect him from dehydration and exposure, or even an assault with something more danger-ous than a mango pip or cooldrink can. Across the road, the parliamentary security guards were looking over at the goings-on at the church with some bemusement. Lights were still on in some of the offices of government behind them, and some BMWs were driving out of the grounds. Can you see my son? Carol wanted to rush up and ask the drivers. Do you get this?

Her feet ached, she was sweaty from the day and hungry. She should find some place that was open, get some food into her. She felt a bit shaky. She sat down on the church steps and considered her options. This part of town was quiet and deserted at night. A few cars passed, slowing down at the sight of a real person hanging from a cross. The robots changed, changed again. The outline of Lion's Head mountain against the glow of the setting sun slowly faded into the night. Shadows between two build-ings across the street yielded up a small cluster of ragged street children who came across the road in bare feet. The eldest looked only about nine years old but perhaps he was older, stunted from a diet of sniffing glue and finding scraps discarded in rubbish bins. His face in the street light was scarred and pinched. 'What's meneer doing?' he asked, looking up at Max.

'He's showing us how cruel the world can be.' As if these kids didn't know first-hand. 'He's asking us to think about kindness.'

'I'm hungry.' The tiniest child put out a small, dirty hand.

'Why you leave meneer there?' the older boy asked, still intrigued. 'Why don't he come down?'

'It's like Jesus, stupid,' another boy chirped. 'You got any money lady?'

'Can you buy something to eat near here?' she asked them.

'Yes, my lady!' another child said, pointing.

She could see lights, some way down the road and yes, there was a Coke sign. A café, still open but she didn't dare walk there with these kids in case they mugged her. Life was full of these situations, where you wanted to help but didn't know how to do so without making things worse. Holding tightly onto her bag, she dipped quickly into the interior and pulled out a note. 'Here,' she said, holding it out. Too late, she saw it was a hundred rand.

'Thank you my lady!' the older boy shouted, snatching it before she changed her mind. The children ran off laughing, in the opposite direction from the café.

Max's head was lolling, his chin on his chest, his eyes closed. His body shook every now and then from the cold, like a rigor of malaria. His naked abdomen, moving softly with each breath, was so terribly exposed.

Why doesn't someone cut him down? the child had asked. Good question – wasn't that what the first poster was all about? In Caesar's day, if someone had taken a condemned man down from a cross they probably would have been put to death too but in this situation nothing was stopping anyone from doing it. Would Max put up a fight to prevent his rescue? Or was he testing his audience, to see how long it took onlookers to do anything?

She walked up the steps and into the enclosure and went to stand in front of her son. The acrid stench of old urine, like the smell in subways, filled her nose. 'Max,' she called, reaching up. 'Max.' She could just touch the small shelf he was standing on. No response. She stretched herself up and managed to brush against his toes. His face was mostly in shadow and her gaze was half-blinded by the security light behind him, but she was sure his eyes opened and that he stared directly, clearly, down into hers.

Siseko was calling from the top of the steps. 'Come inside, Dr Trehorne. Come and get some rest.'

She looked up again at her son but his eyes were closed again. 'I love you, Max.'

Something dripped from Max's face onto her upper lip and trickled into the corner of her mouth. Something salt. The night was too cool for sweat. 'I love you too, Ma.' His voice was quiet but strong; it pierced her that he had broken the performance for a moment, to acknowledge her, to be kind.

Carol followed Siseko through the huge wooden doors and into the dimly lit interior. He showed her the cloakroom, where she used the toilet, washed her face and rinsed her mouth out.

The pews were hard but Siseko had found her a kneeling cushion for her head and an altar cloth for a blanket.

'You okay, Dr Trehorne? I'll wake you if there are any problems, I promise.'

What did an actor know about assessing medical problems? Yet she was grateful for this young man's solicitude.

'Siseko?'

'Yes?'

'Please. Tomorrow, let's take him down. He'll be too weak to resist.'

He hesitated. 'Max told us to leave him until he gives the word.'

The cushion smelt musty and was too hard for a comfortable pillow, compacted by hundreds of repentant knees. It had probably not been washed since the day some church warden's wife had stitched it. It would have to do. Carol put her head gingerly down on it, then lay a long time on the wooden pew, her heart run through, a pain in her gut. Perhaps she was starting an ulcer, although it didn't feel like heartburn. Her belt felt too tight at the waist, she was uncomfortable, she had been putting on weight. Menopause, perhaps.

She released her belt and the button at the waistband of her pants and fished in her bag for an antacid. Then she lay down again and stared up at the struts and arched rafters and the stained-glass windows, lit by sullen street light, the white tablet chalky in her mouth. She could never resist biting them, taking them apart with her teeth, despite the directions on the package insert that advised sucking. Sucking took way too long.

This whole situation was taking way too long. Carol felt crucified too, caught on the cross of her own incomprehension, her own indecision. She lay with thoughts swirling and butting, trying not to let the salt wet that was leaking from her eyes spill onto the cushion.

26.

'Thank you. For fitting me in.'

'That's fine.' Dr Ndlovu held the door open. It was late, after six o'clock; this kind man must have decided to see her in his own time. Carol sat down and worried about his children, never getting to see their workaholic father. They would grow up fatherless, grow wild, undisciplined. They would look for love in all the wrong places. They would hate him. She should warn him, from her own experience.

He waved her into a chair. 'Has something happened?'

'Did you see the *Cape Times* yesterday?'

Dr Ndlovu shook his head.

'Max, he's staging another performance, tied to a cross, crucified, he's crucified himself directly opposite Parliament.' She pulled the newspaper out of her bag, turned it to the front of the arts page and handed it to the psychiatrist.

He read the article, staring a while at the awful photograph. 'Brave man,' he said quietly. He looked at the article again. 'His third day. How is he?'

'He has helpers who get up on a ladder and offer him food and water a few times a day. Mostly he refuses, other than a few sips. He's very weak and the weather is getting colder.'

'How long does he intend staying there?'

'He's told them he'll decide when to come down. What do I do? What on earth is any sane responsible mother supposed to do?'

Dr Ndlovu gave a grunt of sympathy and handed her a tissue. 'Has it ever occurred to you that perhaps your son has a calling?'

'You think he's hearing voices …?'

'No, no, I'm talking about the old religious idea, that you are born in order to fulfil a purpose while you're alive.'

'A calling?'

'People who are called can end up living extreme lives that impact in problematic ways on those who love them.'

'Max isn't religious.'

'The belief isn't only held by people who believe in a god who has a plan for them. It is also a psychological idea, or a genetic one. Take Yehudi Menuhin, for example, or Nelson Mandela. Their lives pulled them into a particular direction, from early on.'

'You're talking about destiny? Or fate?' Carol couldn't help a snarky note from spiking her voice. She had never experienced any invisible rudder directing her path. Everything she had ever done seemed pure accident. She had studied medicine because she was good at biology and science, she'd had a child because the condom broke, she grew lobelia in her garden because Katy had given her some slips. Even Jack, she'd got involved with Jack through an accident.

'Dr Trehorne, I'm not making a case for predetermination as such. I'm merely suggesting that Max's stance might have something in it of absolute necessity, even of heroism. In Xhosa culture, as an example, you have to be called to be a sangoma. It is not something you choose. It chooses you. We fear it, because the training is so tough, much tougher than psychiatry. If you are called you have to obey or you get sick.

'We all know how it feels when we are on a path close to our true natures, whether it is determined by the ancestors or by our genes – which is not as different an idea as one might suppose. There is huge overlap genetically, epigenetically. We also know when we're completely off track. Traditional healers are particularly sensitive to this.'

'Sangomas are called to heal, not to destroy.'

'You think this,' he gestured toward the newspaper, 'is destructive?' He didn't wait for her reply. 'Max is putting his body through extreme hardship but through his uncompromising work we can see something of ourselves and what our society needs in order to heal.'

'Are you sure Max isn't sick, psychologically? I'm so worried

I did something to hurt him and not having a father ...'

'We must be careful not to see all unusual behaviour as pathology.'

'When Max set himself alight in a public place, you considered that pathological. You were very critical of his actions and motives.'

'Are you a reader, Dr Trehorne?'

She wasn't going to confess her penchant for crime fiction. 'When I get to it.'

'Sometimes literature has provided me with insight into what it is to be human in ways that our diagnostic manual of psychiatry can't. Human beings defy being cut up, categorised, examined. Our behaviours resist the microscope and the measuring tape.' He took his glasses off and polished the lenses with the bottom of his shirt. 'I've seen Max a number of times and he doesn't fit a pathological diagnosis. He has some narcissistic tendencies but we all do. His levels of anxiety are not so severe that I could say he has a social phobia or anxiety disorder. He's an extremely functional young man. Look what he has achieved in his short life.' He picked the paper up again and read: 'Trehorne's work will be on show in November at the AARG gallery in New York.'

He folded the paper and put it down. 'Max knows he can come here whenever he needs help. My door is open to him. However, you are the person who has arrived. This is not an easy situation for you. How are you sleeping? Do you need me to prescribe something? An anxiolytic, or a narcoleptic?'

'You know, something about this really irks me. I can hardly sleep for stressing about Max because he's behaving in dangerous ways and I'm the one who has to take medication?'

'There isn't much anyone can do about Max's choices unless he breaks the law, or is actually suicidal, which he isn't. You, however, need to keep yourself well to deal with the strain of the situation. Sleeping well, eating well, these are important. Insomnia can be a symptom of depression but it can also be a predictor of depression.' He picked up a pen and started writing on a prescription pad. 'Your anxiety is normal but not helpful.'

He tore the page off and slid it across the desk to her. 'These pills will help to take the edge off and help you relax enough to sleep. Of course, it's up to you.'

Carol hesitated, then shoved the script into her bag.

'Go and see your GP,' Dr Ndlovu said, 'for a check up if you haven't had one recently.'

Carol wasn't about to admit that she didn't have a GP, not since Audrey emigrated ten years back. She stood, thanked Dr Ndlovu and drove straight to a pharmacy near the hospital.

She didn't want anyone she knew to see her buying pills.

27.

The fourth day there were fewer people outside the church when Carol arrived but it was early morning, and a weekday. She had gone home for a shower after seeing Dr Ndlovu and had slept ten hours straight on his meds. She'd leapt out of bed, horrified by what might have happened while she was sleeping.

Max was still tied to the cross, slumped forward, the strap around his chest pressing into his flesh, his elbows and knees slack, his wrists and ankles held by their restraints. He was not moving but for the slow and regular swell and slack of his abdomen as he pulled air in and out of his chest.

A woman in a blue outfit and head scarf, who was standing in the crowd, started singing in a pure clear voice. *Amazing Grace, how sweet the sound, that saved a wretch like me.* Others joined in, male and female, their eyes raised to Max. The mood had changed; there were no hecklers or projectiles. It felt more like a vigil. Were people going to stand and watch him die? She would give it another hour, then she would do something definitive. Her doctor's bag was in the car.

No sign of Hedley. A thin young woman was perched on a bollard, bent over a sketchbook, absorbed. It was Tamsyn. Her haunches were like a greyhound's; her clavicles above the top she was wearing protruded prominently, fragile as chicken bones. Her head lifted and dropped, lifted and dropped, as she took in the image visually, then brought her attention to the page, setting the crucifixion scene down on paper.

Carol marvelled at Tamsyn's detachment. If this had been Jeremy who was strung up and suffering, way back when they were students, she would have been hysterical, as she had been that time he came home from the police station after a demonstration supporting the End Conscription Campaign. He was limping and spitting blood from a cut inside his mouth. When he took off his shirt to get into the bath, she saw red wheals that had been slashed into his back. She was a mess of guilt about not attending the demonstration herself, fury at what had been done to him and distress about the fact that, although she agreed with what he was standing for, she couldn't bear that he had put himself in danger.

Was art the new form of protest?

The sketch looked fairly conventional, unlike other work of hers. It was well executed with hard, bold strokes contrasting with softer marks, holding tension between cruelty and suffering. Then she noticed a snake coming out of Max's mouth. Was Tamsyn mixing up her Bible stories?

A young man was approaching. His white peroxided hair was shaved nattily at the temples and he had a maroon necktie at his throat. 'Good morning. I believe you're Max Trehorne's mother.'

How did he know? Carol's impulse was to deny it but she realised she would sound too much like the biblical Peter.

He offered his hand. 'Simon Tshabalala from Independent Newspapers. Can I ask you a few questions?' Without waiting, he continued: 'How do you feel about your son's work? Do you support him?'

She could see the headlines: *Artist's mum's agony of tears*, or some such appalling crap. She wouldn't give him the opportunity.

'He is very courageous, standing up for what he believes, unlike most of us who keep our heads down and carry on with what's in front of us while atrocities are being committed.'

'You're a doctor, yes? It must be difficult for you to see him like this.'

'That's a very stupid observation if I may say so. The question has nothing to do with the artwork, which is not about me and how I feel.'

The journalist flashed a glance at her, but recovered quickly and gave a brief nod. 'Right. The artwork. How do you, the doctor mother – which has absolutely nothing to do with it – understand the work?'

Carol contemplated the scene, attempting to see past her own private horror. 'It's … extremely shocking. We no longer bear witness to people dying or being executed, not in public places. Obviously Max is not going to die but he would if left exposed and fasting for long enough. If no one took him down in time.' She was suddenly struck by her son's bravery. 'The title *Cross/Purpose* works with and against what we see. "Cross" implies anger and asks us to look beyond the suffering to the causes of inflicted pain, at how human beings promote and maintain suffering in situations where it is possible, even easy, to alleviate it. The piece asks us, or rather it *requires* us to be angry.'

She swung on the journalist. 'You know, not a single person has tried to intervene, to take Max down. That says something doesn't it?'

He was fiddling with his cell phone. Was he even listening? He lifted his head. 'Would you mind if I quoted you?'

'Go ahead, but I'm not finished.' Again she stared at the tableau of the cross, the banner, the three posters like the three positions on Gethsemane, the kneeling women, with Max as the centrepiece. 'Then there's that word "Purpose". Max's work asks the hard, central question: What life is worth living? What death is worth dying? He takes us right up to the edge of those questions and forces our gaze into the terrifying void. By putting his life on the line, Max challenges our complacency.' She looked towards the magnificent buildings opposite. 'I hope the parliamentarians occasionally lift their gaze from Facebook and look out of their windows.

'Putting the words *Cross/Purpose* together with this awful image of crucifixion, an image that is not derived from fairy tales but from an *actual practice*, Max provokes us into examining how we say one thing and do another, on many levels. Even standing here, feeling appalled by what we are witnessing, we do nothing. What does it take, to wake us up, to stimulate us into doing something that would make a small but significant difference? We look, we shake our heads, we say shame, how terrible and we turn and walk away.'

She could have gone on, she was making all sorts of connections now but Simon put his cell phone in his pocket and shook her hand. 'Thanks so much. Got to head down to the office. Deadline. Good luck.' He turned for another camera shot of Max.

'Which paper?'

'The *Argus*.' He disappeared into the growing crowd.

'That was awesome.' Tamsyn had come up behind her.

'Oh, hi there.' Carol nodded towards her son. 'Pretty grim stuff.'

Tamsyn nodded. 'Max is very … dedicated. What you said to the journalist … I hope it gets into the paper. It'll mean a lot to him.'

'Well, maybe they won't print it.' Carol took a roll of mints out of her bag and offered one. 'This is unbearable. How long are you going to let it go on?'

Tamsyn turned slightly, to hide her expression. 'We're not … really seeing much of each other.'

Not the first time. 'I'm sorry,' she offered.

Tamsyn pursed her lips. 'Anyway. Nice to see you Carol.' She glanced back at Max with terrible longing then stuffed the sketchbook into her shoulder bag. 'I'd better get back to work.'

'Where's that?'

'An art supply shop in Roeland Street. It's how I put myself through varsity.'

'I didn't know.' Carol looked at her with new respect. 'Tell me, why is there a snake coming out of Max's mouth?' She shouldn't get involved.

Tamsyn bit her lower lip. 'It's about how you can find good and bad in the same place.'

'What has …' Carol started, puzzled.

'I've really got to go.' Tamsyn ventured a smile. 'It helps to know you're here, with him.' She glanced up at Max again then wandered away up the road, her thin legs accentuated by black tights and an extremely short skirt.

That evening, when Max had not moved or responded for an hour other than shallow, rapid breathing, Carol insisted they untie him. She'd decided to call in an ambulance or the fire brigade if Hedley and Siseko resisted but both men looked relieved that someone had drawn the line.

They positioned two ladders against the cross and Siseko and Hedley climbed up while church members steadied the ladders below. Hedley prepared himself to receive Max's semi-conscious body as Siseko, wielding industrial-sized scissors, cut through the straps that bound his friend's wrists, ankles and torso. As Max slumped forward, released from the restraints, Hedley received his body over his shoulder like a fireman. He descended with great care, holding his friend's thighs tightly to his chest, the ladder shaking with each step. Carol was surprised by tears pricking her eyes.

Hedley laid his friend gently onto a camping mattress. Max flopped down, his eyes closed, his breathing ragged. While Siseko covered his skinny, stinking body with blankets, Carol crouched next to him and cleaned the grime of four days' exposure to the city off the skin of his forearm. Working quickly, she inserted a drip into a vein and got rehydration fluid running, put a manometer cuff around his other arm and checked his blood pressure: 78 / 52, his pulse weak, running at 108. Temperature was low, 35.7 degrees. They needed to get him into a warm bath. 'Max!' she called, pressing her knuckles into his chest. He grunted, pushed her hand away and his eyelids fluttered briefly. Glasgow Coma Scale of 9. She put a stethoscope to his chest, listened to the life spilling in and out of him. No signs of pneumonia or other infection. She slowed the drip down, concerned about his renal function.

Max moaned as his left leg tensed and shuddered with cramp. Carol would take him home, clean him, send off blood samples to make sure he was out of danger, feed him up, look after him. He would come through again.

As they loaded him into the back of Hedley's kombi, she saw Tamsyn operating Hedley's camera. She had been standing there all the while, filming everything. The scene must have looked something like a painting, one she remembered from Max's art books: the body of the crucified Christ being taken down from the cross, his mother Mary distraught, her arms filled with her son's death.

28.

After three years of Jack and Kraken in her home most of the time, Carol was fed up. She could take men and dogs in small doses but this was too much. Her garden was in ruins, there were large mounds of dog poo on the stoep and a ring of grime around the inside of the bath. There were no rusks left for her breakfast, never mind that she did all the shopping and always tried to ensure that there would be enough for her too, living with two hungry men. That morning, she had come across Max feeding Kraken the very last rusk before she'd even put the kettle on.

If Carol heard 'Blowin' In The Wind' one more time she was going to blow a gasket, whatever that was. Jack only knew three songs, which he never tired of playing. The other two were 'Me and Bobby McGee' and 'Stairway to Heaven'. He had taught them to Max so she was getting a double dose.

The worst part was Jack's moods. He was so unpredictable, critical, so inarticulate about his feelings.

Men are like cigarettes, Carol thought, so easy to start up with and so hard to give up.

Yet there were good days, days when the three of them went up the mountain together, or for a walk to the estuary. Days when the restless, muzzled side of Jack seemed to find a contented place to lie down in for a while.

When they went to the beach, Kraken would immediately hunt for a stick and bring it straight to Max, his soft brown eyes pleading, his eyebrows going up and down in a dance of supplication, his tail revolving like an eggbeater. Max was a pushover and would throw slobbery sticks for Kraken for hours. Carol loved to watch her growing son's athletic body, moving with grace and ease, gathering himself up in a sideways twist, the dog bounding with excitement, then the release of the throw. The stick would arc up, rotating, into the sky and the animal would be off, ripping through the shallows or racing over the sand. He was surprisingly fast and agile for his bulk, already under the stick as it came down to land, leaping and plucking it out of the air as easily as if it were a piece of fruit hanging from a tree. Each time he would trot back triumphantly and lay the quarry down at Max's feet as though presenting him with a priceless gift, and then repeat the begging dance for more.

Watching the endless performance, Carol marvelled at dogs, at how they were so happy with so little. Routine was what they seemed to crave. Give a dog a blanket, food, a pat, a passing stranger to bark at, another dog's bum to sniff and a walk every day and the animal was happy. More than happy: ecstatic. Unlike humans, who got bored and were always ferreting about for something new to do, something to be the first to achieve. The search for novelty and achievement, that's what it was, she decided – the blessing and curse of the human species.

There was some novelty in the routine of their days – events that afterwards Carol considered highlights. When Jack suggested that the two of them camp out on the mountain one night, Carol initially objected that it would contravene Table Mountain National Park regulations.

Jack waved his hand dismissively. 'I grew up in this bush. It was my refuge. Still is. I'm a caretaker of this mountain and no one is going to tell me not to go there any time I like.'

'If everyone camped there …'

'Don't be such a schoolmarm. Everybody doesn't.'

They headed off up the path after work in the early evening, bulging rucksacks on their backs. Carol was worried that they would be seen, either by a ranger or by one of her patients. Only once they had set up camp under an overhang could Carol relax. The night was seeping into the sky, displacing the day, swallowing the detail and definition of fynbos and rock, until all she could see was the ground around the flame of Jack's cooker and the outline of the large bulk of a buttress across the valley. Everything was quiet but for insects, Jack's soft breathing beside her and the slight squeak of his wind-cheater when he moved. When she got up and made her way by torchlight to pee, she could see all the way down to the lit grid of the suburbs through the dip of the ravine. It was surreal to be in such a wild place that felt so remote yet find you were still in the middle of a city.

Jack was sharing his refuge with her; this was no small thing. He would probably have preferred to be up here alone.

'Ah, Max has had a little accident.' Jack's voice sounded strained; there was something he wasn't saying.

'What's happened? Where are you?'

'Somerset Hospital. Casualty.'

'What's wrong?' The two of them had left early that morning; Jack was going to drop Max and a friend off at a skate boarding park in Claremont. Somerset Hospital was on the other side of the city.

'He's broken his wrist. There's a cut over his eye. Not too bad, considering.'

'Considering what?'

'Max was going quite fast.'

'But … where was this?'

'Camps Bay. There's a dead end they use.'

'Let me talk to him.' If Max could talk his condition couldn't be too serious.

'The doctor's busy with him, he's being stitched.'

'I'm coming now.'

'He'll be done soon. We'll see you back at your place.'

'Bloody irresponsible.'

'What?'

'Never mind. We'll speak later.'

The plaster cast was reasonably well applied and the stitches above his brow were neat enough, considering that most of the side of Max's face was one big abrasion.

'Why weren't you wearing a helmet? What the hell were you doing skateboarding on a public road?'

'It's not public, Ma! It's a dead end, no cars go up there. It's perfect for downhill racing.'

'Look at you! You call this perfect? Perfectly stupid perhaps!'

'Everyone goes there Ma!'

'You know I would never allow you …' Carol threw an acid glance at Jack but he had sat down with the afternoon paper.

'You can't stop me doing the things I like!' Max turned and limped into his bedroom, banging the door closed behind him.

'You're too hard on him.'

'Well, you're too bloody soft! He manipulated you, he knew there was no way I'd take him! You knew that.' He's my damn son, she wanted to yell. Don't you take crazy risks with my flesh and blood.

Jack lowered the newspaper. 'I don't like the way you speak to me. Or to Max.'

'I'm upset, for God's sake!'

'Max needs a bit of understanding, not crapping on.'

Carol felt slapped. 'You've never been a parent so don't be so quick to judge.'

'I've never been a mass murderer or a politician either, but I do have opinions about them.'

'I've never been a boy but I do know when they are ganging up against me!'

'Ganging up?'

'You planned this, didn't you? Let's trick stupid Mum who doesn't understand, who is such a spoilsport, who always gets in the way. Let's sneak out when she isn't looking and be naughty.'

Jack's face darkened. 'It was a spontaneous thing.'

'Don't bullshit me!'

He stood and threw the paper down. The pages separated and spilled onto the floor. Who did he think would tidy up after him? 'He's a boy,' Jack said, slinging his rucksack onto his back. 'You can't mollycoddle him.'

'It's got absolutely nothing to do with being a boy or a girl! It's about being sensible. My son could be dead!'

'Well he isn't. Try to be sensible yourself. Life is full of risk.

Every time you get into your car you put your life on the line. Half the fuckers on the road are blind, drunk, demented, or don't have a licence. Max is learning something important, something that can save his life when he really needs it. He's learning about awareness of danger, how to negotiate his way through, how to trust his body. Don't feed him your fear. It's your fear that will kill him.'

He picked up his jacket and left.

Carol heard Max's bedroom door click softly closed. The little bugger had opened it to eavesdrop.

29.

'I'm going to screw this up.'

They were lying in Carol's bed in the half-light of early morning after making up yet again.

Jack had woken her with his hand heavy on her breast and his need nudging her thigh. Despite her drowsiness, she had taken him into her arms and opened herself to him, her hands moving over the familiar geography of his body. She loved the way he was with her sexually – considerate, slow, imaginative. At the same time there was a quality of desperation in the way he turned to her, again and again, seeking comfort. Sometimes his release lightened his mood as though sex was a kind of antidepressant.

'Screw what up?' she asked. As soon as things felt good again, Jack would say or do something to destabilise the moment.

He was silent. Carol reached for him, stroked the flat of his belly over the depression of his umbilicus and down to where the rough hair started at his groin, still damp from their love-making.

'I'm … messed up, Carol. I've worked out a way for myself but I'm not good at … this.'

Her heart went out to him. 'Oh Jack, we're all messed up. Perfection is an illusion. I love you the way you are.'

'Ha!' He sounded bitter. 'No you don't. If I could fit into your idea of things …'

'I've given up on that! Well, I try to …' She laughed. 'I now understand deeply that to love someone you have to learn how to put up with dog shit on your shoe.' She kissed his cheek playfully, trying to shift his mood, get him to play with her. 'Can you put up with my dog shit equivalent?'

'You have no idea. There's something inside me that cannot stand this.'

'What?'

'This!' His hand made a great sweep, taking in her home, all she'd worked hard for and everything beyond. 'All of it. Suburbia. Fast food. People. Newspapers. Cars. Pesticides. Talk radio. Reality TV.' He was tensing up beside her. 'I'm not made for this kind of life, the built-up, fenced-in, medicated, escape route routine.'

'I don't watch reality TV!'

'That's not the point …'

'We don't have to live like that.'

'You do. You're a doctor, you have a kid at school, you live in a city where it's a good idea to have a burglar alarm.'

'You also have a burglar alarm at your flat!' He wasn't making sense. 'Compromise isn't always a bad thing.'

He threw off the duvet, swung his legs over the side of the bed and sat with the long naked stretch of his back to her. 'I don't want to argue. I'm warning you. That's all.' He stood and headed for the bathroom. 'That's the best I can do.'

'Peter's invited us round on Saturday. It's his birthday.' They were having a glass of wine in front of the fire; Jack had his arm around her shoulders. As soon as she mentioned the invitation, Jack removed his arm, ostensibly to poke at the embers and add a few more logs.

'I'll give it a miss.'

'You busy?'

He shook his head. 'No. And I want to keep it that way.'

'Please, it'll be fun. There's sure to be music and …'

'I'm not stopping you.'

'That's not the point. I … I'm asking you to be flexible. For an adventurous man you're pretty stuck in your ways.' She'd intended her remark to be humorous, a light comment, but there was a barb in her voice.

Jack leaned away from her.

'I'd like you to get to know my friends. For them to get to

know you. It's weird, we've been dating for ages but I end up having to see my friends when you aren't around. It's not normal.'

Still no response.

'Don't you think that's weird?'

'Yeah, I'm pretty weird. That's what you've taken on.'

'You're not weird! That's not what I meant. I'm just saying … well to put it straight, I think you're socially phobic. That's not healthy.' Carol didn't want to mention his mouth. 'You don't have to live like that. There's plenty of help, you know, medication, therapy. All you have to do is recognise that there's a problem.'

'Well fuck you too.'

'It's impossible to talk to you about things that bother me. There's no need to become verbally abusive.'

'Can you hear yourself? You should listen to yourself sometime.' He grabbed the remote and switched on the TV. 'Just because I like my own company and am not prepared to sit a whole evening listening to chit-chat doesn't mean I have a fucking problem.'

There were trapdoors. She was always trying to second guess their location, the triggers; they would be enjoying a great evening, then one of them would say something, or do something and suddenly they had fallen into a cold, incomprehensible place. All that warmth and ease would shatter, lying in shards around them.

Jack would disappear for days, often after an argument. She would call him on his landline and his cell phone and get an electronic voice telling her to leave a message. She would go round and ring his bell, or drive past his flat at night to see whether a light was on. Darkness. No reply.

'Where were you?' she demanded, arriving back from work one evening to find him cooking dinner as though nothing had happened.

'In the bush.'

'Why won't you tell me you're going away, where you're going and for how long? I've hardly slept with worry.'

He slowly added a fistful of sticks of pasta to the boiling water, watching as they softened into strings. Took a swig of his beer. Didn't even look at her. The air seemed to have hardened around him.

'All I'm asking for is a note. It's really inconsiderate, buggering off like that.'

'I'm a free man. You're a free woman.'

'What about your clients? You're running a business, you can't just …'

'If they want me, they have to wait. I'm not like you, letting patients rule your life.'

That stung but she knew better than to argue her point. She tried another tack. 'I care about you, Jack. I need to know you're okay.' She felt herself heating up again. 'I also need to know how many people will be home for dinner.'

He stared at her as though she had gone mad. 'Just assume I'm okay,' he said, throwing some salt into the pot. 'I was absolutely fine my whole life until I met you.' He went over to the television and turned it on, catching the end of the news. Slumped down on the sofa and sat drinking beer, watching some cricket highlight.

Carol picked up a block of cheese he had left on the counter and started grating it miserably. When Jack was in a mood, whatever she did or said was the wrong thing, so she was always tiptoeing around, waiting for the next detonation. It was too difficult, living like this. She was starting to behave in ways that she didn't recognise.

She went over and switched the television off. Stood between Jack and the screen. 'Jack,' she pleaded.

'I was watching that.'

'Please, I want to –'

'Switch it back on.'

'You said you're going to screw this up, remember?' Her voice was climbing, wobbling 'It doesn't have to be like this, we can work things out –'

'Stop telling me what I can do and when I can bloody well do it! Now switch the fucking TV on!' She stood there, horrified by how much hatred there was in Jack's voice.

'It happens to be my television! I am so sick of you taking me and my things for granted.'

Jack grabbed his rucksack and jacket, went to Max's bedroom door. Knocked and opened it. 'Come Kraken.' Kraken came bounding out. Jack raised a hand. 'Bye Max.'

Then Jack was out the house, leaving the front door open and the pasta bubbling on the stove.

Max appeared from his room. 'Where's Jack gone?' There was an edge in his voice.

'To his flat, probably. Who the hell knows?'

Max's face went blood red. 'Why do you always fuck everything up?' he spat, going back into his bedroom and banging the door.

30.

After that argument, Jack didn't come back after the usual three or four days. Carol steeled herself. Perhaps that was it. The two of them had been going round and round in circles for some time, and now Jack had turned her own son against her. Max was sullen, resentful, uncommunicative.

One evening Max wasn't home by the time Carol got back from work. She rang his cell phone but it was on voicemail. Her first thought: Jack's back.

Jack answered his landline. She felt something lift to hear his voice.

'It's Carol.'

'Ah.' Extra non-committal. What to say? The man was so extreme. He hated small talk, people asking 'how are you' when, according to Jack, they didn't give a damn.

'How are you?' she risked, meaning it. 'How's the man I adore?'

An intake of breath on the other end of the line. Her neck began to pulse. The guy needed to be on medication for rudeness.

'Max!' he called. 'Your mother.'

Then her son's voice. 'Ma, it's serious.'

'What?'

'Kraken. He's really sick. The vet says he's got … what's he got, Jack?' A pause. 'Heart and kidney failure.'

'Oh, I am sorry. Poor dog. That doesn't sound good.'

'He's really –' Max stopped, his voice thin to the point of breaking.

'Can I speak to Jack?'

Another pause. 'He's busy, with Kraken. Trying to get him to eat.'

'You probably haven't noticed the time. It's late darling. I'll come and fetch you.'

'I can't leave Kraken!'

'It's school tomorrow. There's your homework. Jack knows how to care for his dog.'

'Ma –'

She heard a sob. Max hadn't cried for over three years, not since the accident, not in her presence. 'What is it?'

'Kraken's going to die.'

'Yes, I suppose so. So sad. He's such a great animal.' Carol had become fond of the dog but her main thought was, wonderful, now I can start gardening again.

'I'm not leaving him –' Max's voice cracked and wavered.

'You can see him tomorrow, every day, after school.'

'School's a waste of time.' He was starting to sound like Jack.

'That may be but you need that little piece of paper at the end of the twelve years to take the next step in your life.' And, she wanted to add, I'm spending a fortune on your education. 'I'm coming to get you now.'

Jack opened the door. His face was haggard. 'Hey,' he greeted but didn't touch her.

'Hi there,' she said, a churn starting up.

'Come in.'

The sweet, acrid stink of urine hit the back of her throat as she stepped inside. Jack went into the kitchen, his movements unusually slow and stiff. Kraken was lying flat on some egg box foam and a blanket, a towel folded under his hips. Max was sitting on the floor next to him, stroking his flank. The dog raised his head with some effort at her approach and whimpered. Carol crouched next to him and scratched his huge brow. His eyes were dull and he looked as though he was putting most of his energy into pulling air in and out of his chest, but he managed to whump his tail once or twice on the floor before dropping his head back down. 'Oh, Kraken! What's happened to you?'

She looked up at Jack who was filling the kettle. He shook his head. 'Nothing they can do,' he said gruffly. 'Kraken got ill, while we were in the bush. I couldn't …' He leaned on the kitchen counter, his body bent forward in pain.

She stood. 'You hurt your back?'

He shrugged off her concern. 'I took too long.'

'Jack had to carry Kraken back to the bakkie,' Max explained.

'I'm so sorry.' She could picture him struggling alone through the wilderness carrying his sick animal. You shouldn't have left me, she thought. If you keep running away, if you avoid and denigrate the people and places where you are loved, where there's real help, you arsehole, this is what happens.

As Jack reached to take the tin of tea down from a cupboard, he jerked and tensed with pain.

'The pain's going down your leg?'

'Yep.'

'I have to stay and help.' Max insisted. 'Kraken can't even turn by himself.'

Kraken's rib cage stuck out more than usual, the bones sliding up and down under his pelt with each rapid breath. As she watched the dog released a small spurt of stinking urine onto the towel. She reached over the sink and opened a window. Turned to see Max pulling the towel out and wiping Kraken clean, getting dog urine onto his hands. Nausea choked her.

Jack handed her a mug of tea. Not enough milk. After more than three years he still couldn't get her tea right.

'When are you going to put him down?'

There was a terrible silence.

'Would you kill me, if I was sick?' Max demanded.

'Of course not, it's different with a dog.'

Max's voice was trembling: 'No it's not! You don't get it Ma.'

Jack had turned and was hobbling through to his bedroom.

'I do get it, actually. I understand how lucky animals are, that we are allowed by law to be humane to them, unlike your Gran who had a miserable paranoid existence because we couldn't do what was right and end her suffering. Some of my patients, many of them young and likely to live for ages, have terrible incurable conditions they no longer wish to live with.

'Look at Kraken, Max! Just look at him! The poor creature. If he's going to die, the kindest thing we can do is to help him along.'

'It's not Kraken you're thinking about,' Max glared, 'it's you. You don't want the bother of looking after him. He's not suffering, he knows Jack and I love him. Hey, Kraken.' The dog managed one whump of his tail.

'Well, there many different ways of showing love,' Carol said. 'I hope one day you graduate from dogs.' She picked up her mug and went through to Jack's bedroom. Hesitated at the door. In all the years she had never slept over at Jack's. She couldn't handle the dust and disorganisation; also Kraken slept on Jack's bed.

He was lying down with a stack of pillows under his knees and his eyes closed.

'Can I come in?' She went to sit on the end of his bed which was no more than a mattress on the floor. 'Can I give you a rub? Or arrange a physio?' He didn't respond. 'I can offer you an anti-inflammatory injection, if you like. It would give me an opportunity to see your lovely bum again.'

He said nothing. Carol sat sipping her bitter tea, desperate for milk. Through the grimy bedroom window she had a view of the shopping mall signs on the wall over the road. No wonder he hated the city. She had provided an alternative, a lovely, cared-for home overlooking the vlei with greenery and birds, but he had been too critical, too difficult, to appreciate that.

'The thing about dogs is you can trust them.' Jack's eyes were still closed; his hands lying clenched at his sides. 'They show you what they are feeling using their whole body. They don't say one thing while doing another. They're the most honest creatures on earth.'

Why was he telling her this? 'It's so sad. What can I do, Jack? To help.'

A pause. 'Nothing.'

'Why is it so hard for you to ask for help when you obviously need it?'

Again, silence. His tea was getting cold on the floor next to the bed. He was too sore to move; she should dig around in the kitchen drawers and try to find a straw.

'You don't really want to help, you want to control.'

'What?'

'Doctors always think they know best. Put the dog down, prescribe painkillers. Be civilised, sterile, functional, rational. What you lot don't understand is that pain is a major part of life. Now, if you don't mind, I need to sleep.' Wincing, he slowly pushed himself onto his side, facing away from her.

Should she point out that the so-called honesty of dogs seemed to include crawling back, again and again after being kicked, or sinking your teeth into someone's throat if you didn't like them? That his interpretation of her offer of help and his refusal were in themselves controlling? That it is a significant achievement of the modern world that we no longer have to suffer without respite?

It was pointless. He would interpret whatever she said or did to fit his idea of who she was. 'Control is not always such a bad thing,' escaped her mouth. 'Especially where rudeness is concerned.'

Carol walked out of the bedroom before he could respond, straight past Max, without looking at him. She let herself out. Let them mess up their lives as they wished. She was finished with being a punchbag.

31.

'Do you ever think about Jack, what happened to him?' Carol asked her son. After five days recovering from *Cross/Purpose*, mainly lying around, eating and sleeping, Max was up and about. Carol had made him porridge with honey, cinnamon and stewed apple, just as he liked it. He was sitting in a patch of sun at the table outside, eating hungrily.

He considered her question. 'Sure.' He scooped up the next spoonful, avoiding her gaze. 'We used to email. I haven't heard in a while.'

'You never told me –'

'Ma-a, I don't have to tell you everything. Besides, you two didn't get on.'

'We did get on!' No response. 'We were together for three years.'

'Yeah, well, I remember a lot of shouting.'

'Have you … seen him?'

Max shook his head. 'He moved to Kwazulu-Natal. To his sister.' He scraped his bowl, getting the last out. 'Then he went to the Tsitsikamma a few years ago. Since then I haven't heard much. He's living on a remote farm. Pretty much a recluse, out of contact. No internet.' He put the bowl on the table, leaned back and linked his fingers behind his head, his elbows angling. 'One day I might go up there and find him.' There was a seam of longing in Max's voice.

'You know where he is?'

Max gave her a warning glance. 'Forget it, Ma.'

'I wasn't –' but of course, she was. Despite all the drama, there was still that tug.

Max started rocking on the back legs of his chair, like he used to as a boy. Carol was about to tick him off when he said,

'I tried to run away with Jack, you know. When Kraken died and the two of you split up. When he left.'

The truth was intolerable. 'Oh. What happened?'

'He brought me back home.'

'I don't remember.'

'You weren't there.' Why wasn't she there? 'Jack made me promise to stay with you until I was old enough to leave. Finish school, that kind of thing. He said if I still wanted to come and live with him then, I could.'

Bastard, thought Carol. Couldn't get his act together to have his own child, so he tries to steal mine. 'So? Why didn't you?' Hoping for some indication of love, even a scrap would do.

Max shrugged. 'Time passes, stuff happens.' He stood and began to walk into the house.

'Take your bowl and mug with you. And mine too for that matter.' Why did kids turn their mothers into stuck records? 'You're not so weak you can't do a bit of washing up either.'

'Sure.' He came back to the table and put her bowl on top of his. 'I'm feeling great this morning. Time to go home.'

Although it pained her to hear him call his horrid, dark, rented accommodation 'home', Carol was also ready for him to leave. Tamsyn had slept over a couple of nights which Carol had tried to discourage, saying the patient needed rest, but the truth was that the laughter from behind Max's bedroom door made her feel lonely in a way she never did when living alone.

Although Tamsyn tried in her ineffectual way to be a considerate guest, there was a curl of dark blonde pubic hair in the bath. A red splotch on a tile, like hard blood. Nail polish. Cigarette stubs in her agapanthus bed outside their window. She'd heated up frozen pizzas one night that were so tough and tasteless Carol had thrown hers away. One evening she'd presented Carol with a bunch of hibiscus flowers which she recognised from the neighbour's hedge.

'I thought the two of you had split,' she'd quizzed Max one morning after Tamsyn had left for work.

'We have,' Max said.

She's like a dog, Carol wanted to say. Keeps coming back.

32.

Carol stood in front of the massive central salt water tank in the Two Oceans Aquarium. She remembered the kelp forest from her first visit years back. It swayed slowly in the currents generated somewhere backstage, with an array of large fish and sharks silently patrolling the reef, gliding in wide circles with shoals of smaller fish flicking their mass of silver bodies this way and that, avoiding the predators.

Today, a huge multicoloured creature like a giant jellyfish floated on the undulating surface of the water, its long, uneven tentacles trailing down into the body of water. It consisted of an amalgam of broken plastic refuse – crates, bottles, containers, netting, rope, bags, implements, shoes, toothpaste tubes, toys, straps, packaging. Small fish darted in and out of the fronds as if it were a chunk of floating vegetation. It was a shocking aberration, a wanton despoiling of a pristine ocean environment.

On the wall next to the tank was a large poster.

PLASTIC POLLUTION AND THE 5 GYRES

Just a generation ago we packaged our products in reusable materials – glass, metals and paper. Nowadays, most of what we consume or use comes packaged in petroleum plastic, a material designed to last forever yet it has no value once the product is delivered and is thrown away.

The short-term convenience of using and throwing away plastic carries a very inconvenient long-term truth. We currently recover only 5% of the plastics we produce. What happens to the rest of the plastic water bottles, cups, tubes, utensils, electronics, toys and gadgets we dispose of daily? Roughly 50% is buried in landfills, some is remade into durable goods and much of it remains 'unaccounted for', lost in the environment where it ultimately washes out to sea.

Plastic pollution is a growing plague, clogging our waterways, damaging marine ecosystems and entering the marine food web. Much of the plastic waste we generate on land flows into our oceans through storm drains and watersheds. It falls from garbage and container trucks, spills out of trashcans or is tossed carelessly.

Sunlight and wave action cause floating plastics to fragment, breaking into increasingly smaller particles, but never completely disappearing. This plastic pollution is becoming a hazard for marine wildlife and ultimately for us.

Our oceans are dynamic systems, made up of complex networks of currents that circulate water around the world. These large systems, coupled with wind and the earth's rotation, create 'gyres', massive, slow rotating whirlpools in which plastic waste can accumulate.

The largest, the North Pacific Gyre is roughly twice the size of the United States of America. Plastic trash in the gyre remains for decades or longer, pushed in a slow, clockwise spiral towards the centre. There are four other major oceanic gyres, with several smaller gyres in Alaska and Antarctica.

44% of all seabird species, 22% of cetaceans, all sea turtle species and a growing list of fish species have been documented with plastic in or around their bodies. When marine animals consume plastic rubbish, mistaking it for food, this can lead to internal blockages, starvation and death.

Also of deep concern is the potential human health impact of toxic chemicals entering the marine food chain through plastics.

Take this challenge: walk into any shop and try to fill a trolley with products that are not made from, packaged, or labeled with plastic. Though some products, like plastic bottles, have a recovery plan, most do not. We must demand zero tolerance for plastic pollution. Reducing our consumption and production of plastic waste will go a long way towards protecting our seas and also ourselves.

FOR MORE INFORMATION ABOUT WHAT
YOU AND YOUR COMMUNITY CAN DO,
PLEASE TAKE A PAMPHLET.

Peter, at her elbow. 'So what do you think? Art, or propaganda? How can something be so beautiful and horrible at the same time?'

The great mass of plastic in the tank was moving slightly under the influence of the currents like a breathing, sensate creature. 'Suddenly, making music seems to be the most ecologically friendly occupation in the world,' Peter sighed. 'All a musician does is disturb the air with rhythm and sound and then it's gone.'

Back home, Carol took the lid off her rubbish bin. A mist of fruit flies lifted out of the stink of rot. She stared at the contents. Plastic bottles and packaging, her old toothbrush, plastic bags, an empty tissue box, newspapers, chocolate wrappers. Polystyrene trays. Bones and scraps from last night's meal, vegetable and fruit peelings.

The discarded history of her thoughtless life.

Where would it go? Rifled through by the destitute on Monday mornings, then squashed into the back of a rubbish truck. Then? Out of sight, out of mind.

In the bathroom she found a box of latex gloves and took out three pairs. Pulled them onto her hands. It was time to perform some serious surgery on her attitude.

Carol found a couple of cardboard boxes and placed them next to the bin. Again, she opened the lid. Penetrating her disgust, she bent and picked out a toilet roll and put it into the box that would go to cardboard recycling. Then she plunged her hands into the mess and started sorting in earnest, what could be recycled and what could be composted.

Looking for redemption, it occurred to her.

33.

Max was up to something again. Carol could tell by his distracted air, by how unavailable he was. One evening he arrived at her place wanting some spray paint canisters from the garage where he'd left them years ago. She stood watching him rummage through old boxes.

'I'll put the kettle on,' she told him.

He came in and sat on the stool at the kitchen counter, sipping a mug of coffee, his leg jigging. Since *Cross/Purpose* the colour had returned to his skin, he'd put on a decent amount of weight and he was looking robust again. Incredible, Carol thought, what the body can survive.

'Can I test them out?' he asked, picking up a canister and shaking it, the ball inside going clack, clack. He pointed the nozzle at the kitchen wall, his finger ready.

'No! Of course not.'

'You'll regret it when I'm famous,' Max grinned, putting the canister down. 'A few artistic marks of mine will increase the value of this property enormously.'

'I'll risk forgoing that. What's the spray paint for?'

'Trying out a couple of things.'

'You're such a dark horse. Is it for a video performance? For that gallery in New York?'

'Yep. And the Goodman.'

'Spray paint is a bit passé, don't you think?'

'Not the way I intend using it.'

Carol's throat tightened. 'Please tell me. Maybe I can handle it better if I know what you're planning.'

'No you won't!'

'It's that bad?'

'It's brilliant.'

She went with him to the gate to say goodbye. A weird contraption of a car was parked across the road. The front bumper had been refashioned, and had another bumper welded above it so that the vehicle appeared to have a mouth that was either laughing or sneering. Attached to the car boot was a pointed devil's tail made out of metal that flicked upwards in provocative, yet cartoon-like curves. 'What on earth have you done to your car?' She'd helped him buy it a few years back, so strictly speaking it wasn't his to do with what he pleased.

'You'll see.'

'You *can't* drive around like that. It's against road regulations, the cops –'

'No one has stopped me.'

'That's because they're bloody incompetent, not because it's allowed!'

'Ma, Hedley's waiting.' Max threw the box of canisters onto the passenger seat, wrapped his arms around her briefly, kissed the top of her head and got behind the wheel. 'Love you!' he said, without looking at her as he turned on the ignition and revved.

Then he was gone.

Carol threw herself into recycling waste at work.

'We can't have this!' she protested. The bin was stuffed with computer printouts, plastic wrappings and containers from medication stock, cans and newspapers. 'I'm going to put paper recycling bins in every room.' She pulled on some gloves and started sorting the items into cardboard boxes.

Zubeida was watching her with an amused smile.

'Come on, Zubeida, we have to set an example to our patients. How can we tell them to look after their own health when we don't care about the health of the planet? It's incredible, how we're happily shitting in our own nests.'

'Besides wanting to save the planet, what's going on, Carol?'

'Why does this have to be about something else?'

'Doctor?' It was Naledi, looking in at the kitchen door, surprised to see her employer up to her elbows in the rubbish bin and knee-deep in boxes. 'Your next patient's here.'

It was Witness Phoswa, a taxi driver in his forties. She'd been treating him for hypertension for years.

'Have a seat, Witness. How are you?' He looked well.

'Doctor.' Witness rubbed his hands on his thighs and shook his head. 'I need to know my status.'

'You mean HIV?' He nodded. 'Has something happened? Something that's made you worried?'

'No,' he said. 'I'm a married man, but we all need to know.'

'Do you have any symptoms? Weight loss? Diarrhoea?'

'No, doctor, I feel good.'

'I'm curious, why have you come for testing today?'

He shook his head again. 'I saw a play a few nights ago and it stayed with me. About a man who didn't know his status and all the trouble it caused for him and for other people.' He cleared his throat. 'So, I decided. I am here.'

'That's fantastic. What play? Where is it on?'

At teatime she told her colleagues. 'Pity our waiting room isn't big enough to stage anything,' she said.

'We should put up posters for theatre productions like that one,' said Xoliswa.

'You know, my girlfriend is in children's theatre,' Trevor added. 'In Germany, theatre groups get doctors to prescribe shows for children. They write out a prescription and that goes towards a discounted price at the door.'

'Theatre as medicine. That's so exciting!' Xoliswa cracked open a cooldrink.

'I've started recycling, by the way. Please put that can in the right bin.'

'Sure, sure.' She took a sip. 'There're some books I'd like to prescribe my patients too. *Emotional Intelligence*, for example, and *The Power of Now*. We should start a lending library.'

'Good idea,' Trevor said. 'There's this bookshop in London where you get interviewed about your work stress and chronic illness, and things like your travel plans and childhood traumas. Then they draw up a list of books, both fiction and non-fiction that can help you understand and deal with things that affect you.'

'That wouldn't stand up in court.' Ralph snorted. He affected a feminine tone of voice. '"I went to see my doctor with this pain in my chest Your Honour and she sent me off to a bookshop."'

'Do you ever read anything other than journals, Ralph?' Carol wondered aloud.

'Thrillers. They keep my adrenalin up.'

'Together with your blood pressure.'

Ralph shrugged. 'Someone has to keep the pharmaceutical industry in business.'

34.

'Max, I've had an idea. For an artwork.'

'Yeah?'

Even over the phone Carol could hear the doubt in his voice. 'Can we meet? Talk about it?'

'I'm helluva busy right now.'

'It's a good idea. I promise I'm not wasting your time. I'll throw in breakfast.'

When she arrived at the coffee place she'd suggested, he was already sitting at a table outside with a large plate of scrambled egg, fried tomatoes and toast in front of him. 'Sorry, I couldn't wait.' He'd shaved his head as well as his beard. He looked like a youthful film star or a criminal.

Or a Buddhist monk. If the long hair and beard was preparation for crucifixion, then was this new look for a role in another performance? What dangerous things did Buddhist monks do other than self-immolate? Feed themselves to vultures?

Carol ordered coffee. Max seemed to have forgotten why they were there. He was far more interested in his scrambled egg. 'So, Max, as you know, many of my patients are killing themselves. Unwittingly, of course. If I try to reason with them it usually doesn't work. It's astonishing how unhelpful facts are when it comes to changing behaviour. Then recently, Peter dragged me off to the installation at the aquarium. Have you seen it?' Max shook his head. 'Well it made me aware of my own unhealthy habits around waste. Do yourself a favour, go and have a look.

'And then, a patient came in asking for tests as a direct result of a play he'd seen.'

She waited for a response; Max was concentrating on wiping his plate clean with a piece of toast. 'So?'

'So-o, I thought I could commission you to design and install an artwork in the waiting room at our practice. Something about our bad habits and our reliance on medication instead of lifestyle change. A conceptual piece that would catch the attention of my patients. You,' she drew a deep breath, 'are really good at getting people's attention through your work, making them feel and think.'

Max was looking at her in a new way, as though she had suddenly and surprisingly morphed into an interesting human being. 'Cool.'

'I'd have to clear it with my colleagues and Ralph can be a stickler. You'd have to take into account that there's not a lot of room. And it couldn't be gross.'

'Come on Ma! Eating or drinking yourself to death is gross! You can't tackle a gross subject without doing something disgusting.'

'There are degrees of grossness in art, as in life.'

Max slumped back and rolled his eyes. 'You can't commission me to do a conceptual piece and then start telling me what I can't do!'

'In the setting of a GP practice, it does no one any good if a work is so disgusting people don't or can't get the message ...'

'I'm an artist, not someone who promotes propaganda!'

'Max, please. There'll be children in the waiting room and conservative people, people who've never set foot in a gallery. Some of them have never been exposed to modern art, installations, performances ...'

He started on another piece of toast. He was losing interest.

'Don't get me wrong. I understand the piece has to be provocative, but it should be, you know, tastefully offensive.'

'Hah! That's a good one. So? You have an idea?'

'Nothing concrete. Something visual – an image that confronts the patient about their lifestyle choices while they're waiting to see the doctor. Like, I don't know, a mirror with a sign above it, saying "Heal Yourself".'

'I've got all these deadlines ...'

'I'll pay you.' She knew he needed the money. Carol took

the rejected rocket off his plate and chewed the peppery leaves. 'If I can afford you.'

'What do you mean, a work of art?' Ralph asked, piling his plate with drumsticks and wings.

Trevor bent to inspect the platter of food the drug rep had provided for their lunch. Chicken pieces, pale pink sliced tomatoes and potato wedges arranged on a bed of limp lettuce. He pulled a face. 'I'm not sure I can do chicken again today.'

Ralph settled himself into a chair. 'Are we talking sculpture? A painting?'

Trevor cleared his throat. 'What Carol's son might have in mind is not what most people would regard as art. Going by his previous work.'

Ralph's eyes widened. 'Oh, *that* son!'

'I only have one son, Ralph.'

'It would be so great.' Xoliswa poured boiling water onto her instant soup, 'What does Max have in mind?'

Carol shook her head as Trevor offered her a plate. She'd lost her appetite of late, not a bad thing, as she'd decided she must do something about her midlife midriff discomfort. 'The waiting room should be more than a space for waiting. It could be an educational experience. We don't have room for a theatre performance but art could work.'

'Cool!' Xoliswa exclaimed. 'At the moment all the patients do there is read articles about multiple orgasms in the latest *Men's Health* while eating sweets.'

'Isn't your son's work pretty damn …' Ralph searched for a way to say it, 'shocking?'

'His performances tend to be, but this would be a conceptual piece.'

Xoliswa was struggling to get the flesh off a drumstick with a knife and fork. 'What's the difference?' she asked.

Carol smiled, recalling how Max had explained this to her. 'Conceptual art is when an artist throws tea trays into a ditch. Performance art is when the artist throws himself into the ditch along with the tea trays, wearing a tiara and wielding a hammer while singing the national anthem.'

Xoliswa and Trevor laughed.

Ralph blinked. 'I don't get it. How is that funny?'

'That would wake things up around here!' Trevor chuckled.

'Why would we want someone doing something ridiculous in our waiting room?' Ralph said.

'That example was a joke, Ralph.' Carol flattened her voice, trying to stop her irritation poking through. 'Max isn't stupid. His work is about holding up a mirror to show us how we abuse others and ourselves.'

'Art can be powerful,' Xoliswa chipped in. 'I've seen some dance performances that tear your heart out.'

'We don't want to upset our patients,' Ralph grumbled. 'There are some beautiful watercolours on the walls. They help people relax.'

'We also have the TV on, with violent children's programmes and stressful soapies,' Trevor remarked.

'What does Max plan to do?' Xoliswa asked.

'He's working it out. Something to do with a curtain and mirrors. I've told him he has to take into account that our patients are mostly not from the art-going public. That he's not to upset children or old conservative doctors.'

Ralph was fishing around in his locker. He stopped and glared at Carol. 'You're one blink away from my age, my dear.' He brought out a bar of chocolate. 'Money would be better spent on improving our educational posters.'

Xoliswa was washing her hands. 'My patients think that facts only apply to other people. I vote for trying something new.' She checked her watch. 'I've got to go, patient's waiting.'

Trevor stirred his tea. 'Let's go for it. Tell Max to submit a plan and a budget.'

Xoliswa grabbed her stethoscope. 'Ralph, it's not as though an art installation is an injection and once it's in you can't take it out again. Excuse me.'

'What's this going to cost?' Ralph peeled the chocolate bar and sank his teeth into it.

'Don't worry,' Carol reassured him, 'I'm paying.'

35.

Max came round after clinic hours to check out the space and measure up. 'This corner would be good,' he suggested. 'We'll have to move a couple of chairs.'

'How long do you think it'll take?' Carol asked.

'A week or two. Got to fit it in between other projects.' He snapped the metal tape measure back into its case and wrote something down. 'I'll need as many samples of vitamins as you can lay your hands on.'

'What for?'

'A bead curtain.' He gestured towards the entrance to the passage to the consulting rooms.

'Make sure no small child can choke, Max.'

'Don't worry, I'm an expert beader.'

'I've never seen you bead anything in your life!'

'When I put my mind to something, I make sure I become an expert. You'll see. No children or animals will be harmed in the making of this artwork.'

A day later her cell phone rang. She didn't recognise the number.

'Hello?'

'Hi, Carol?'

'Who's this please?'

'Tamsyn.' Was that a sob?

'Hi.' Carol couldn't help feeling suspicious. 'How are you?'

'Can I come round?' No doubt about it – she was crying.

'Sure.' Carol knew she shouldn't get involved. 'How about … tomorrow morning?' she offered, looking in her diary. 'Ten a.m.? I'm not working this weekend.'

'Please, don't tell Max.'

Tamsyn's hair was now a screaming red with her fringe hanging in her eyes. She'd put on some weight, but there were dark rings under her crystal blue eyes. She sat on the edge of her seat, cupping her mug in both hands, her elbows on her knees, her shoulders hunched, as though trying to warm herself with the heat of the beverage. Carol sipped her tea and waited.

Tamsyn put the mug down on the coffee table. She cracked the knuckles on both hands, one after the other. The sleeves of her jersey were too long and the ends frayed as though they'd been chewed, but perhaps that was the fashion now.

'So what can I do for you?' Carol had gone into doctor mode.

'I'm sorry to disturb …' Tamsyn started, 'I didn't know …' Her eyes blinked then screwed closed. Her head lowered, her mouth pulled into a wide grimace and she began to cry, great heaving sobs.

Carol found a packet of tissues in her handbag and ripped them open. She went to sit next to Tamsyn on the sofa, offering her one. 'What's happened?' Cigarette smoke and lavender.

'You won't tell Max?'

'I'm a doctor, we know how to keep confidences.' Behind all the makeup, Tamsyn was quite attractive. Carol had an impulse to lift her hand and brush the hair out of the young woman's eyes, as a mother would. Where was Tamsyn's mother? Why had she not gone to her own family?

Tamsyn was fiddling with an earring, staring at the floor in front of her. 'I'm pregnant.'

Carol couldn't stop the recoil, her intake of breath, the horror spilling into her face. Tamsyn's abdomen, she now saw, was pushing at the waist of her dress. She was sitting next to a woman who was carrying her son's baby. Her first grandchild. 'You … you haven't told Max?'

'Oh, he knows.' Her son had told her nothing. Tamsyn blew her nose, studied the snot in the tissue as though trying to read the future, then screwed it up into a soggy ball. 'He doesn't want it.' Her eyes brimmed again. 'He says he can't have kids and all that, his thing is his art, a baby would … get in the way.'

Carol was suddenly on Tamsyn's side. Bastard. Just like his father, she wanted to exclaim. Just like Jack, too. Men want all the pleasures of sex without any of the responsibilities. They plant the seeds – babies, or relationships – then walk away from the hard task of tending to the consequences with love.

'I understand what he's saying,' Tamsyn continued, wiping her cheeks with the backs of her sleeves. 'I should've known, he's never … only I …' She put her face into her hands, sobs shaking out of her, her shoulders collapsing. 'I hoped,' she pulled another tissue out of the packet, 'maybe having a kid would make him want to be around.'

'Around as in around you? Or as in … wanting to live?'

'He's wild, like he doesn't care. I'm so scared. His next two performances … well, I don't think he'll make it.'

'What's he up to?'

'He did a dry run the other night, for *Shoot The Messenger*.'

Carol wanted to ask more, but she also didn't want to know.

'This must be so kak for you. I'm only twelve weeks gone and already I feel like, you know, protective towards this kid.' Tamsyn wiped her eyes with her snotty tissue. '*Shoot The Messenger* is supposed to be about being vulnerable, about security, inequality, stuff like that. Max walked through Mannenberg in the middle of the night with like nothing on except white underpants and a halo made of Christmas lights. Holding a placard like at a demonstration, but this is a combination of a dartboard with a hippy peace sign flashing on it.'

Carol could see the half-naked young man, his skin unnaturally illuminated, walking barefoot and exposed through the dark alleys and glass shards of gangland. It was tantamount to asking to be shot. 'What happened?'

'The cops picked him up, maybe someone saw him and phoned. They thought he was a psycho. Hedley had to go round to the station and explain.'

'Where's Hedley in all of this?'

Tamsyn gave a short laugh. 'He's worried about how to film it without the fucking camera equipment getting nicked. They're working on sponsorship for a GoPro. Or a flying camera, what do they call it? A drone. But they, like, cost megabucks and some gangster might take it out of the sky with a bullet.' She started worrying a thumbnail with her teeth.

'And Max's car? What's he planning there?'

'I'm not sure. He and Hedley are always doing stuff in the garage. I think … I think they're going to crash it.' She pressed a fist to her mouth and shook her head, a brief shake as though to rid herself of the thought. 'I want my baby to have a dad. Maybe Max is right, I should get rid of it.' Her voice hardened. 'But that would feel like he's won. If I keep the baby, it's a fuck-up,' Tamsyn continued. 'If I like … get rid of it, it's also a fuck-up.'

I'm going to get stuck with this kid, thought Carol. At my age, starting with nappies and bottles again. Poor baby. It didn't ask for this.

Tamsyn turned to her. 'Are you sorry you had a kid on your own?'

Carol hesitated. 'Never.'

'Even now? Even if Max dies and messes you up for the rest of your life?'

Carol wasn't going to think about that. Tamsyn looked at her hand sandwiched between Carol's. 'Sometimes I think I must keep the kid so I have something to remind me of Max –'

'For God's sake!' Carol snapped, pushing herself up from the sofa.

Tamsyn grabbed Carol's hand, gripping it hard as though it was the last piece of flotsam left to cling onto. 'You think things would've worked out different if Max grew up in a proper family?'

'What do you mean?' The room went a bit dizzy, so Carol had to sit again; pulled down by this crazy situation; she was filled with the fear of being pulled under.

'If Max had a father, maybe he'd want to be one.'

'Oh please, it's much more complicated than that.'

'I also didn't have a dad, not really. My aunt fostered me but she didn't want to. My mother died when I was four and my father –' she shrugged, 'got busy with other things.'

The thread of unwanted children, passed down through the generations. 'My dear Tamsyn, there is no such thing as a "proper" family. I can tell you that any configuration of relationships and living arrangements carries all kinds of difficulties. Sometimes what looks like so-called normal – two parents, two kids and a cat – hides the most appalling abuse.'

Tamsyn loosened her grip on Carol. 'You know, you're actually quite cool. I used to be scared of you.'

'Why?'

'You always made me feel stupid. You look so, like … fierce.'

'I can be fierce. Right now I'm feeling pretty fierce towards Max.' Carol wished it was five so she could have a drink. 'Anyway, why the secrecy? Why can't I talk to him?'

'He said I shouldn't tell you, not yet. Not if there isn't going to be a baby.'

'You're the one carrying the consequences, so why does Max get to call the shots?'

'Please, you said you wouldn't –'

'You afraid of Max?'

'He'll get angry.'

'So? Let him get angry!'

'Then he'll leave.'

'He's left you so many times, Tamsyn! I'm surprised you come back for more.' The same old problem, embedded in all love songs. *I can't doooo without yoooo!* Hadn't she felt the same whenever a relationship started showing signs of disintegrating, even as an older woman, even with Jack? The sudden loss of a secure footing, the feeling of coming adrift. The fear of being alone, of loneliness and being unloved. 'You'd rather try to manipulate him into staying? Why the hell didn't you use contraception? It's the bloody twenty-first century!'

Tamsyn bit her lips; she gazed up at Carol with big scared eyes like a small stray chocolate-box puppy asking to be taken in. For goodness' sake, the child had had the guts to put herself through university so there must be mettle to her.

'I don't know what happened, I was on the pill. This baby feels like something new, something unspoilt in a fucked-up situation. I want to do the right thing by it. I don't want any more damage.'

How to explain to this child that everyone who has a baby expects things to turn out well. She felt ill. 'If you decide to have the abortion, I'll come with you. If you decide to have the baby, we'll speak to Max, all right?' To Carol's discomfort, Tamsyn put her arms around her. 'But decide soon,' she recommended, disengaging herself as soon as she could. 'If you delay much longer, it'll be too late and the decision will be made for you. Tamsyn?'

'Yes?'

'Are you on vitamins?'

Tamsyn nodded. 'I saw a doctor.'

'Good. And it's a really bad idea to smoke if you're going to keep it. Or drink, or take any kind of drug.' That's my grandchild in there, she wanted to add. 'If you really want to protect this child, take it seriously.'

The sleeve of Tamsyn's jersey had dropped back during the hug, revealing parallel scars, hard wheals across her forearm. Tamsyn saw her staring and quickly pulled her sleeve down. 'That was long ago,' she murmured. 'I'm much better now.'

After Tamsyn had left, Carol poured herself a whisky, then grabbed her phone and called up Max's number. Bugger her promise; telling him what she thought of him was more important.

But then she might lose the new and fragile trust that had sprung up between her and Tamsyn, which, if she decided to keep the pregnancy, would be essential. She didn't want to end up like Katy, with no access to her grandchild.

She put the phone down, fuming. She would store up her speech, Carol decided, let it build pressure. When the right time came, she would let Max have it.

36.

Nothing. Carol heard nothing from her son. Nothing from Tamsyn either, for four long days.

At work and in the street, she became more aware of pregnant women and tiny babies. At home she wandered around, finding it hard to concentrate. She put on music – the late Beethoven quartets or Led Zeppelin – and turned up the volume, then lay on the couch with her feet up on the armrest and a scarf over her eyes.

She couldn't stand not knowing how things would turn out. There would be consequences that affected her and yet here she was, helpless, a mere receptacle of whatever other people decided about their lives, about death.

'She's got a sore ear, haven't you my lovey?' Lillian Grootboom sat on the examination couch and lifted her three-year-old granddaughter onto her knee. 'This kind doctor is going to make it all better.'

'No!' the child shouted, hanging onto her granny's neck, her large eyes swimming.

'I'm also a mommy,' Carol explained. 'You don't have to be scared of me.' She took the otoscope off the wall mount. 'Have you seen my little light? If you put your finger on it, the tip will shine red.'

'Oh, look!' exclaimed Lillian as the little girl pointed her finger and touched. Her face relaxed when she saw the blood-red glow. She turned her delighted face to her gran. 'I'm a witch!'

'A witch with a magic finger!' Lillian chuckled. 'You'll have to tell your baby brother to be careful.'

By the time the child left, with a dinosaur sticker on her dress and medication for an ear infection, she was smiling and agreeing to come back to see Carol again. Carol was behind in her appointments but she sat quietly at her desk for a moment, feeling the ache of wanting the kind of relationship with a child that Lillian had. Once upon a time Max had been a sweet little thing too.

'Dr Trehorne?' Sally on the phone from the pharmacy down the road.

'Good morning, Sally. What's up?'

'I have a script here, for a Mrs Lindiwe Mbotwe. For Lisinopril twenty milligram tablets four times a day.'

'Oh for goodness' sake, sorry. Change that to once daily please.'

Thank God for these quality controls. That was the second wildly incorrect script she had written that week. She had to do something about her state of mind before she inadvertently killed someone.

Poor baby. Poor little girl. She was convinced it was a girl that Tamsyn was carrying. A granddaughter. Here was an opportunity to start again by entering the important arena of caring for children as an older and hopefully wiser person.

When Carol had found out she was pregnant, she'd made an appointment with a psychiatrist who was sympathetic to young women in trouble and who was prepared to subvert the law, risking his own licence.

She'd sat in his stuffy office, her breasts aching, needing to pee.

The elderly man with more hair in his moustache than on his scalp, had looked at her kindly from the other side of the desk and picked up a pen. 'How do you spell your surname?' he'd asked. 'We need to get all the details right.'

As Carol spelt it out, he'd fitted her name into the blocks on the form.

He'd raised his eyes. 'Now, you are in no mental state to proceed with this pregnancy, isn't that so? You are planning suicide due to a major depressive disorder? Insomnia, poor appetite, suicidal ideation. You know what to say.'

He'd rested his arm on the desk, his fountain pen pointing at the form, waiting for her reply. A buzzing had started up in Carol's ears, getting louder, a thin scream.

'No,' she'd heard herself say. 'No, doctor. I think I'd commit suicide if I went through with it.'

Carol could have given the baby up for adoption. She could have carried on with her life and tried to forget about it. She could have been free to socialise and to meet the right man with whom she could have had two kids and a cat. But there was something in her that knew she'd have to go through with this messed-up blessing.

Unlike Tamsyn, she'd had the security of a proper degree and a well-paid job. She'd had parents who, after they'd recovered from the shock and disgrace, had fallen in love with Max and his whole-body chuckle. They'd helped her out with the tough things about having a child on your own – the monotony, the stress, the loneliness, the washing. The sleep deprivation.

She reached for the phone and dialled. 'Tamsyn?'

'Oh, hi Carol.' She sounded guilty. Was it too late?

'Have you –?'

Silence. 'No, not yet. I – I just can't.'

'Keep it. I'll help you.' Carol would show her damn son what responsibility and love looked like. 'Now that that's decided, can I talk to Max?'

37.

Max agreed to meet her for a walk in the forest. This particular mountainside held memories of when he was a baby. On her afternoons off she'd drive to the reserve, put him in the baby carrier and sling him onto her back. He'd throw his head back, gurgling and pointing at the tall tops of the trees going past as she walked.

It was twenty-three years later. Good thing we don't know what life has in store for us, thought Carol. We wouldn't have the guts. They walked up next to the stream in silence. Max strode along not looking at her, his hands in his pockets.

'So,' Carol started, 'what are you going to do?'

'What can I do?' Max kicked at a stone, sending it crashing into the undergrowth at the side of the path.

'Don't bloody well play the victim here. It takes two to make a baby.'

'I thought she was still on the pill, Ma! You're not the only one who's pissed off.'

'Mistakes happen. Babies happen. It's a call to wake up, to grow up.'

'Jeez, Ma, don't dump your shit on me!'

'If you bring a child into this world, you need to take responsibility for it.'

'I never wanted to bring a child into this world, you know that!' No, she didn't. 'If Tamsyn wants kids, that's her business.'

'But you …'

'You're not listening. She used me! I wasn't the one to go off the bloody pill!'

'It makes me so mad. The woman takes the responsibility for contraception and if she makes a mistake, she has to carry the responsibility for that too!'

'It wasn't a mistake! There's a side to Tamsyn you don't know. The most responsible thing is abortion.'

'Would that have been the best thing for you? For me to abort you?'

'I wouldn't have known then, would I?' He shook his head, as though dealing with an imbecile.

'Trouble is, you think that abortion is like getting rid of a wart. There are consequences to everything, Max. No matter what you choose.'

They stormed on up the forest path, Max with his long legs keeping a little ahead, as though trying to escape her.

'You didn't force my father to do the so-called right thing,' he threw over his shoulder. 'There were no consequences for him.' Was that bitterness in his voice? He stopped, turned and glared at her. 'Do you understand what it means for me to take on a kid? I would have to go and get a bank manager job. That would kill me. So, choose. As you point out, there are consequences to everything. This kid will either have an absent father, or a metaphorically dead one.' He carried on walking, Carol straining to keep up.

'Maybe actually dead,' she threw at him, 'the way you're behaving!'

'My life is my art. I can't do that and be a good father, the kind of father I'd want to be if I wanted to be one. It's not fair, this decision is out of my hands and now you're trying to get me to promise all sorts of things that I told Tamsyn, right in the beginning, that I was not up for.'

'You're a narcissistic child, Max, people like you shouldn't be allowed to have sex, bringing more misery into the world.' She knew was going too far, but she couldn't stop her bile spilling out.

'You think Picasso wasn't narcissistic? Or Lucian Freud? They put painting first, before the people closest to them, but they weren't only living for their own selfish pleasures. That's what you don't get because you've never had one artistic bone in your body.'

'Will you stop!' Carol was out of breath and a terrible stitch had started up in her belly. 'Stop! You're going so fast. That's the kind of thing you do, you don't consider anyone else, and I don't care if you're the most famous artist in the whole bloody world, if that makes you unkind and inconsiderate, it means nothing! You hear me, nothing.' She had come to a halt in the middle of the track.

Max stopped and stared at her, his face distorted by an emotion she didn't recognise. 'Unbelievable. You're just like Tamsyn. Well, I won't be manipulated. Do you understand?'

38.

A few days later, Carol was driving back from town on the highway, the windscreen wipers slashing away at a downpour. Again she was obsessing about Tamsyn and the baby, worrying that she had offered help out of some mad sentiment. She would end up like one of those exhausted, resentful grandmothers that she saw fairly frequently in her practice – chained to bringing up their grandchildren because the next generation was too immature or addicted or crazy to be decent parents.

The off-ramp to the hospital was coming up. On an impulse, she took it and made her way to the visitors' parking lot. She ran through the rain, signed in at security and then took the stairs to the psychiatry outpatient department. If Dr Ndlovu wasn't there or was unavailable, she would make an appointment.

The sister was preparing files for the following day. Carol recognised her frizzy blonde hair and protuberant eyes from previous visits. Someone should tell her to have her thyroid checked, she thought.

'I'm sorry,' she replied to Carol's query. 'Dr Ndlovu left last week.'

'Left?'

'Say, aren't you a doctor? The mother of the artist?'

'Yes. Max Trehorne. I'm Carol.'

'How's he doing?'

'Okay, thanks.' She didn't want to get into it. 'Has Dr Ndlovu been transferred to another hospital?'

'He's left the rotation.'

'He's qualified?'

The sister looked at her patiently. 'He's resigned. He's no longer a psychiatry registrar.'

'Why?' It felt like a personal betrayal. 'He was so good –'

'You can get your son an appointment with someone else,' she said, waving her hand towards the end of the corridor. 'The booking office is still open.'

'No … I –' Carol decided not to explain that the appointment was for herself. 'No, thank you.' Still she hesitated.

'Anything else, doctor?' The sister picked up a pile of folders, about to leave.

'Is Dr Ndlovu … ill?' Carol persisted. The sister hesitated. 'I want to thank him for helping us. Is there any way I can get hold of him?'

The sister narrowed her eyes. 'You could email the department and they can send your message on. It might be a while before he gets back to you.'

'He's ill then –'

The nurse laughed, glanced about her. 'I shouldn't really tell you this,' she said quietly, smiling in anticipation as though sharing a really good joke, 'but Dr Ndlovu has gone to the Eastern Cape. Can you believe it, he's chucked up everything to go and train to be a bloody witch doctor.'

39.

'My colleagues want to know about the installation,' she told Max on the phone. 'It's still on?'

'Give me another week, okay?' They were being cautious with each other. 'I've started. Not feeling inspired at the moment.'

'Difficult times.' Trying for non-committal. Non-judgemental. 'Hey, Max.'

'Yep.'

What to say? 'I love you.'

'Right. Yes. Got to go.'

Max had arranged to come one evening after the clinic had closed to install the artwork. The next morning Carol arrived before anyone else, fearful about what she might find. Her name was at stake and if Max had strung entrails from the lights or was wandering around naked with a flashing light on his head, she was the one who would be held responsible.

She was relieved to see that Max's car wasn't outside the building. She parked and let herself in. Over the passageway to the consulting rooms was the multicoloured bead curtain made of vitamin pills hanging from a large mouth affixed to the wall above. The mouth belonged to the painted head of a distorted and androgynous figure whose bloodshot eyes were raised in either agony or ecstasy. The strings of pills were being vomited from or being consumed by the mouth. A halo of cigarettes radiated out from the icon's head. On the forehead, in a meticulous font, were the words: *NOTES FOR SLOW SUICIDE*.

Alongside was a full-length mirror framed by a collage of chip and sweet packets, chocolate wrappers, cigarette boxes, wine sacks, biscuit containers. A chair was positioned in front of the mirror and a pair of headphones hung from a hook on the wall alongside.

Between the curtain and the mirror stood a rubbish bin, with a large sign on it: *PLEASE TAKE ONE.*

Cotton name tags, like she those she used to label her school clothes, were attached to the curtain strings at intervals between the pills and capsules. On each, in a plain font, were diagnoses:

High Blood Pressure
Diabetes
Heart Attack
Asthma
Cirrhosis
Stroke
Insomnia
Depression
Emphysema
Lung Cancer

She stood in front of the mirror and saw a middle-aged woman who was losing her waist. She sat and clamped the headphones to her ears. Different soundtracks funnelled into each ear; into her left was the sound of heartbeat and breathing, both of them disturbingly rapid and irregular, while an electronically generated voice in an anxious but monotonous drone fed a slow litany of words into her right: … cake … bomb … crowds … chocolate … sex … lonely … sleeplessness … debt … traffic … fat … cigarettes … heart attack … break up … cancer … ageing … abortion … infertility … road rage … in-laws … bully … theft … break in … security … murder … unemployment … panic … rape … haemorrhage … nightmares … corruption … incontinence … rust … damp … loss … death … drugs … addiction … alcohol … abandonment … advertisement … gagged … snakes … starvation … burn out … homophobia … tyranny … climate change … extinction … nuclear war … paedophilia … breast lumps … impotence … suicide … pollution … toxic … chemical weapons … insanity … ozone layer … depression … torture … mutilation …

Carol pulled the headphones off and slipped them back on the hook. It was hard to take the barrage, while looking at her image. It was enough to give anyone high blood pressure.

She opened the rubbish bin, glad to see it looked clean. It was filled with apples and folded pieces of paper. *PLEASE TAKE ONE* – the notice was repeated on the inside of the lid. Rummaging around in the bin, she felt like a homeless woman looking for food, or a child taking a lucky dip. She took one and opened it. *LAUGH* was written on it. Quickly she folded it again, dropped it back and picked out another. *SING*. She kept returning the pieces of paper and choosing new ones until she found one she was prepared to live with. *CLEAN AIR*. Then she worried about her state of mind. Why hadn't she wanted to keep *LAUGH, SING, SERENITY*, or *HEALTH*?

'Morning, Doc.' Naledi was coming through the front door, followed by some patients. Geoff Hattingh and his wife and Nkululeko Xama. Also Cassandra Gelding. They stared at the mirror and curtain, curious.

'Good morning.'

'What's that?' Geoff wanted to know, taking his spectacles out of his breast pocket, pushing them on to read the writing on the icon's forehead.

'It's an artwork, Geoff. Back in a mo.' Carol escaped to the kitchen to make herself a cup of coffee while Naledi got the folders out. Anxiety was running round in her. What would her patients and the staff think?

While waiting for the kettle to boil, Carol decided that she liked what Max had produced. Stuff what anyone else thought. She pulled her phone out of her bag, dialled his number. Voicemail. He must be sleeping. 'Well done,' she told voicemail. 'That even gave *me* something to think about.'

40.

'That pill curtain's so cool!'

'You think so?'

Cassandra folded one long leg over the other as she sat down. Her fresh unblemished face was so full of health and vigour, Carol couldn't tell yet why she had come in. 'I was in London last year,' the young woman said, 'and there was this conceptual piece at the British Museum, long rows of pills and stuff woven into netting, stretching down the hall. At first you hadn't a clue. Then a notice explained it was all the prescription medicines an average person takes over a lifetime, from when they're babies to when they die, vaccines, antibiotics, blood pressure tablets, the pill, stuff like that. They didn't even include all the over-the-counter medicines, which would've amounted to way more. They were in long rows, in the order a person takes them. It was bizarre, all that stuff we put into our bodies.'

'Sounds powerful.' She wondered whether Max knew about it.

Cassandra grimaced. 'So ironic. I'm here to get my regular stash.'

'What's up?'

'Just a repeat. Contraception.'

'Well, a pill a day keeps the babies away. Nothing wrong with that.'

'So weird. It feels like magic.' Cassandra laughed. 'I know there's hard science behind it, hormones and enzymes and things, but it still feels bizarre, that you can take this teeny tiny red bead every day and it's enough to stop a sperm and an ovum from hooking up.'

'We're so lucky to live in this age. You can't believe what women used to shove up their vaginas to try to prevent

226

pregnancy. Come sit on the bed so I can take your blood pressure.' Carol wrapped the cuff around her patient's upper arm. 'You think art could change people's habits?' She could smell cigarette smoke.

'Yeah, sure.'

'Could a work of art make you stop smoking for example? You obviously know that in a decade or two you will probably need those long rows of prescription meds if you carry on.'

Cassandra shrugged. 'It's that word "probably" that gets in the way. I've cut down, doc, honest. It's hard when your boyfriend lights up in bed next to you. He's not at all interested in quitting.' She smiled. 'What am I supposed to do?'

Her next patient was a man who said he had a rash in his groin.

'That mirror!' Guy enthused, as he dropped his pants. 'I took a selfie of the reflection.' He was already pressing buttons on his phone, with his jeans around his ankles. He showed Carol the screen. 'Whose idea was it, Carol? Isn't your son that artist?'

Carol could barely hide her pride as she explained how the work had come about. 'You think it'll make an impact?' she asked. 'Make people reflect?'

'Sure. Look what I got.' He pulled a piece of paper out of his shirt pocket and unfolded it. *MUSIC*. 'I was thinking the other day, that I must pick up my trumpet again. And those apples. We've come so far from Eden.' He cupped his genitals in one palm, pulling them aside. In the crease of his groin was the hallmark red edge of a fungal infection. 'Just don't tell me that's an STD.'

Carol bent to take a look. He should be lying on the bed, in good light. It would be more dignified, but the diagnosis was obvious. 'No, it's Dhobi's itch, a fungal infection. Why do you ask about STDs? Have you been taking risks?'

'Well, you can't necessarily trust people. None of the women I'm sleeping with admit to sleeping with anyone else.'

Carol's next patient came in wanting her ears syringed. Nandipha was a heavy woman and as she sat down, the chair squeaked with the strain. 'Doctor!' She banged her hand on the desk resolutely. 'I am always avoiding myself. Even when I brush my hair or wash my face. I don't even have a mirror in the bathroom. Today, I walked into the waiting room and I thought, who is this fat woman, standing in here? Why is she looking at me like that?' She shook her head, her cheeks wobbling. 'I got a big shock.' Her face broke into a grin. 'So, okay. From today, I'm going to cut out the sugar and the starch, like you always say.'

'I'm so pleased, Nandipha. If all my patients take care of themselves it means I can retire early.'

'Ha haaa!' Nandipha laughed. 'Oh, no, Carol, we don't want you to be doing that! You must always be here,' she banged on the desk again to emphasise. 'Here! Helping us. Right here, for our blocked ears and sore knees.'

'Now that you're going to lose weight, your knees won't be so sore. Also, if you stop using those damn ear buds, your ears won't get blocked. Then, when I retire, we can meet over a cup of coffee instead of because of your painful joints.'

Levona came in with a streaming head cold. 'That mirror is a great idea for kids,' she sniffed. 'Kept my little one busy while we waited.'

'Well, that's not for entertainment. It's to get our patients thinking.'

'I did wonder, if I stood on a chair and pinched a couple of cigarettes off the wall, whether anyone would notice –' She threw back her head and wheezed with laughter, phlegm rattling in her throat.

By teatime, the haloed cigarette saint with the pill curtain vomit had been removed.

'What's this?' Carol asked Naledi.

The receptionist glanced anxiously down the passage, 'Sorry Dr Trehorne but Dr Longman told me to take it down.'

Ralph wasn't in his usual spot in the tea room so Carol knocked on her colleague's door.

'Come in.'

Ralph was at his desk, working through a stack of results.

'Excuse me, Ralph but why did you –'

He twisted round in his seat. 'Carol, it was bloody irresponsible. I have such a struggle as it is, getting my patients to take their medication and that ... that ... I don't even know what to call it, it's certainly not art. Why would anyone think that a mouth spewing tablets would encourage patients to take them?'

'The whole idea –'

'That mirror and the rubbish bin can stay, they are harmless enough, although they do take up space and you know how busy the waiting room gets by the end of the day.'

'It isn't harmless!'

Ralph's brow lifted. 'You want to do harm?'

'No, no, Ralph don't be obtuse –'

'I'm being practical!'

'We've got such different ideas about health care, we might as well –'

'The wrong idea about health care can cost some idiot his life! The so-called art in there is just fun and games. Your clever artist son has no clue about the serious issues involved.' He shook his head. 'We can't leave pills around in a waiting room! Use your sense.'

'They're vitamins! Vitamins! Knotted to a string, not "lying around"!'

'Excuse me.' Trevor, at the door. 'I'm not sure our patients need to hear this.'

As Carol turned to leave, a pain skewered her belly. She bent over, winded by the stab.

'You all right?' Trevor took hold of her elbow.

Carol straightened up and forced a smile. 'Absolutely fine.' She made for the door, faint and sweaty with pain. She managed to get down the passage to her consulting room and grabbed her bag and keys. It was just a wind, a big fart building from the bean stew she'd eaten the previous night, or maybe it was stress. Either way, she'd had enough.

On her way out she told Naledi to reschedule her patients who were booked for the afternoon.

41.

Carol didn't make it home. Every time she applied pressure to the accelerator or the brake, the pain in her abdomen intensified to the point she was afraid she might pass out behind the wheel. She pulled over. Perhaps it was appendicitis. She was sweaty with nausea, bent over the wheel, waiting for the wave to pass. Just in time she managed to fumble the car door open and heave an acrid mess onto the tar; pain rammed deeper into her belly with every retch.

'Lady?' A car guard in an orange bib was leaning over her, his face wrinkled with concern. 'Can I help?'

'No!' Carol groaned. 'Give me a moment.'

Then there was a woman's voice, someone on a phone and someone else trying to get her to drink a glass of water and after a while there was the siren and flash of an ambulance and she was being taken to hospital.

There wasn't much of a history Carol could give the young doctor with spiky hair who introduced herself as Trudy. Just a feeling of bloating for some time, how long was it? Perhaps even months, which she thought was due to stress, or mild constipation. Or irritable bowel syndrome, which she'd had as an adolescent. Also a little tiredness. Occasional pain of late but this last episode had been the worst by far.

'Nothing a good fleet enema won't sort out,' she reassured the young thing through a haze of pain, watching a nurse prepare to take blood and put up a drip. Lying on her back with her knees bent relieved the pain slightly but it was still unbearable. She turned her head away and steeled herself for the needle.

Doctor Trudy placed the flat of her hand on Carol's belly and pressed her fingers down, starting near the spleen, away from the worst of the pain. Slowly her fingers palpated around Carol's abdomen, getting closer, then her hand was over the pain and pressing into it, squeezing a grunt out of Carol. When she released the pressure, Carol cried out in agony, tears springing to her eyes.

'Sorry,' Trudy said, writing something down. Carol knew what it was – the doctor had elicited rebound tenderness, the sign for peritonitis. The membranes in her abdominal cavity were inflamed. It had to be appendicitis, even though the thermometer hadn't registered a fever. 'Are you allergic to anything? Can I give you pethidine? I'll also prescribe an anti-emetic.'

A swirl of opiate entered her arm, soothing the ache, blurring her. Strange, Carol mused, how that pointless little wormy appendage could suddenly become an angry inflamed snake, or maybe it was a rat that had somehow found its way into her sewerage system and was trying to scratch and gnaw its way out. Or perhaps it was the old hurt that had been hiding in her heart for years that had slipped, dropping like a bomb into her belly, about to explode. The pain started squealing – she could actually hear its plaintive voice which she knew was her own, even though she was always very careful not to sound plaintive in any circumstances whatsoever – the pain whined on and on, a pity pot, complaining: see what I've been carrying all these years, the disappointment, the loneliness, the brave attempt to live a decent life.

The doctor was saying something that sounded like rap poetry but Carol couldn't follow, so she nodded and then they were wheeling her down a tunnel somewhere with the neon strip lights flashing their bright stripes like the white painted lines of a highway passing, why were they driving in the middle of the road? She wanted to warn them that Max might be coming the other way but she was distracted by a dull ache tucked into a corner of her body, were they going to operate? Was it possible to cut pain out? How would a surgeon find something as vague as pain? Carol was trying to remember from her medical school days, what did pain look like, perhaps like the rat? Or a ragged-toothed saw?

She was gliding on her back into a dimly lit room and a strange man was beside her, saying something and lifting her hospital gown – where had that come from? Where were her clothes? He was smearing some cold goo on her belly. Pressing a hard, plastic knob into her abdomen, sliding it around and over the burning hurt, again and again, as though he wasn't quite sure. Pointing at the screen, at a large blob floating amongst the squiggles. 'Your ovary,' she heard, then his voice swam away again and she closed her eyes.

'Mum!' Max was standing by the side of her bed in a room with a large TV glaring down at her from a wall opposite, two immaculately groomed women arguing silently and sulkily with each other on the screen. On the left were white curtains, pulled back, hanging from a rail above. A door stood ajar behind which she could see the corner of a bath. A bag of fluid hanging from a hook on the ceiling, with a tube winding down to the back of her hand.

Hospital. A private room. She had never been a patient lying in a bed before.

It was coming back. Her belly. She tried to sit up but was stopped by a sudden slice of pain. This hurt felt different, what had they done? Something was sticking to her skin. She lifted the bedclothes and pulled up her hospital gown. A long strip of white plaster, applied above her naked and shaved pubis, over what only could be an incision. Even breathing was a little sore.

'What did they do?' Looking at Max, scared.

'They found a lump. On your ovary.'

'But who ... I didn't sign consent!'

'I signed. You were given pethidine, so you couldn't. You were talking to a blue baby on the ceiling.'

She tried to remember, there had been a baby in trouble … 'I was just a bit sore, it would've settled –'

'It was an emergency, Ma. The surgeon said the ovary had twisted. The blood supply was cut off. They couldn't wait.'

'Which surgeon?' Someone had been rummaging around in her insides. It was a horrible thought. A stranger had seen bits of her she didn't even know she possessed, not really. She didn't identify with what she'd seen in the autopsy rooms and operating theatres, those lengths of lumpy tubing attached to filmy membranes with blood vessels crawling all over them; those glistening bulbs and slugs of organs.

'Dr Klein.'

She'd heard him lecture before and had spoken to him over the phone when referring patients. A tall man with good hands; she remembered him arriving out of the fug at some point, was it after the ultrasound? Carol watched a small air bubble travel down the drip tubing and into her arm. Torsion. Of the ovary. That was something that happened in textbooks. She'd only diagnosed one case in twenty-six years of practice.

She turned her head to Max. He was different today, as though he was really looking at her. She put out her hand and he took it, held it. 'See the lengths I have to go to get you to visit me?'

Max gave a half-smile. 'How're you feeling? Can I get you anything?'

'A double Scotch and some Baked Alaska.'

'Ha! They obviously didn't cut out your sense of humour.'

On the screen a manicured woman in a red hat was shouting silently at a man in a tuxedo. 'Please, turn that off,' Carol asked. Max took the remote and pressed a button. The television image collapsed and disappeared. 'So what else did the good doctor say?'

Max averted his eyes and shrugged. 'He said he'll be here around seven.' He checked his cell phone. 'It's five now.'

What had happened to the time? Her eyelids felt weighted, they kept threatening to close. She was uncomfortable on her back, so she tried to turn but the knives started up again. 'Ask the sister to get me more painkillers darling. Something stronger than Smarties. I've decided to really wimp out for a while.'

Carol knew the term. Surgeons call it a case of 'open and close'. Like a book, only you get the full complicated story in a glance. Lay people call it 'riddled' as though what's obvious contains a mystery.

There was the gangrenous ovary, twisted on its stalk, which had had to be clamped and removed as a life-saving procedure. It was possibly the ovary that had provided Max with life that had reared its cancerous head.

Dr Klein had explained from the foot of the bed – as though her malady was contagious – that the tumour had seeded itself around the lining of her belly in rough patches and there were several tumours in her liver.

He had the report from the frozen section sample, done while she was still on the operating table. High grade. Poorly differentiated. The extent of the spread meant it was inoperable.

Just like that. Carol remembered how her neighbour had snapped her fingers at her birthday party, going on about how your life can change in a second.

Max was stroking the back of her hand as though it was an animal precious to him.

'There's chemo,' Dr Klein had offered. 'We'll have to wait for the operation site to settle before you start treatment but in the meantime I've made an appointment with Dr Naidoo in oncology. You know her?' She was an oncologist that Carol had spoken to on occasion over the phone, colleague to colleague, about other people, patients. 'She will talk it through with you.' He closed her folder and slipped it back into its slot in the trolley. 'Assuming all goes well, you'll go home in three days' time. You'll need to take it easy. No driving for six weeks. You need a sick note?'

Carol gave a nod. For insurance, so she would have an income while she was off work. Wasn't there a clause, something about a pay-out for dread disease? An insurance for managing her dread.

It's dreadful, she wanted to exclaim to Max. You've made a baby. What's going to happen now? How will we bear this?

What on earth was she going to do for six whole weeks? She would get Trevor to pick her up on his way to work. She would manage. She had to get back to her desk, back to her patients. She was not going to give up that easily.

42.

Max moved in. Carol knew he didn't really want to be looking after his sick old mother. And she was feeling old. Sore and weary. Max shopped and fed her and fielded visitors like Stella and Greg who only ever seemed to arrive when there was a scandal. He also worked away at his IT job on a laptop on the kitchen counter. Carol found it comforting to drift in and out with the click, clicking of the keyboard down the passage.

Dr Klein had told her she should 'mobilise early', meaning walk around, get things going again, but she found it hard to scrape enough energy together even to sit up in bed long enough to eat the watery, lumpy soup and the cheese sandwiches Max prepared for her. Maybe it was the painkillers, zonking her out. Maybe she had years of sleep to catch up. Or perhaps she was depressed. It wasn't fair, to come to this, after trying so hard all her life. It felt as though she had hardly even started and here was the horizon, closing in unexpectedly.

How many patients had she seen through cancer, surgery, radiotherapy, chemo? At least a hundred, over the years. Some did exceptionally well, bouncing right back, carrying on as though cancer were a minor setback. Others died quickly, even though every possible therapy had been thrown at them. Yet others grumbled on for ages, dipping in and out of relapses and remissions.

She knew, despite Dr Klein's encouragement, that poorly differentiated ovarian cancer that had already metastasised had an extremely bad prognosis. Crying didn't help but she couldn't stop herself, soaking her pillow when Max was not in earshot. What had happened to the five stages of grief? She could do with a bit of denial.

They had given her support stockings at the hospital to prevent deep vein thrombosis and pulmonary embolism after surgery, but she couldn't be bothered to pull the ugly things on. Pointless. Rather go quickly with a big chunk of clot choking her than die slowly with hair falling out, nausea, pain, uncertainty.

Pumi came into the bedroom carrying a tray. 'Molo, Carol.' She put the tray down on the bedside table and Carol caught a sickening whiff of hot chocolate, a muffin on a saucer next to it. The last things she felt like. Pumi stood with her hands on her hips, looking down on her employer. 'This is the first time I find you in bed in over eight years!'

She should get up but some essential part of her workings had locked. 'I'll be up in a minute,' she said.

'You stay there!' Pumi ordered. 'Sometimes the doctor must be the patient, so you know what it's like for us.'

She was still in bed hours later. Max appeared at the door. 'Come on, Ma. Let's go for a stroll down the road. It's not often you have a handsome young man to lean on.' He handed her a dressing gown. 'It's a great day outside.'

'I am not walking around the neighbourhood in my dressing gown and slippers like some old lady!'

'Those are your associations. I would look at you and think, wow, there's some relaxed chick! She's her own person, she doesn't give a toss what people think. I want to be like her.'

She pushed herself up and shuffled on some loose-fitting clothes. Max knelt to help her get her shoes on.

She caught a glimpse of herself in the mirror near the front door as she passed and was dismayed to see how fine wrinkles had collected in the hollows of her cheeks where she had lost weight. Her hair had become a dull brown, as though life had already gone out of it. Soon the little she had would come out in clumps on chemo.

Outside was much bigger than she remembered. Carol walked along the verge of the road, careful of the wincing pain in her belly, not wanting to strain the stitches. Her arm was linked through Max's, hooked up to his youth, his energy, his life; he kept reining himself in to keep to her slow pace.

Sunlight bounced brightly off walls and postboxes and off the strap leaves of agapanthus bordering the road; shadows skulked under hedges and parked cars. Sunbirds chirruped and flitted in the protea bushes, her neighbour's tabby cat lay in the middle of his driveway, twitching the end of his tail, perusing the world through half-open eyes, the buzz and whine of the construction team renovated number 18.

They walked in silence. There was so much that could not be said.

Carol stopped. 'I need to go home,' she told Max, even though they had only walked two blocks.

Max helped her up the steps to the house and into bed. Maybe this was it. Her purpose was over. She'd brought a replacement into the world, brought him up and now that he was independent it was her time to move on, making space for the next generation.

Peter arrived with an arrangement of protea flowers and her favourite chocolates and stood behind her, massaging her shoulders as she sat in her dressing gown at the dining room table. Carol took one of the chocolates out of its wrapper and slipped it into her mouth to please her friend, but the chocolates didn't taste as delicious as they usually did. Had the cancer got to her tongue, wrapping its tendrils around her taste buds, preventing her from enjoying anything ever again? Horrid feeling and she wasn't yet on chemotherapy.

Her body felt unfamiliar, invaded.

'Have one.' She offered Peter a chocolate over her shoulder.

'No thanks, they're for you. You need fattening up.'

'I'll go easy on them, or I'll split my stitches.' Once she'd been called to a patient's home after he had had an operation because his abdominal incision had come apart. He was sitting in a chair, the long pink tubes of his intestines lying in his lap.

Carol put the box of chocolates down on the table and pushed it away. Her hand didn't look like the one she remembered. It was so pale and thin that the few sun spots she'd developed

238

showed more prominently than usual. 'I'm dying, Peter.'

His hands stopped rubbing the muscles alongside her spine. He came to sit in front of her and took her hands in his, looking directly into her eyes. 'You'll have chemotherapy, that's what the chemo's for, to make you well.'

'Yes, right.' She looked away, needing someone to talk to, to have a real conversation with about all this, couldn't Peter see? It was crazy, having to pretend she was stronger than she was so her bloody friend didn't get upset.

She played along for a while, chit-chatting about Peter's work, the weather, skirting the unpleasant mess that life had deposited in her path. Before long she told him she needed to rest. The effort of pretence had used her up.

Trevor came over with Zubeida. Carol heard Trevor talking to Max in the lounge, she could only hear snippets: 'Sorry about – should have known –'

Max, retorting, 'Well, it's not okay. You can't –'

Her son appeared at the door, furious. 'You've got visitors. Want them in here?'

'I'll get up.' She swung her legs over the side of the bed, reached for her dressing gown. 'What was that about? I heard you say something.'

Max was jabbing at the top and bottom of the light switch repeatedly, flicking the light on and off. 'Stop that, darling.'

'They took *Notes for Slow Suicide* down. Your colleagues are a bunch of retro retards.' Max glared at her. 'If they'd tampered with the *Mona Lisa*, they'd be in jail by now, but they think it's fine to pull my work apart. I didn't even have time to get Hedley to film it, what with you in hospital and all this.' He waved an arm at the sick bed, the bottles of pills. He turned; the door to his bedroom slammed.

Trevor and Zubeida were standing in the sitting room clutching a bouquet of flowers and an enormous card.

'I'm sorry,' Trevor started. 'Max only found out about that now.'

'Want some tea?' she offered.

'I'll make it.' Zubeida was already in the kitchen.

'The rest is doing you good.' Trevor had found a vase for the flowers. 'I've known patients who've beaten this thing,' he encouraged.

'I've never known anything to get you down.' Zubeida took a packet out of her bag. 'Homemade koeksisters,' she announced.

Carol smiled and nodded and bit into the twist of sweet fried dough. She couldn't be bothered to argue. Dr Naidoo, her hand on Carol's arm, had told her that even with chemo, she had a five per cent two year survival rate.

Katy arrived with an enormous teddy bear, shaped so it could be used as a continental pillow. 'You should know me better,' Carol said. 'I've given up having men in my bed.'

Katy looked between the teddy bear's legs. 'Hmmm pretty androgynous bear, this one. Low to non-existent sex drive. He won't bother you at night, don't worry.'

'Looks like an allergen trap to me,' Carol remarked, ruffling the bear's plush pile. 'You trying to kill me off with sneezes?'

'Love always comes at a price,' Katy pointed out. 'Anyway, stop moaning and get out of bed you slut. It's another gorgeous day. Best time of the year, April. Let's go for a walk before you haven't got any muscles left.'

She was feeling a bit stronger, so Katy drove her down to the beach. 'Let's go down to the Fish Hoek end,' Carol suggested. She didn't want to think about Daniel today, although she already had.

Life on the beach swirled around her, full of energy. People walking their dogs, others setting off in kayaks through the sluggish breakers, the blades of their paddles winking in the sunlight, children pushing their spades into the sand. Had she already arrived at the outer edge of her life? Three women about her age jogged past, laughing. All this would carry on after she had gone. No one would miss her.

A wave washed over her feet as she walked; it felt refreshing. She had the urge to plunge into the sea. It was ages since she'd felt the tug of wild water on her whole body. Why had she insisted on living so high and dry, she was dry as bone, dead already. Water could bring her back to her senses. She needed to feel her life, to really experience life before it left her.

Or she could let the water take her, wash her out to the sharks. Not a bad way to go as ways went.

Her friend was rabbiting on beside her. 'So my son-in-law phoned me and asked me to come round for tea. He said family is too important to let our differences get in the way. It's a flipping miracle but you know, I'm not good at miracles. What does one even do in a Muslim house? I've heard you have to take off your shoes.'

'You're going to see your grandson? That's such a breakthrough. What happened?'

'I got down on my knees and prayed to Allah to intervene. I felt certain He wouldn't want little Abdullah growing up without me.' Katy took her sunglasses out of her bag and put them on. 'Wish me luck. I'm almost ready to convert so I can have a relationship with this little tyke.' She glanced at Carol. 'How's Tamsyn?'

Carol shook her head. 'I haven't seen her. Neither has Max, although he did message her to let her know I was ill.' She'd wanted to phone but was too afraid of not being able to control her emotions. 'I'm so pleased for you Katy. Just practise zipping your lip, okay? Turns out life is so very short. At least your family's healthy. At least you are too.'

'Oh Carol! Surely it can't be that bad? You were so well.'

Carol bit her lip. 'The worst thing is that chemo has a microscopic chance of success with this kind of cancer. The bloody irony is that even if I go all out, trying to survive even a few more years, the treatment itself wrecks your life. I don't see the point of that.'

'Girlfriend! You can't do this to me!' Katy had stopped walking and grabbed Carol by the shoulders. 'You have to try everything!' she insisted. 'You have to. You can't give up.'

Carol looked away over her friend's shoulder at the familiar contour of blue-hued mountains on the other side of the bay. 'I also want to see my grandchild,' she muttered. 'I'm determined to hold out till the birth.'

'You're going to see that kid graduate from university, Carol! Flipping hell, girl, stop talking like that!'

'Sure, all right.' She was tired. 'I need to turn back.'

When Carol got home, she found Max in the garage. He'd been setting up a studio with an old easel and a trestle table for his paints, sponges and brushes.

'Good to see you painting again.' He turned to her, a brush in his hand; red had splashed on the front of his t-shirt. He was painting a hunk of meat displayed on a plinth, reminiscent of Francis Bacon. Carol saw that he'd been working from a raw side of beef he'd positioned on a stool in front of the easel, lit by a desk lamp.

'Max! Isn't that …' It was the roast she had put in the freezer months back, now thawed out and posing.

'Yep. I'll pop it in the oven when I'm done.'

Above the painted flesh was a Rorschach-shaped clot, with lighter red drips running down the canvas. Dried ones, turning brown. Red on Max's fingers. Carol looked back down at the front of his t-shirt, put a hand out and lifted it. In the second that it took Max to pull away, Carol caught a glimpse of a vertical cut just below his navel that was oozing blood.

'What have you done?' Carol asked, aghast.

'It needed blood.' Max gestured at the painting. He picked up a rag and wiped his fingers.

'Max, please, not now, not here, give me a break from all this.' She reached for the arm of a garden chair and sat down.

He looked down at her, his face expressionless. 'Perhaps this isn't the best time to tell you.'

'What?'

'Tamsyn had an abortion. Yesterday.' He turned back to studying the canvas, then picked up a polystyrene tray on which he had mixed some paints and dipped the tip of his brush into some lurid green. With a confident scrubbing gesture, he made a mark that hovered like a candy floss cloud above the clot.

43.

One night a man in a hood chased her through a dream. It was one of those nightmares where her legs wouldn't work properly; she felt as though she was wading through thigh-deep mud. The man was gaining on her, and her whole body was tense with fright. He had something, a knife, or a gun. When he caught up to her, he grabbed her hand. She was trying to scream but no sound came out. Gently, he placed a small, exquisite white bloom in the middle of her palm. A frangipani flower with a golden centre, The edges of the petals were starting to turn brown, yet the flower was still giving off a powerful scent, one she remembered from her grandmother's garden.

On waking, she was filled with yearning for the wonderful woman who hadn't lived long enough to know Max. Her garden had been a child's paradise, overgrown with shrubs, trees and creepers that carried an enormous variety of blooms. Any time of the year the garden was a dazzle of colour and there were tunnels in the foliage where Carol loved to make little squirrel homes and fairy bowers.

The dream flower stayed with her throughout the day, in an ache of loss, a reminder from her Granny May. She had not given up living when she'd got ill, even though for a good few years she'd had to go to the hospital three times a week, spending hours attached to a dialysis machine. Carol loved how her gran kept the other patients enthralled with her madcap stories of the early days of her marriage when she and Carol's grandfather sailed a yacht around the world without knowing much about sailing at all.

She must make the most of her limited time left, even while the edges of her petals were fading.

Carol started walking every day, something she had not had time to do for years. Down to the vlei she'd wander, through the wetlands along the wooden walkways and over the bridge. As she recovered she went further, all the way to the beach. Being outside, surrounded by light and living things, helped her mood. Even the soil felt alive as she pushed a finger into the earth around a potted plant to see whether it needed watering.

The soil, to which she would return. She knew about digestive systems and chemical cascades and bacterial action, but how was it that the quiche she swallowed for lunch could somehow turn into muscle and bone? Then how her muscle and bone could become compost or ash?

Throughout her career, Carol had been present at so many deaths, both violent and peaceful. It was miraculous the way an animated body displaying all the tics and habits of character suddenly became drained of life force, leaving a cold carcass unable even to close its own eyes. That was what she dreaded: people watching as she struggled and died. Better to live in a nomadic culture where the frail were left alone under a bush to die.

There was no getting round it. She needed to make a will and funeral arrangements, to sort out her drawers and keep on top of her bills. She needed more exposure to the sun to thaw the fear wedged like a cold ice in her chest. It was the end of April; winter was on its way.

Max had been putting more effort into the food department and Carol had been eating thick, nourishing soups, paella, omelettes. She was becoming stronger and putting on weight.

Her operation site was healing and her appointment for chemotherapy was approaching. Would Max stay on? He was restless, although after each session in the garage, working for hours on end, painting a series of abortion pieces, he would emerge calmer.

No sign of Tamsyn; Carol thought every day about phoning her but couldn't quite summon the energy to do it.

Max's car, with its ridiculous lips and forked tail, was sitting in her driveway. Had he given up on the car project, and *Shoot The Messenger*? Carol was afraid to ask. Fear wasn't good for her, winding itself up in knots.

On her next walk she turned up the mountain path towards the neck. It took a while to get up the slope, stopping and resting on the way, but eventually she made it and stood looking back over the golf course to the sea on the other side of the peninsula. *You haven't got an artistic bone in your body*, her son had accused her. She could still hear his tone, still feel the way it had cut her. Was it true? She'd been good enough at drawing at school but had given it up in favour of the sciences. In her day art and domestic science were only taken by the girls who couldn't do physics and maths.

It was too late to start drawing again. Max wouldn't take her pathetic efforts seriously.

She was feeling good, so she went back down the long way, through Kalk Bay. As she came to Main Road and walked along the raised pavement over the subway to the beach, a disturbance caught her eye. Sea gulls were flapping and squawking around a mound lying on the sand. It was a man, going by the trousers and the boots, lying still as the dead with an open newspaper covering his face and chest. At first she thought it was a homeless person but the boots were in good condition. His arms were flung out either side of his body and there were chunks of white stuff scattered over his abdomen, on his pants and held loosely in his hands. Pieces of loaf. Sea gulls were landing around him, feasting on the bread, having minor squabbles, agitating their wings, jerking their heads to swallow a chunk and hurrying back to peck at another morsel.

Carol stopped for a while, staring. A young couple, with ice creams held to their mouths like microphones, slowed down beside her.

'Is he dead?' the woman joked, concentrating on licking the drips.

'Looks like a sky burial,' laughed the man as they sauntered on. 'There'll only be bones in the morning.'

Carol kept looking at the man on the beach for any sign of life. Should she intervene? Was this life? Or art? Or death? How could one tell the difference?

The gulls scattered, squawking, as the man rolled over and carried on sleeping.

'I've brought you something.' Peter lifted a heavy present onto the dining room table, wrapped in pink paper with little angels on it.

'Don't you think that's a bit inappropriate, Peter?'

'What?'

'Those angels.'

'You'd prefer devils?'

'Neither! I'm not ready to die yet.'

She tore the paper open. Inside was a packet of brown clay. 'What's this?'

'You've got time now.' Peter went into the kitchen and emerged with a large wooden chopping board. 'Pull off a piece and get your fingers into it. You won't believe how much better it makes you feel.'

'What, pinch pots?' She made a face.

'Anything you like. Any shape that arrives through your hands. The clay will show you what to do.' He opened the tie at the neck of the bag, dug his fingers into the wet clay and pulled a chunk off. 'I'll wedge some for you, that part might be too rough on your stomach muscles.'

'Wedge?'

'It gets the air out, in case you want to fire whatever you make. Air bubbles make the clay crack.'

'That's my chopping board!'

'Clay washes off.' Peter was bending over the lump of clay, leaning his weight into it as he repeatedly squashed it in a rolling movement under the heel of his hands. 'Don't fret, darling. When you're better you can join my class and learn to use the wheel. It is the most satisfying thing in the world to make a perfectly cylindrical vessel.'

After Peter had gone, Carol sat looking at the irregular clump of clay on the board. It still bore the imprint of his palms. She didn't know where to begin. It was too late. She had left everything until it was too late and now she was useless, pointless. Hopeless. She herself was about to turn into fucking clay.

She picked up the clod and hurled it at the wall.

'Do you know Marina Abramović's work?' Max asked. Carol shook her head. 'I've downloaded the documentary of her retrospective at MOMA. Want to watch?'

They settled down in front of the TV with a bowl of popcorn and glasses of wine. Carol's moods were swinging all over the place. Right now it felt wonderful to have these moments with her son. While Max was fiddling with the remote, getting to the right place, she put a hand on his knee. 'Thank you,' she said.

He settled an arm round her shoulders. 'Watch this,' he said. 'I've seen clips of it on YouTube. We studied her early work at varsity.'

Performance art. Carol might have known. The artist, sixty-three at the time of the making of the documentary, was looking gorgeous. The documentary showed her coaching thirty young artists who were going to re-perform her early work. She herself would perform one new piece, *The Artist Is Present*, sitting on a chair without getting up once for the entire duration of the museum's opening hours, six days a week for three months. Opposite her would be another chair and anyone in the audience was invited to come and sit in silence, and meet her gaze.

It was a curious idea for the public to come and stare at the artist as though she herself was one of her works. It was so different from her earlier performances, also depicted in the documentary – running naked into walls, repeatedly slamming her beautiful young flesh into concrete, or taking up a knife and stabbing the spaces between the splayed fingers of her other hand, faster and faster, horrifyingly fast There was also an awful scene where Abramović cut the cross of David into her abdomen with a razor, over other scars – this was not the first time she had performed this piece on the tender underbelly, where babies and cancer grew, and where Max had opened himself and mined his body for raw material.

The artist was being interviewed, smiling at the camera. She explained that for most of her life she had been seen as fringe at best or else an aberration, someone who should be locked up in an asylum. Perhaps this was why Max had invited her to see the documentary.

She nearly excused herself, pretending she needed to go to bed, but Max would be gone soon, back to his flat. Soon she would be gone too, and it would all be over. So she stayed, to be close to him. There was something compelling about this woman and the artistic expression to which she had devoted her whole life. The artist's stamina, her endurance. The courage she displayed early in her career in choosing poverty rather than abandoning her vision was impressive, as was her persistence in the face of public derision.

The preparations for the retrospective were complete. Marina, in a plain red gown that covered every inch of her flesh except for her face and her fingers, took a seat on a chair that had been discreetly modified into a commode. The public started arriving, waiting in long queues outside the gallery then running as the doors opened to be the first, to have a chance. The old, the young, the scrawny, the plump, people from all walks of life came, hoping to sit in front of Abramović and to make eye contact in silence. As the security personnel ushered a visitor away at the end of their turn, Marina would lower her eyes to prepare for the next, then would raise them for a fresh encounter with the new individual opposite her. She was really paying attention, turning the act of looking into a way of making herself open to receive whoever was in front of her. Her communication was fearless, direct and curious, without judgement, a look that was filled, very movingly, with something that appeared to be love.

The Artist Is Present was the name of her piece.

Nobody had ever looked at Carol like that, without reserve and with great kindness. A yearning started up in her; she also wanted to sit in front of this artist. Despite Abramović's own profound lack of mothering, and without being a mother herself, she had managed to develop this capacity, if only in performance.

Had Carol ever looked at anyone like that? Had she ever looked at her own son so openly, so unhurriedly? There had never been enough time and yet here, this woman was just sitting, breathing, looking, in silence, for three whole months.

Thousands of people were arriving to sit across from her. Amongst them was Ulay, Abramović's lover and artistic collaborator from the early days of her career. As she lifted her eyes and saw him, Marina broke into tears. She leaned forward and took his hands in hers. They sat and regarded each other, over a lifetime, across all the pain and pleasure that they had shared, across all those things that cannot be said. Then she let his hands go, he stood, and he left.

Why had Ulay come back? Why did anyone decide to return?

Where was Jack? She was filled with a desire to see him, one more time, to say … what? Sorry? No, she wasn't sorry.

Carol could hear his voice clearly: 'What you doctors don't understand is that pain is a major part of life.' Jack hadn't been able to see through the barricade of her ways to where she was most hurt. Tamsyn too had recognised Carol's fierceness but not what it had hidden.

The artist has to be a warrior, Abramović was saying. *The artist has to conquer her own weaknesses.*

Carol wanted to do that. Before she died, she wanted to do something that even vaguely approximated Abramović's courage.

44.

'Take me to the cave.'

Max stopped chewing his muesli and stared at her. 'What cave?' he asked, chopping more banana into his bowl.

'I want to go into Boomslang Cave.'

'That's quite a climb, Ma. I'm not sure –'

'I've been walking every day. I'm fitter than you think. I can't walk as fast as you, so I'm asking a big favour. It might even take all day, but I'm determined.'

'Let me get this straight, you want to go into Boomslang?' Carol nodded. 'You hate enclosed spaces, remember what happened last –'

'Please. Just this one thing, Max. I need this one thing from you.'

They drove to where the path left the road and climbed up the slope into the nature reserve. Max was silent behind the wheel of Carol's car. She kept glancing at him, trying to read his mood.

'What's up?' she asked.

Max looked over his shoulder as he reversed into a parallel parking place. He switched off the engine and grabbed his rucksack off the back seat. 'Nothing,' he said. 'Let's go.'

The first section of the path was the most arduous and Carol had to rest a few times, sweating, a little cramp starting up under her diaphragm.

'You all right?' Max was being sweet, reining in his impatience.

'I'm fabulous, thanks!' Smiling up at him. She hadn't walked this track in a long time, not since that afternoon with Jack. Max must be thinking of him too. Only when they got to the inter-section of paths up at the stream did her son's mood lighten.

'Well done, Mother!' he remarked, taking his rucksack off. 'To think, you could hardly walk down the road a month ago.' Carol warmed with pleasure as though she was a child being praised.

Max put his hands on the earth near the edge of the stream and lowered his mouth to the water, emulating the way animals drink, as he'd always done when on the mountain. 'Want some?' he asked, leaping up and bringing her a scoop of fluid in his cupped hands. There were flecks swimming in it; Giardia perhaps. Then she thought, fuck it. She put her lips to her son's flesh and managed to sip some water as he tipped, some spilling down her chin.

It was so good to drink in the taste of the earth, so unlike what came out of municipal taps. Living water, Jack had called it.

They stopped again for a rest before they reached the mouth of the cave. Max brought out the thermos flask and they sipped tea and dunked rusks while looking over the enormous blue sheen of False Bay. The small pill container Carol had put in her pocket before they set out was digging into her thigh. She took it out surreptitiously and slipped a tablet into her mouth. A beta-blocker for nerves, for the cave.

'Ma.'

'Yes?' She knew what was coming.

'I'm going to have to move back to town soon.'

'Of course. I'm surprised you've stayed so long. And delighted,' she added, in case he got the wrong idea, 'that you stayed. So long.'

'Three more pieces have to be finished by August,' he explained. 'That requires a lot of work and preparation.' Carol nodded, not trusting her voice. Three more extreme works in the next three months. Chances were that Max would be dead before she was. 'You'll need someone to help you,' Max continued, 'shop for you, drive you to chemo. I've asked Peter if he could move in for a while.'

She supposed she could put up with Peter straightening her paintings and rugs for a few weeks. The ill could not be choosy.

'Thank you,' she managed. 'Good luck with your work.'

She struggled a bit in the last stretch, stopping several times.

'We can go back,' Max advised. 'You don't have to go all the way.'

But she did have to. She heaved her body up to the sandy clearing at the opening of Boomslang Cave and stood looking at the dark mouth partially obscured by bush. She knew she mustn't stop too long in case paralysis set in, so she turned to Max. 'The light, please.'

He felt around in the rucksack and pulled out a headlamp. 'It's very safe, Ma,' he said as he helped her slip the elasticised band around her head. 'You really don't have to worry. There's only one way in and one way out. No deep pits to fall into.' He was trying to help but there was no way he could understand the terror. 'The first part is low, you have to crawl for about fifteen metres. Then it opens up, you'll see, it's magic.'

It was totally unnatural, thought Carol, as she bent down and took a first few tentative crouching steps into the narrowing tunnel towards the black void. Her breath tightened, there wasn't enough oxygen. What if she got stuck, or rocks fell on her?

What if she died?

Laughter gasped out of her.

'What now?' asked Max, behind her, his light moving across the rocky walls ahead.

'Hysteria, darling. A classical Freudian response when confronted by the desire to penetrate dark holes.'

Before long the roof was so low Carol was forced to get down on her elbows and knees. The sandy floor was damp and very cold, and by the light of the headlamp she could see the rocky walls run with streaks of wet black. The line of her scar pulled. Her knees were protected by long pants but the rough, icy sand scraped against the skin of her elbows and forearms. Her ears were screaming, her throat was dry, too dry to swallow. Focus on the light in front, showing the way, she instructed herself. Don't even think of the tons of rock above, waiting to fall in and crush you.

'What's up, Ma?'

She'd stopped, her muscles frozen. 'I've got to get out!' The words stuck to the back of her tongue, came croaking out. The heavy black was pressing, and the horror of darkness, of not being able to see what lay ahead, was unbearable. 'Please, *please*, I have to … we've got to –'

'Ma, listen to me. Breathe and listen. You're doing really well. I mean it. You are amazing.'

'I have to get out … *please!*' This was such a bad idea.

'The fact is it's far easier to go a short way forward than to try to reverse. Another metre and we'll be in a space as big as a cathedral.'

'I'm sorry, I –' Nausea pushed at her throat. She mustn't vomit here.

'Just put one elbow ahead of you, then the opposite knee. Then the other elbow and the other knee. Make like a dog. Think of Kraken, Ma. Imagine you're Kraken and you can't wait to get to the magical cave.'

In front of her Kraken's great square head appeared, tilting from side to side, his great steak tongue hanging out of his muzzle mouth, laughing at her. His forequarters went down, his rear end in the air; he looked at her with his eyebrows twitching, his soft brown eyes pleading to play. Then he turned and was trotting away down the tunnel. Her limbs had thawed and she was following him.

Before long the tunnel opened out into a space large enough to stand. She clambered to her feet. The cave certainly wasn't of cathedral proportions. Now she was no longer so cramped her panic subsided. Her legs were a bit wobbly, so she sat down on a rocky outcrop and brushed at the wet, muddy knees of her trousers.

Max emerged from the passage, pushing the rucksack ahead of him. He got to his feet, fished out Carol's windcheater and handed it to her. Pulled on his own. 'Well done. You were a champion.'

'I'm not sure I want to be here long.'

'Hang on, the best's to come. Kill your headlamp.'

'Why?'

'Just try it.'

He switched his light off; after a moment's hesitation, Carol followed suit. Pitch black. Carol had never been inside such utter darkness before. There was water, somewhere, dripping. Her own breathing, shallow and fast. Otherwise, silence. Her panic was rising again.

'I used to come here with Daniel.' This was the first time Max had mentioned his friend since he'd died.

'Yes, I remember. With his father.' Breathe. Be present.

'No, just the two of us.'

'You were only … how old were you?'

'The first time, about ten. Eleven.'

'But you told me –'

'You didn't have a clue what we got up to. You believed all our lies.'

'What!' Shut up, Carol scolded herself. Just listen.

'Daniel was the best.' Max's voice was so soft she could hardly hear him. 'He knew everything, how to tie knots, how to tell the time with only a stick and the sun, how to make bombs.'

'Bombs!'

'Yeah, we nearly set Trappieskop alight once. Remember, I came home with burns on my hand.'

'You said it was from a braai.' What a gullible, distracted fool of a mother I was, thought Carol.

The sound of Max swallowing. 'Can I ask you something?'

Carol's heart lurched. 'Sure.'

'I've always wondered why you didn't come to Daniel's funeral.'

Hadn't she? She couldn't recall. 'I … I don't know.' Of course, Max had gone with Daniel's parents.

'I hated you for not being there. I was angry with you for years, wondering whether you would have bothered to come to mine if I'd died.'

'Oh, Max.' She remembered now; Daniel's death had been too painful. She couldn't face the parents, so she'd made an excuse. Patients, she'd explained, feigning regret. Nobody could object if you couldn't go somewhere because you had to do a house call, particularly if you said the patient was dying.

An image appeared out of the blackness of a fist punching a hole in a door. That strangled cry of rage. 'Oh Max. I'm so sorry. I was ... so messed up.' Should she tell him how every time she went past the dunes she'd leave something in memory?

Her son switched his headlamp on and bent his head over his rucksack. He took out a packet containing tea light candles and positioned them all on ledges. A flare as he struck a match. As the flame touched each wick and it caught, the light became brighter until the cavern was lit with a golden glow.

Max draped a dishcloth over his forearm and bowed. 'I would like to invite you to a celebratory lunch.' Out of the rucksack came a tablecloth, two plastic wine glasses, sparkling white wine and sandwiches. Carol took one gingerly in her dirty fingers and lifted an edge of the bread. Sardines in mayonnaise.

A huge swelling of appreciation expanded in her chest. 'Thank you,' she mumbled. 'This is amazing. I've never –' she looked around at the cave, at her dirty knees, at the sandwich in her muddy hand, 'had champagne with sardines before.'

'Really? It's served in all the best restaurants, as our friend Katy would say.' He popped the cork and handed her a glassful.

'After this,' Carol warned, lifting her glass in a toast, 'I'll probably fall down the bloody mountainside.'

'Way to go.' Max snorted.

'What are we celebrating?'

'You're the coolest mother on the planet, Carol. I want you to know that.'

That undid her. Tears dripped down her face; she wiped them away. 'Oh, Max, I've made so many mistakes –'

'Nothing wrong with mistakes,' he retorted, biting a sandwich. 'I make a living out of them.' He glanced over. 'So do you.'

A dark shape swooped past, a silent flap of black plastic. Carol tensed. 'What was that?'

'Bats.' Max raised his head and looked around, trying to spot them. 'Amazing creatures.'

Carol was suddenly afraid. 'Are we going out the same way?'

'Nah, there's a way out over there.' Max pointed to what looked like an alcove at the opposite end of the cavern. 'That way we can walk out upright as true homo sapiens, all the way to freedom.' He was appraising her. 'You know, you look good with dirt on your face.'

'Thank you. Amazing what it takes to get a compliment.'

He paused, thinking. 'I've got it!'

'What?'

'How we can get rich quick. We introduce a new range of cosmetics based on cave dirt and bat shit extract. We package it in expensive containers and call it "Originals". Or "Cave Credentials". Or "Primitive Urge". We can charge a bomb. Retire early.'

Laughter was mixing with chewed sardines; bubbles were getting up her nose. 'How can life be so sad, so terrible,' Carol spluttered, 'and so perfect all at the same time?'

Max shrugged and topped up her glass. 'That's why we drink. To enhance pleasure, to generate great lousy ideas and to forget pain.'

He brought out a packet for dessert. 'Uh-oh,' he lamented. 'Looks like I sat on these.'

'What were they?'

'Two little milk tarts.'

'Oh, looks aren't important. It'll taste the same.' Carol spat on a forefinger and wiped it on her shirt in an attempt to clean it, then stuck it into the mush of cinnamon custard and bits of crust and sucked it off. It melted on her tongue.

She couldn't put it off any longer. 'Max –' she started.

'Yep?'

'You know – I'm dying.'

He looked away. 'We all are, Ma.'

'So I've been thinking.'

'What? Again?' Max, trying to lighten things up, trying to steer her away from setting the truth down in front of them.

She reached her hand out and grabbed his wrist with some force. His gaze swung back to her, surprised. 'Don't be like the others. Especially not you.' She let go of his arm, needing to let go of him, to let go of everything.

'What?' he sounded twelve years old again. 'You couldn't have got up here if … look at you …You're great –'

She had to press on. 'My prognosis is so bad it's not certain I should even try chemo. Even if I decide to go through with all that, with what one has to endure – these are hectic drugs – I won't increase my life expectancy much.' A lump in her throat was interfering with her swallowing. She paused, wanting him to take it, to take it in. 'Sorry to spoil the party but this is as real as it gets.'

Water, still dripping somewhere near. She had forgotten for a moment that they were embedded in soil, surrounded by the wet heavy dark. It now felt comforting. Perhaps she would be able do it after all: to die. Millions, even billions, had done so before her.

Max dipped his head, scuffed at the dirt with his boot. 'Death is not the problem. At least, not for those who are doing the dying.' His voice caught; there was a pause as he struggled to control his face. 'It's only difficult for the people left behind.' He breathed in deeply, remembering. 'I was so nearly dead, that time with Daniel.'

'Yes, thank goodness Jack –'

'No, I'm saying something different.' Max's voice was urgent. 'When the tunnel fell in on us … on me … I tried to struggle against the incredible weight crushing me. It was completely pinning me down, I actually couldn't move at all, yet I was fighting with all my might to break out, break free. Instinct, I guess. Then I realised it was pointless. I stopped trying to escape. I remember thinking, this is it. Stay awake, be curious. Go with it. An awesome feeling of calm came over in me, an incredible lightness, a complete sense of peace. Then I must have passed out.

'I've never been able to get back there, to that place. Not even close. It's reserved for the dead.' He started packing their picnic away. 'It's like the best trip ever, like you've got this stash of drugs that get released into your system when your body knows it's going. It must be where ideas of heaven come from, when people come back from the brink and report on the experience. I'm not afraid of dying. You don't need to be either.' He switched his headlamp back on and started blowing out the candles, his lithe body bending toward each flame, the tiny fire bracketed between his face and his cupped hand, the flame vanishing into smoke with the release and eddy of his breath.

She would miss him so very much. 'Max?'

'Yes?' His voice wavered.

'I want you to use me.' It was clear to her now.

He stopped putting the candles into the bag, his expression hidden behind the glare of the flashlight on his forehead. 'What do you mean?'

'I want you to use my death.'

45.

Carol had never visited the Goodman Gallery before. Peter drove up the ramp into the parking garage and pulled into a bay. Despite their being fairly near the elevators he insisted on lifting the wheelchair out of the back seat and pulling it open. Carol couldn't quite muster enough strength to lever herself out of the passenger seat, so Peter put out a warm hand, so full of life and music, and took a gentle hold of the cold bones of her own. She'd always assumed that Peter would die before her.

Two young men were coming towards them. Hedley was behind the video camera, filming this moment for the documentary about the show. And Max, the right side of his face abraded and bruised, was swinging his body forward through crutches, his right lower leg like a limb out of a sci-fi movie. A metal exoskeleton was protruding from his shin – an horrendous contraption of bars and bolts, holding his shattered bones together.

'Howzit, Ma.' Max leaned on his crutches, swinging his torso on the pivot of his hip to kiss his mother on the lips, something he had only started doing since the cave. 'We're ready for you.' Carol lifted a hand to her son's hurt cheek, immensely grateful she hadn't been required to dispose of her child's ashes as the final act of her life.

They pushed her to the lifts, Carol feeling exposed and vulnerable in her pyjamas and dressing gown. She was grateful that she was seated on the way up to the third floor – it meant that she was not confronted by her face in the mirrors fixed to the walls of the lift. Her countenance had become strange to her, wrinkled and pale. Her thighs no longer touched each other as she sat, her knees were swollen bone.

The glass doors to the Goodman were closed. It was 9.10 a.m. and the gallery opened at 10 a.m. There was a movement from inside and a bulging man in a smart olive-green jacket came over to the door. He unlocked it, slid it open and flapped his hands in greeting. 'Oh, Dr Trehorne, at last! I'm Robert. So lovely to meet you! What a brave woman, what a talented son.' He gestured round the space, avoiding her eye. 'Let me show you round.'

'Peter?' Carol gestured urgently to her friend; he handed her a plastic container. 'Excuse me –' Heaving. It was happening more often nowadays. A string of thin dribble, clung to her lip. A teaspoonful of bile was running around in the bowl. Someone handed her a tissue.

'Oh, my,' Robert twisted his head this way and that, not knowing where to look, a bit green himself, 'Don't you worry, all's fine in love and art, I always say.'

Max found an anti-emetic tablet in her bag. He rubbed her back affectionately as she put it under her tongue. Robert ran up with a glass of water. 'Here you go my dear. Wait till you see some of the artist's recent work. It's enough to make anyone throw up.'

'Hilarious, Robert,' Max retorted. They were bantering with each other but there was an edge in Max's voice. 'My mother needs to lie down.'

'Of course! Of course! Come this way.' He swept across the room to where a partition screened off a corner of the space.

'Wait, please,' Carol asked, looking around. She felt light-headed but less nauseous. She first wanted to see the show. The title was displayed on the wall: *DEATH IS PRESENT*, next to a notice asking visitors not to touch any of the artworks.

Near the entrance was a sculpture that bridged the space between floor and ceiling at a slight diagonal. It was a metal ladder twisted like a double helix. One of the rungs was broken as though a heavy workman had fallen through, which also suggested a chromosomal abnormality. The piece was called: *Accident (self-portrait) I.*

'Well, you didn't get that chromosome from me,' Carol snorted but Max was busy with Robert and didn't hear her joke.

Peter laughed. 'Oh, I reckon most of my rungs are gone by now.'

On the floor next to the sculpture was *Accident (self-portrait) II*. Black tyre marks skidded to an abrupt halt, the tread starting faintly and getting darker and more pronounced to where they ended in an edge halfway across the room as though encountering a cliff.

She felt Max arrive back at her elbow and smiled up at him. 'I am so proud of you. How did last night go?' She had been too nauseous to attend the opening.

'Well, I suppose, in that it was the perfect wank.' Max pulled a face and looked around at the show. Mounted around the walls were large video screens displaying the performance pieces. *Burning Man* was there and *Food/Fast;* also *Holy Tablet* and *Cross/Purpose*. 'We'll see what the reviews have to say. Wankety-wank.' He gave a sharp laugh. 'I never dreamt I'd end up selling out like this.'

'It's a great show,' Peter commented. 'I don't see you losing your edge.'

'I want to get out of this damn thing and have a look,' Carol said. Peter helped her stand. Leaning on his arm, she moved closer to a triptych called *Scraping/A/Living*. Carol recognised two of the three pieces from the garage: paintings depicting meat on plinths, Rorschach clots and luminous clouds. The third panel was a video of two looped clips in a split screen: the first was a blurred image of something she didn't recognise initially, then identified as an extreme close-up of gloved fingers which were repeatedly pushing and pulling a steel instrument into and out of a fleshy opening; every time the instrument was extracted, bits of clot and what looked like a tiny limb came out with it. Alongside this ran a clip of a thin and naked young woman, standing in the middle of a demolition site, who was painting a mural on a badly damaged wall. Chunks of broken brick and stacks of planking lay in piles around her, there was broken glass at her bare feet, and in one corner of the frame a huge yellow grader was parked, at a slight angle. The naked artist was touching up a perfect, half-opened rose with utmost care and attention on a portion of wall that still retained some plaster.

It was Tamsyn. Carol could just make out parallel scars on her arms and thighs.

She turned her head away from the distressing images and the worry that Tamsyn was back in Max's life, and saw the video of the car crash on the other side of the room. The title of the piece, *Adrenalin Junk Blood Heap*, was painted on a twisted car bumper mounted below the screen. Peter had only informed Carol about the performance once it was over and Max was in hospital.

The newspaper Katy had brought round reported that Hedley had sold a huge number of tickets for *Adrenalin Junk Blood Heap* on Facebook. The event promised the audience a ringside view of the staged accident with the undertaking that, if Max died, they would be presented with a small vial containing the artist's blood and a piece of the wreckage.

The video screen of the performance was split into three looped clips that ran concurrently: the one on the left was filmed from the stands using a hand-held camera; you could see the car's progress from the point of view of the spectators as the vehicle built up speed around the track. The middle clip was captured by a static camera trained on the crowd, and the third on the right was shot from inside the car, over the shoulder of the driver. That frame vibrated into a queasy blur as he accelerated round the track and then headed at terrifying speed towards the barrier. The spectators silently gasped their horror and delight as they watched the car driving directly towards the cement barricade and then ploughing into it, the back wheels lifting from the force of the impact, the car flipping, crashing down on its side, slewing, then skidding along on its roof, steam and smoke pouring out of the concertinaed bonnet until it came to a standstill. The clip on the right blurred and whirled, then came to a stop with the world upside down.

There were headphones hanging on hooks in front of the videos; Carol briefly considered listening as the clip of the car crash started up again but couldn't face the awful sound that must accompany it. Max's car with its devilish leer and tail, adorned with flashing Christmas lights, once again driving faster and faster around the small track, with the audience cheering and screaming, baying for her son's blood, followed by the horrific smash and crumple of glass and metal as he hit the barrier. How had he survived that, only fracturing a tibia, fibula and a cheek bone?

'*Artist With Nine Lives*', was the headline in one newspaper.

Nailed to the wall next to *Adrenalin Junk Blood Heap* was a white sheet which bore an indistinct imprint of a figure with a recognisable face, arm, part of a hand and a leg, as though a bloody body had been wrapped in it. Above it, in neon lights, was the title of the work: *Killarney Shroud*.

On the same wall were two more performances on video. A man in white underpants illuminated by a prickled crown of Christmas lights, walked slowly through a starkly lit cemented area between run-down tenement buildings, holding a lit cage in which fluttered a white dove. He was filmed from a high vantage point, his head held in a circle with cross-hairs as though a sniper was following his progress, ready to pull the trigger. That must be the Mannenberg one, she realised, about shooting peace or something. The title: *Shoot The Messenger*.

In the other he was dressed in red and scaling the side of what looked like the Taal Monument. The camera zoomed into his face; he was screaming something. Presumably one could discover what if one donned one of the headphones hanging next to it. The piece was called *Speaking In Babel*.

Carol's energy had deserted her. 'Come on,' said Peter, hooking his arm through hers, 'let's get you comfortable.' He helped her settle into the wheelchair.

'I have to wee,' she said. Peter pushed her to the toilets, following the signs.

Peter hesitated at the door. 'Want someone to come in with you?' She'd had a nurse aide at home in the afternoons for the past two weeks so that Peter would not have to help with intimate practical details like showering, but she was still adamant that she was capable of going to the toilet by herself.

'Of course not!' She stood but didn't have the strength to push the door open, so Peter leaned against it.

Carol's features in the bathroom mirror were surprisingly familiar, as though the crannies and collapses of her mother's face had crept under her skin, replacing the smooth contours with her mother's aged ones. Better to go this way, reflected Carol, knowing what you were doing.

She leaned unsteadily on Peter's arm as he led her across the gallery towards a partition with *DEATH IS PRESENT*, the title of her piece as well as of the whole show, written on it. A notice invited members of the public to take turns sitting with a dying woman for up to fifteen minutes at a time, in silence and without touching her.

Behind the partition was her deathbed – a single bed in the centre of an area demarcated by red tape stuck to the floor. Max was sitting and unpacking the bag she'd brought, placing the contents onto a bedside table and onto the carpet.

A human skull was suspended over the bed, sparkling unnaturally as it caught and reflected light. Pieces of glass, or translucent beads, were stuck over the crown.

She hadn't expected a skull even though Max had told her he was thinking about suspending something as part of the work. He had explained that *DEATH IS PRESENT* would not only reference Abramović's work but also Tracey Emin's controversial conceptual piece where she'd displayed her unmade bed as a work of art, with all its mess and detritus, in which she had lain around for days suffering from profound depression. Her original work had had a noose hanging above as part of the installation.

'Not a noose,' Carol had objected when they'd discussed it. 'Our work isn't about depression and suicide.' So here instead was a skull regarding her with empty sockets. Quite a shocking thing, perhaps referencing a work of Abramović's where she'd lain naked with a skeleton lying on top of her. Or maybe it referred to that piece by Hirst. Since Carol had decided to participate, she had been doing some research on the days when she'd had enough energy, looking up conceptual and performance art pieces. She had come across Damien Hirst and the furore around the diamond studded skull.

'The encrusted skull,' she asked. 'Is it broken glass or plastic?'

'Bling! I got these plastic bracelets at a five rand store.'

'Oh, that's a clever aside!' Carol exclaimed. Max smiled, pleased his mother had got the reference to Hirst's work. 'I brought my bling along too, as you asked.' She waved at her bag. 'I'm afraid it's not quite enough to cover my skull when I pop off.'

He had found her necklace and earrings, as well as her lipstick and moisturiser. He placed them on the bedside table which also held a lamp, a glass of water, a box of tissues and a container of wet wipes. A plastic bowl was nearby in case of vomit. Also lying next to the bed was a heap of medical journals, topped by *Palliative Care*. She recognised them from a stack in her office that she'd been wanting to get around to. A huge pile of knowledge that was absolutely no good to her now.

Katy's enormous teddy bear sat smiling benignly on the floor next to a wastepaper basket. A commode was parked on the other side of the bed.

'I'm not going to use that!'

'This is your space, Ma,' Max reassured her. 'You do whatever you want. We are here to support you.'

She sat beside him as he took her medication out of the bag and placed it on the table. Morphine and anti-emetics. Laxatives to counteract the constipating side effects of the painkiller. Her toothbrush, toothpaste, dental floss, her facecloth, a change of underwear. A packet of adult nappies that she'd started using at night after an accident.

'*This is not about you,*' Max had emphasised while they were planning the performance and those words rang clearly in her head, kept ringing. At the time his words had stung, but now she understood that he was treating her like a colleague, an artist. She'd overcome her shame and had told Peter to pack the nappies. Her son was placing the evidence of her incontinence and weakness on the floor.

It didn't matter anymore. All those petty embarrassments and arguments, all the frivolous agendas that had driven her life, everything was evaporating in the face of this last sequence. Better to be brave and revealing than to hide away, whimpering, in shame and defeat.

He hooked her stethoscope onto the end of the headboard. So ironic. Physician, heal thyself.

As Max grabbed hold of his crutches and levered himself up off the bed to make way for her to lie down, she saw he had placed some straps of liquorice on the bedside table. Her favourite confectionary, and it also helped with the nausea. Her many small resentments had become irrelevant, yet these tiny acts of kindness meant so much.

She collapsed down onto the pillow, not bothering to take her dressing gown off, lifted her legs with effort and pushed them under the covers. A load of cold sat in her bones. Between the sheets was a hot water bottle for her permanently icy feet. Balancing on his good leg, Max plumped up her pillows and tucked her in. Then he took a few crutched swings backwards and surveyed the overall effect. 'Anything missing?' he mused, half to himself.

'A bottle of J&B. If Emin can have booze in her bed, so can I.' It was a joke; she had lost the taste for alcohol since she'd been ill. Now that she no longer had to worry about whether she was becoming an alcoholic she didn't feel like drinking.

Max was laughing. 'Throw in a couple of joints too, good for nausea.'

Robert came around the partition carrying a tray overflowing with an embroidered cloth. He was followed by a man in uniform, and Hedley with his camera. Max made space for the tray on the table.

'A cup of tea and homemade rusks for you, lovey,' Robert crooned, 'courtesy of the management. Do you eat wheat? Good. There are so many dietary foibles nowadays, it makes catering impossible!'

He swung round to introduce the security man. 'This is Josias, our bouncer and general strongman. Josias, this is Dr

Trehorne, our most valuable item in the exhibition. Don't let anybody steal her.'

'Don't worry, Josias, I'm alarmed. If anyone tries to run away with me, I'll scream.' She put out her hand and shook her guard's hand. 'Please call me Carol,' she insisted.

Josias gave a slow nod of respect and held onto her hand for a moment. 'We must agree on a sign, Miss Carol, if somebody is making too much trouble with you, or if you want anything.'

Carol nodded and took a sip of her tea. She liked the idea of this well-built man with broad features and a considerate handshake looking after her. She had wanted one all her life. 'My guardian angel,' she said with satisfaction.

Robert took a look around the partition towards the entrance. 'It's a quarter to, people are waiting outside already. Got to toodle-oo.'

Carol lifted her right hand and waved by twisting her wrist like the Queen of England. 'Our secret signal,' she explained, 'not to be confused with the wave when I actually depart.' Josias gave a little bow and took up his position at the edge of the demarcated area.

Max sat down in the wheelchair next to the bed. His right eye was disconcertingly bloodshot from the recent blow to his face in the car accident and the subsequent surgery to push his facial bones straight but his left eye was also reddening. 'You know, you can pull out at any point.' His voice wobbled, his eyelids were blinking. 'You don't have to do this. We could take you home right now.' He was crying openly, quietly. He reached for a tissue. 'I knew these would come in handy.'

Hedley was on the opposite side of the bed, filming. Couldn't he stop for even one moment? But she understood that this was the nature of the piece, these intimate, hidden moments laid bare for the world to see. Strange to think that her image would continue to die, again and again, on the internet, long after she was gone.

'Don't worry about me, Max. I'd rather be here with you than at home with Peter, sweet as he is.'

He blew his nose one more time and threw the used tissues on the floor.

'There's a bin,' reprimanded Carol.

'Yes but *this isn't about you.*' Max teased. 'Emin would be horrified by your neatness.'

Carol was suddenly overwhelmed with exhaustion. 'Let's start,' she said. 'Let's do this thing.'

Max checked his cell phone, then called out to Robert: 'We're starting. You can open the doors any time you like.' He took his mother's hand in his. 'Thank you.'

'The sign says you're not allowed to touch the artworks,' reminded Carol.

'I have always been the exception to every rule,' Max retorted.

46.

As she gazed at her son's face, she was surprised to find him almost unrecognisable, now that she was taking the time to really notice each freckle and hair. She had frequently been so critical of him; now she felt only curiosity and a deep affection. She thought she saw his pupils dilate and a surge started up between them. Millions of particles were washing across the space between them, as though travelling along lines of magnetic force, their eyes locked, their faces pixelated with light.

She must be hallucinating from morphine drops or from having thrown up her breakfast.

Concentrate. She'd lost the thread. How to do the difficult, simple thing of pausing long enough, being present enough, to look with love and regard. She blinked and her son was a stranger, different. She blinked again and he was recognisable.

The sliding doors of the gallery gave a low rumble as they were pushed open. She heard shoes squeaking on the floor and a staccato of laughter and talk as people entered. Carol was aware of movement in the periphery of her vision, aware of coughs and stares but she kept gazing at her son. Her eyes were dry, she was blinking, her breath was in knots. People were looking at them, at the injured artist sitting at the bedside of his dying mother.

Carol was afraid of their pity, their disgust. She was worried that she might smell of decay.

Too soon, Josias stepped forward and put a hand on Max's shoulder – the sign that his fifteen minutes was up. Max paused a moment longer, his face vulnerable and open, then he got up without touching her and swung away on his crutches, relinquishing the seat.

Carol shifted onto her elbow and took a sip of her cold tea as the first member of the public came forward and took the seat in the wheelchair. She looked up into the face of a young woman who appeared to be of Italian descent with long, dark hair and a distinctive nose. Attractive, except for her irritating sniffing and the way her mouth hung slightly open. You need to treat that allergy, Carol wanted to explain. A shot of steroid up those nostrils every day will improve your bunged-up life.

Carol lay down and tried to settle into a relaxed gaze. The woman was wearing a St Christopher around her neck and had fine dark hairs at each corner of her mouth. Her cinnamon-brown eyes were apprehensive or sad, or perhaps peaceful. She sat straight and still, her long hands lying loose in her lap.

Who are you? Carol wanted to ask, filled with a curiosity she had never allowed herself in her busy consulting room. Why have you come here dear one? What are you looking for, as you sit with me in silence and look? What am I looking for?

There were visitors who kept coming back to her mind after she'd been taken home at the end of the day. For example, the old man who had a tracheostomy. Although it was covered by a scarf, Carol could hear the tell-tale hoarse breathing sounds. His spotted and sinewy hands shook on his stick and he bent forward towards Carol with a look of such longing she thought that perhaps she knew him from somewhere, a patient maybe? Or perhaps he wanted to swap places with her and lie down and die. She almost pulled back the covers and invited him to join her.

There was the problem of patients who had heard about the show. Tertia Brimley, someone who would bully the reception staff into squeezing her into a fully booked day for a non-emergency, was the last person she wanted to sit with. Carol was tempted to wave like the Queen and have Josias drag the bitch away. Carol escaped Tertia's tears by closing her eyes and feigning sleep.

'You don't have to do the Abramović thing of staring at every visitor,' Max had advised when they'd planned the work. 'The intention here is different. The public is invited to witness something that we normally ignore. You've often said, it's incredible how many people think that the subject of death is morbid. We live as though it doesn't exist.'

He was pacing her lounge, on fire with ideas. 'Your job is to present them with the truth. That is the artist's work. So, if you are tired, sleep. If you are hungry, eat. If you want to vomit, then vomit. Any time you need the toilet, one of us will take you.' He stopped, snapped his fingers. 'In the afternoons, we'll have Busiswe come.' Busiswe was the nurse aide. Carol wasn't sure the solemn older woman would want to be part of a performance. 'She can change your sheets.' Max paused. 'How do you feel about having bed baths? At the gallery?'

Carol's mind tightened with fright. 'I don't need bed baths yet.'

'Okay, we'll decide that if it comes up.' Max waved the thought away and came to sit on the coffee table in front of her, her knees inside his. He took hold of her hands. 'You must understand, performance art is the antithesis of acting. Whatever you do, you mustn't act.'

Carol jerked awake to find a young woman with a red dot in the middle of her forehead regarding her. It was Dr Naidoo, her young oncologist, her smile wide and red with lipstick. Was this a consultation? Carol wiped her mouth in case she'd been dribbling. Already Josias had his hand on Dr Naidoo's shoulder; how long had she slept? The doctor smiled sorrowfully at her and walked away. There was a crowd behind the tape, many waiting for a turn.

Wait, Carol wanted to call after her colleague, her doctor. I missed your visit. My whole life I've been sleeping. Don't go now.

Next was an older woman with a pale complexion and grey teeth. The shoulders of her apricot cardigan were sprinkled with dandruff, as though she'd walked through a light fall of snow to get here. She stared at Carol through large pink-framed spectacles, her lips working, holding back tears. Carol wanted to put out a hand to comfort her. She wanted to explain that she mustn't worry, that worry only created more problems. Everything would be fine. But talking was not allowed, only the quality of the look and the considered weight of silence.

She felt ill and tired despite her nap and it was only the fourth day. Two and a half more weeks to go, if she made it that long. This was too exhausting, trying to bolster everyone up, trying to let them know that it was okay to die. *Leave me alone*, she wanted to shriek. This was exactly why people didn't die in public but were sealed up in hospital, or in their own homes, rebreathing their own breaths. This was a terrible idea and she should demand to leave now.

Carol lay crying quietly, beyond caring about the angular young man seated at her bed, nor the twenty-odd members of the public, staring. It was the first time since primary school, when she'd wet her pants in assembly, that she had cried in front of a crowd.

This is not about you, proclaimed a gruff voice. Something heavy was pressing on her chest, interfering with her breathing. She looked up; Kraken was on her bed with his great paws over her heart, looking down at her, his gentle, sentimental eyes shining, reprimanding her through sloppy jaws. *Even your death is not about you*, he insisted. Any moment a long string of dribble would land on her face.

'Get off!' Carol told him angrily. 'You *know* you're not allowed.' She was struggling with the bedclothes, the animal was pinning her down.

'It's okay, Ma.' Max, beside her. Carol looked again and the dog had vanished. 'Where is he?' she asked, frightened. It wasn't possible for such a large animal to disappear so fast.

Josias was leading the angular man away. Maybe he had something to do with it. 'Where is he?' Carol called after him.

Then she was being trundled to the car in the wheelchair and taken home, lying on the back seat.

'I can't do this anymore.' Peter and Max had had to lift the wheelchair up the front steps to bring her inside. Max crouched in front of her and looked up into her face as she wept. 'It's okay, Ma. I understand. You've been incredible but this wasn't a good idea. You're not well. I'm so sorry.'

'It isn't you!' Carol sobbed. 'It's me. Me!' She hit her fist against her bony chest. 'I wanted to do this and I've failed. I'm a failure. How hard can it possibly be to lie around in a bed!'

'Performance demands huge endurance,' Max insisted. 'It's emotionally and physically exhausting. You have to be fit to do it. This isn't fair on you.'

'Let's get you something to eat,' Peter intervened. 'Then take some medication. You haven't been sleeping properly, that can make anyone feel terrible.' Peter's own eyes were ringed with tiredness. 'We'll talk about it in the morning.'

Carol drifted off in the dark warmth of her room to the sound of Peter playing a piece she recognised as a Brahms' intermezzo, and woke in daylight to barbed wire knotted under her ribs and rain thundering down on the roof. It was a Sunday, the gallery was closed, so they had a day off. She took a dose of morphine, her hand shaking with the effort but too proud to call for help. Perhaps it would rain the whole week and she would have an excuse to stay where she was.

She slipped in and out of sleep; at one point she was dancing with a young boy, at another she was alone in a wasteland, a freezing wind scalping her.

A man familiar to her was sitting on her bed. Someone was holding her hand. Was it Jack? Or Max? 'What's the matter?' the man asked. 'You were shouting.'

'Why did you leave me?' she asked, rising and clinging to him.

Monday broke clear and sunny, although there was still a winter nip in the air. Carol felt a little stronger. She had woken at 5 a.m., and lay in bed listening to the robins outside the window. She was thinking about *Cross/Purpose* and the nature of suffering.

She insisted on getting up for breakfast and managed some thin porridge, then patted her lips with the serviette. 'I want to go in,' she declared.

Peter raised his eyebrows at this; as the two men cleared the table, she heard them having words in the kitchen, their voices low and insistent.

They came back to the dining room as a unified front. 'We don't think you should,' Max said. 'Not today.'

'Have you forgotten,' Carol said, weak with fury, 'what the hell this is all about? Did you imagine that this would be easy?'

So many people. Carol could not believe the number who arrived every day. Some came to wait their turn to be with her; others sat cross-legged on the floor behind the boundary tape to witness from the edge.

A middle-aged woman, the purple stain of a birthmark covering half her face came forward, her greying hair in a plait down her back. She nodded a greeting and lowered herself into the wheelchair. Then a man with loose skin around his eyes and a butterfly tattooed on his forehead. A girl with a shock of tight curls and a mouthful of braces, who jigged as she sat and stared with her fresh, curious face. A young man came to sit whom she recognised from somewhere – it was Siseko, Max's actor friend from *Cross/Purpose*. He sat very still with tears pouring down his face.

How are you, Carol wanted to ask him. How kind of you to come.

Someone was calling. Carol woke with a start. She found herself staring straight up at a small black hole set into bone. The underside of the skull. The puncture where the spinal cord emerged was making a sucking sound, tugging at her like a noisy vacuum cleaner.

Her abdomen was full of dull ache as though she'd eaten the contents of a tool box; a sharper pain was digging around under her ribs. Her skin and her urine had become darker. She'd been taking both morphine and an anti-emetic more regularly.

Her death was spreading.

Someone was beside her. She turned. Sitting in the wheelchair was a man who resembled Jack. His hairline was receding;

the hair that remained was cropped short. The skin of his neck was scraggier and sunburnt at the back. They were supposed to have grown old together.

His eyes were resting on her with affection.

No, not Jack. It couldn't be. He would never appear in public, in full view. Certainly not in front of Hedley's camera, not in an upmarket gallery. Never.

Yet there was the scar, unmistakable, puckering his upper lip.

'Jack.' Her body broke into joy. She turned her head, looking for Max. Her son must have engineered this, first bringing Kraken to her and now Jack. Had he done this for her sake?

Or had he done it for art, for the documentary, for his CV?

Did it matter?

No Max anywhere. Only the eyes of strangers, their focus on her, staring out of their fragile, invincible bodies, sitting and standing, arranged around the periphery like a frieze or a painting. Carol turned her gaze back; for a moment she could not find her old lover. Had he fled, away from the face of her illness, away from the crowd? Blinking, refocusing, she realised he was still there, his brown eyes on her, his irises flecked with light, the intransigent hardness gone out of them.

'Oh Jack!' she cried, laughter spilling as she tried to extract her thin, unsteady arms from under the weight of the duvet; wanting to reach out so she might take him in her embrace and hold him. The fragile basket of her chest was releasing the pain of happiness in great sobs, her skeleton shaking and shaking under the loose fabric of her skin. 'I never believed this would happen.' Carol's voice wavered on the air like a frayed prayer flag.

Jack's palm settled warmly against her cheek, his eyes calmed her. A rip tide had started up in the room; it was gathering her up in its current and was pulling her. She no longer felt the desire to struggle and relaxed, letting the wash take her all the way out.

For more about Modjaji Books and any of our titles go to
www.modjajibooks.co.za

Printed in the United States
By Bookmasters